NickGyver

Book One

The Battle between Light and Darkness

NickGyver

BOOK ONE in the Adventure series of the battle between Light and Darkness

NickGyver Revealed
The Battle Begins

A Science "Faction" Series

By: *Ideas and Concepts LLC*

Copyright 2005

Copyright © 2006 by Nicolus Jameson
Copyright © 2005 by Ideas and Concepts, LLC

NickGyver
by Nicolus Jameson

Printed in the United States of America

ISBN 1-59781-923-9

Although this novel is based around factual material, the characters, some incidents, some cities and dialogue, except for incidental references to public figures, products, or services, are imaginary and are not intended to refer to any living persons or to disparage any company's products or services.

All rights reserved solely by the author. The author guarantees all contents are original and do not infringe upon the legal rights of any other person or work. All rights reserved. No part of this book may be reproduced in any form or by any electronic or mechanical means, including information storage and retrieval systems, without the permission in writing from the publisher, except by a reviewer who may quote brief passages in a review. The views expressed in this book are not necessarily those of the publisher.

Unless otherwise indicated, Bible quotations are taken from the Amplified and King James versions of the Bible, using The Layman's Parallel New Testament. Copyright © 1970 by Zondervan Publishing, and the Hebrew/Greek Study Bible by Spiros Zodhiates. Copyright © 1991 by AMG International, Inc.

www.xulonpress.com

Table of Contents

Acknowledgements - Without these people
there would be no book series xi

Introduction/Fore Word- about the author 17

Chapter 1 - Foundations of Electromagnetic
Energy – FOE or FRIEND??? 29

Chapter 2 - The principles and effects of lightning 48

Chapter 3 - The "Nick" of time 61

Chapter 4 - The Imperfect Sun 77

Chapter 5 - NickGyver Revealed 91

Chapter 6 - Nick builds a reputation 109

Chapter 7 - Ions: Vitamins of the air 125

Chapter 8 - Attracting and repelling shock of the
Century 151

Chapter 9 - A return to Vitamins of the Air 165

Chapter 10 - A Warm Welcome for NickGyver 179

Chapter 11 - Another WARM Welcome for
NickGyver 199

Chapter 12 - Fire from Heaven 221

Chapter 13 - Nick's Mountaintop Experience 241
Chapter 14 - Nutrition and the Mind 253
Chapter 15 - Samantha Vies for Independence 265
Chapter 16 - Bioentrainment & So what about the
 Mosquitoes? 275
Chapter 17 - Angels of Light 297
After word - The author shares how the novel
 relates to his life experiences 323

-Acknowledgements-

*M*ost of all, I want to thank my Heavenly Father for direct insights, inspiration of story plots and scenarios as direct and often immediate answers to prayer regarding my book series. The author also wants to thank the following people for support to write this novel series:

For financial backing in the costs for publishing the first book of the series:

>I thank Harry Nelson of Paramount Plumbing and Heating from Duluth, Minnesota and
>Kimberly Sannes of Compass Rose, a civil engineering firm from Duluth, Minnesota

I thank the following authors for insights:
>Playfair and Hill, "Cycles of Heaven."
>Ronald W. Clark, "Einstein – 'The life and times'."
>Leo F. Buscaglia, PhD., "Living, Loving and learning."

I also thank the people who contributed to the Public Domain information on the Internet regarding Nikola Tesla that I compiled over the past twenty years.

Also notable references:

Heinz R. Pagels, "The Cosmic Code – "Quantum Physics as the language of Nature."

Stephen Hawking, "The Universe in a Nutshell."

Isaac Asimov, "The Neutrino – Ghost Particle of the Atom."

NickGyver

Book One

The Battle between Light and Darkness

NickGyver Revealed
The Battle Begins

I choose this day to serve you, to obey you, to seek your face, to love you, to honor you and to worship you. I choose the fear of you Lord.
Proverbs 1:29

There are many choices we must make each day. Who do YOU choose to serve today?

Other books in this series to date include:

Book Two - *The Battle continues with Anti-Relativity*

And

Book Three - *The Evil of Sulocin*

Introduction

The stories in this Christian novel adventure series are based on facts and theories from the author's research and others who will be recognized and given credit for their work throughout the book.

Many of the incidences in this novel series are from the author's actual personal experiences. A number of the inventions or ideas represented in this novel series may either be in process of or have patents pending by the author's corporation, Ideas and Concepts, LLC.

The technical lectures in the college or political settings in this book are the author's sole creations from actual college research and lectures he has given as part of technical degree studies. The letter that the main character Nick receives from the New World Order is an excerpt from an actual letter received by the author.

The author's background of expertise includes electrical, computer networking and systems design, and electronics engineering degrees, 13 years of teaching technical courses at technical colleges, Certification in Network Plus Professional, Certified Electronics Technician, licensed Master Electrician in two states and 30 years of specialized electrical contracting in all types of construction.

The author may overwhelm the "just curious" reader with more technical jargon and theories than they would ever care to read, but you can be assured the information has been worded in as simple to understand language as possible.

If you enjoyed the "Left Behind" series, you will love this series possibly even more. For those technical readers who love the TV series of X-FILES, MacGyver, STAR TREK and STAR WARS, you will glean the needed information from each chapter to bring credibility or plausibility to the author's stories.

The stories of the NickGyver series are fictional, although fact based. If you like plausible science fiction, mystery, intrigue, loads of extremely funny situational comedy involving jokes and puns, heart warming emotional scenes and an opportunity to witness a real threat to our world be constantly overcome by the power of God's word, inspired technical wisdom and angelic intervention, you would like to be encouraged in ways to strengthen your family bonds and how to deal with the temptations and trickery of Satan, then this is the book series for you!

The characters portrayed in this novel are fictitious although all references to Nikola Tesla and his accomplishments are accurate to the best of the author's knowledge.

Any reference to any family members of Thomas Edison are strictly fictitious and in no way portray any intent of the author to slander them if they existed. The concept of Edison's living relatives no matter how remotely related are just part of the story plot.

The following true story actually happened which "sparked" the author's curiosity to do research on other effects of electrical radiations on the human body, which in later years prompted this novel series. For those of you who appreciate a more technical description of what goes on in electric systems that cause damage to humans at the cellular level, continue reading after this short, but true story of the death of one boy and severe sickness of his brother due to low frequency electric fields surrounding them in their bedroom. If you choose to skip the technical explanations that follow, fine. Just jump to Chapter One with the stories to follow and enjoy!

Here is the story of death and sickness under the bed........

As a Master Electrician and electrical contractor, the author got a call one day from a father who was a very knowledgeable doctor. He had concerns that his old Knob-and-tube wiring (common wiring from the pre-1940's) left in place after the house was modernized was the possible cause of Leukemia which led to the death of one son and another son recently diagnosed with the disease and was undergoing treatment. This call had been referred to the author by the local power company where one of the author's technical friends worked as an electrical engineer. The author's friend offered to assist him in getting down to the bottom of the possible cause of the death and present illness of the doctor's remaining son. He arranged to loan the author sensitive instruments to measure ELF's (Extremely Low Frequency Radiations) and also provided him with an established level of ELF as a reference thought to be safe, to compare existing readings with. The second floor bedrooms had not been rewired when the rest of the house had been remodeled so it was logical and probable to test the ELF levels there, especially in his sons' room which had the same tenants over the years. Upon removing the furniture and mentally recording the furniture placement in his mind, the author recorded an ELF level of over 3000 in the floor under where the bed once sat. The ELF levels gradually diminished to around 300 about 6 feet from that spot. For your information, a level of 10 ELF measured in milligauss was considered at that present time by health authorities to be a safe level. His thought to effectively reduce the ELF level to an acceptable level involved removing the knob and tube wiring under the floor and re-routing the wires to junction boxes in the walls using modern romex (plastic sheathed wire) wiring. After rolling back the carpeting and removing sections of the plywood floor he was able to re-route the wires to new junction boxes in the walls. Subsequent ELF readings were less than 10 throughout the floor area in that bedroom so the author's project was a complete success with a reduction from over 3000 down to levels as low as 2 milligauss under the bed location.

Just for comparison, the Earth's natural ELF reading is around 43 gauss and you might ask why the Earth's magnetic field doesn't cancel out that which is produced by internal knob-and-tube wiring? Well, it's not the same frequency as the Earth's so it can't.

The following is a technical explanation of why low frequency radiations can be deadly under the right circumstances. If this doesn't interest you, jump to the first chapter and enjoy the story lines to follow!

Soviet scientist A. S. Pressman has done a lot of work studying the effects of electric and magnetic currents of all strengths on living systems and written an important book on the subject. He has found that EM (electromagnetic) fields can have a marked effect on living tissue even when the power applied is so weak that no thermal effect at all can be detected. It is interesting to note that as the power applied is increased, the effects on the human body are actually decreased! Lower levels of EM accompanied by ELF (Extremely Low Frequency) waves, which by the way may be the cause of low level electromagnetic radiations, have been found to be the cause of damage at the cellular level. This often results in changes to the cellular structure, DNA modifications and neurological changes in the transfer of normal electrical signals throughout the body. Some typical resulting diseases are; Leukemia or other blood anomalies, cancers and the author doesn't rule out the possibility of diseases such as Parkinson's or other nerve-related diseases. Now that your attention is hopefully aroused, you might be asking what some possible sources of low-level EMs and ELFs are? To understand the cause of EMs and ELFs, a lesson in basic electrical and magnetic theory is helpful.

As electricity in any form whether alternating or direct current passes through a conducting wire or through the air as transmitted radio/TV signals, it causes a magnetic field to be developed around the conducting medium. It's intensity or how far the magnetic wave extends from the wire or conducting medium is directly proportional to the amount of electrical current (commonly referred to as AMPERES) being carried in the conducting medium. The more current, the farther EMs and ELFs are spread out from their source affecting subjects farther away from the source of the damaging radiations. You may all have thrown a rock into a lake or pond and seen the rings spread out from the center of the impact in the water.

Such is likened a magnetic wave which radiates out from a current source. The larger the rock you throw, the farther the resulting rings will travel. The same as the more power (current through a conducting medium), the farther the electro-magnetic wave will travel.

All Matter, including air is made up of building blocks called ATOMS. Each atom contains its own solar-like system (like orbiting planets and moons). An atom consists of a nucleus and orbiting electrons around it. The nucleus consists of positively charged particles called protons and also neutrally charged particles called neutrons. The negatively charged electrons are held in their orbits by the attracting force of an equal number of positively charged protons in the nucleus. This is analogous to our own planet orbiting the Sun, except that involves magnetism along with electrical charges.

When an electrical force (a voltage) is applied to a conducting material, the force overcomes the electrical charge force holding the electrons in orbit and they are caused to get excited and jump to another atom nearby in a vacant spot between other electrons. If this electrical force (a voltage) is continually applied to the atoms in the conductor, a cascading effect will result in a continuous transfer of electrons from one atom to the next, which we refer to as electrical current flow.

Electrons are very small! It takes 3.6 times ten to the 36th power electrons, (for those of you who can't comprehend scientific notation, I will write out the number in full: 3,600,000,000,000,000,000, 000,000,000.000,000,000) passing by one point in one second to be equivalent to one ampere of current.

Early forms of house wiring installed in the days before 1940 used a technique called "Knob and Tube" which utilized individual electrical conductors. Either the "Hot" or "Neutral" wire but not both together were pulled through bored holes in the framing members of a house using ceramic sleeves (the tubes) in the bored holes and a ceramic knob where the wire was anchored to enable other wires to be spliced to it.

Now hopefully you recall the magnetic field which is created when electrical current flows through conductors.

One more added bit of information is that just as our Earth and any magnets have NORTH and SOUTH magnetic poles or polarities, so the do conductors when current is flowing through them.

The direction the current flows in the wire determines the magnetic polarities of the magnetic fields developed and extending out from the conductor.

This said, you should deduce that the magnetic field produced around the "HOT" or source current wire will be opposite that produced around the "NEUTRAL" or return wire.

To make matters even more interesting, house current reverses direction and polarity every 1/60th of a second. That's why they call it "alternating current"!

Our modern wiring practices run both the HOT and NEUTRAL wires together in the same plastic sheath or conduit so the magnetic fields developed around each wire effectively cancel each other out, since opposites cancel both electrically and acoustically (with sound).

Experiments were done using animals to find out the effects of magnetic fields on their bodies. One experiment which placed small magnets around a cow's udder, proved to actually increase the fat content of the milk compared to previous milk fat averages.

Pigeons navigate by sensing changes of the Earth's magnetic field through magnetic field receptors under their wings. Their brains memorize the magnetic field patterns of the Earth and use that information to travel from place to place without getting lost. If it snows, they have to perch somewhere and wait 24 hours before they can again sense the magnetic fields on the surface of the Earth.

This fact was confirmed when small magnets were placed under the bird's wings which messed them up in their travels.

Light waves are actually a form of magnetic waves, although in the higher frequency ranges. Ultraviolet light waves coming from the Sun are actually repelled magnetically as they attempt to pass through the Van Allen radiation belt about 500 miles above the earth's surface. The main reason our radios work world wide is because the radio electromagnetic waves beamed into the sky from radio antennas are repelled by the ionosphere, a magnetically charged area high in our atmosphere. The radio waves effectively bounce off the ionosphere and are redirected to other continents below on the Earth.

It has been found that strong magnetic fields can actually retard healing in a body by causing a decrease in the formation of antibodies, although carefully controlled amounts of magnetic field strength make it possible to control unwanted cell growth as in certain types of cancers. In some instances magnetic fields generated by high frequency currents improved metabolism in test subjects.

Dr. E. Stanton Maxey, a surgeon in a Stuart, Florida hospital, found that human brain rhythms can be altered without the person knowing it by the application of weak magnetic waves. EEG's taken showed that rhythms in the subject's left brain hemisphere altered at once, remaining altered as long as the artificial magnetic field was applied. He explained that the intrusion of weak magnetic waves into our brains may help explain the causes of some accidents ascribed to pilot or driver error. Waves that can pass through metallic structures, such as cars or aircraft cabins, may influence mental activity in certain persons, prolonging their reaction times and decreasing their sense of awareness, creating ideal preconditions for an accident.

In 1962, using super cooled measuring instruments, the Russian histologist A.G. Gurvich's theory was confirmed that all cells give off and absorb ultraviolet light as a controlling mechanism of the cell. He proved that ultraviolet light caused cells to divide. Professor L. L. Vasiliev of the Leningrad Institute for brain research claimed he could cause nerve cells to give off ultraviolet light by electrical stimulation. An interesting experiment was done where identical tissue cells were placed in sealed glass containers separated by quartz to allow ultraviolet light to be passed from one container to the other. When the scientist introduced a virus to one container, the cells in the other container not open to the air of the other container also showed virus infection as if the virus was passed in the photon flux of ultraviolet light passed between the containers. One other doctor, V. Schjelderup, even suggested that when the virus appeared to be transferred from one container to the other through the medium of ultraviolet light waves, it was not actually the real virus but an electro-magnetic representation of it! But curiously, it had the same effect in contaminating the cells of the separated container with the disease.

This gives me the fuel for the basis of part of my story, plausible but did it really happen or could it be happening even as you read this?

Chapter -One-

Foundations of Electromagnetic energy - FOE or FRIEND???

*P*rofessor John Jameson stood before his class of 120 avid students for another of his technical lectures. He began to speak.

"Think for a moment about a typical day you or someone you know may experience. You finish your work day, turn out the OFFICE LIGHTS, take the ELEVATOR down to the parking lot where you UNLOCK and START your car with your REMOTE key chain fob. You get into your car, turn on the RADIO and drive toward home somewhat distracted by all of the NEON and FLUORESCENT LIGHTS advertising everything under the sun and having to negotiate all of the TRAFFIC LIGHTS along the way. You arrive home and hit the REMOTE again to operate your GARAGE DOOR OPENER. You go into the house, get a soda from the REFRIGERATOR, sit down in your MASSAGING EASY CHAIR, turn on the TV with a REMOTE and SWITCH CHANNELS to watch the weather channel which touts a seven day weather projection because of RADAR. In your short trip home you experienced just a small part of a not widely known inventor's contribution to mankind by the name of NIKOLA TESLA.

Because of my wide electrical and electronics background and training, I was drawn to do an extensive study on the inventor who made all these things possible. I am about to persuade you that Nikola Tesla is perhaps the greatest contributor to our modern day life than any other inventor.

He unearthed the foundations of electro-magnetism, literally!

Born in 1856, Yugoslavian-born Nikola Tesla was more than an inventor or a producer of new devices, he was a discoverer of new principles which even today have been only partly explored. He was a very rare creative genius. Our creator GOD who is the author of all technology gives to whom he pleases insights and visions of creative inventions. To Tesla, our Creator was very generous. Let's look first at Nikola in his early childhood.

Nikola always credited his amazing memory capability and his inventive ability to his mother who devised many household labor saving devices.

At age 4, he developed a crude water wheel from a round slab of tree trunk, a branch through a hole he made in the center, resting in a cradle made from other branches, fastened to a rock and suspended in a brook. He improved that idea into a steam turbine engine and a water turbine for generating electrical power in his later years.

At age 7, a new 16-man manual water pump for putting out house fires was to be demonstrated to his small community but they couldn't get it to work. Nikola didn't have the faintest idea of how the pump worked but got an intuitive flash of knowledge that told him to go to the hose in the river and straighten out the kink in the hose. He was the hero of the day!

At age 9, he experimented in original methods of power production. It was a sixteen bug-powered engine. He used sixteen June bugs connected with thread by a little glue in groups of four to each of four arms of a miniature windmill. The windmill drove a pulley about the size of a pea which was connected to a larger pulley. When the June bugs flapped their wings the large pulley developed surprisingly large torque.

At age 10, he entered college and discovered how he could harness the strange power he possessed at early childhood which he previously saw as more of a nuisance beyond his control. If he thought of an object, it would appear before him as a three dimensional form looking as if it were actually solid. It was often difficult for him to distinguish between vision and reality. He could perform unusual feats in mathematics. If he were given a math problem he was able to vision a blackboard on which the problem was written with all of the operations and symbols used in working out the problem. Each step appeared more rapidly than he could work it out by hand on his slate. He could give the solution almost as quickly as the whole problem was stated! His teachers soon ruled out the possibility that he was somehow cheating and were more than amazed. He studied twelve different languages and found them very easy to learn. In addition to his native language, he especially excelled in German, French and Italian. He loved to read so this opened up for him great stores of knowledge. He found he could recall at will whole pages of any book and read them word for word in his mind when he needed to consult a technical resource.

Even as a boy, Tesla was an original thinker and never hesitated to think thoughts on a grand scale.

At age 13 while in the mountains and involved in a snowball fight, he saw how a snowball, weighing a few ounces could start an avalanche. This convinced him that there are tremendous forces locked up in nature that can be released in gigantic amounts for useful as well as destructive purposes. He also saw a flash of lightning and thought that lightning controlled the rain and if one could produce lightning at will, the weather could be brought under control. Why could he not produce lightning, he thought? Tesla entered manhood with a definite knowledge that nameless forces were shaping for him an unrevealed destiny.

Nikola's view of himself was as merely an automaton (robot) that followed the directions he was supernaturally given to produce his inventions. He did not credit himself or his brain for any of the things he has done.

At age 19 he studied electrical engineering in Austria. At that time the only known electricity was direct current earlier discovered by Thomas Edison. Before he received his DC motor and generator as part of his studies, he was convinced the whole system could be simplified and improved. He had a vision of rotating electric and magnetic fields and this led him to develop the concept of the alternating current induction motor and AC generator as we know it today. There were not any supporters of his ideas though, but many critics. Tesla's college professor devoted his normal lecture time one day to talk about Nikola's proposed alternating current motor idea. He methodically picked it apart, one point at a time, demonstrating its impractical nature, ending with this statement, "Mr. Tesla will accomplish great things, but he certainly never will do this. It would be equivalent to converting a steady pulling force like gravity into rotary effort. It is a perpetual motion scheme, an impossible idea."

Nikola's ability to see things that he conceived in his mind as solid objects before him, which he considered to be a great annoyance in his childhood, now proved to be a great aid to him in trying to solve obstacles ahead. He could visualize these devices in three dimensions. Time after time, he created visual motors, able to trace the coils and see the changing currents until he made one that functioned as he knew it would. He worked out the design of AC generators, motors, transformers and all the other devices for a complete alternating current system. His mentally constructed devices were run-tested mentally for weeks, after which time he would examine them for wear. He could see if a rotor was out of balance or if something vibrated when it shouldn't. His memory would retain every detail. Five years later he would actually build the working models.

After graduation from the University of Prague, he found it necessary to become self-supporting. He heard about Alexander Graham Bell's new invention, the telephone and that a central station was to be installed in Budapest, Hungary. A friend of the family was the head of that enterprise.

Self assured, he traveled to Budapest expecting to be immediately employed as an engineer. When he got there, he discovered that the project was still in the discussion stage, so there was no job open for him. Of course, he had to support himself since he had no money to return to Yugoslavia, so he took the best job he could find working as a draftsman for the Hungarian Government. When they saw his outstanding abilities, they put him in charge of designing and making calculations and estimates for new telephone installations. A year later they put him in charge of the new telephone company when it started.

At age 25 while there in Budapest, he made his first invention then called a telephone repeater, which we now call a loud speaker. After a year, with a letter of recommendation from his college professor, he got a position with Continental Edison Company in Paris where he was eventually assigned the job of troubleshooter (basically to repair the blunders the company made in installing electrical powerhouses and lights).

While there, he had the time and machine shop equipment available to actually construct his alternating current motor. He was able to build it without working drawings, since he could project a picture before his eyes, complete in every detail of every part of the machine. He remembered exact dimensions which he had calculated mentally for each item. He did not even have to test parts through partial assembly because he knew they would fit.

When he was 28, he was invited to New York to work with Thomas Edison. That relationship didn't work out very well since Edison used trial and error to develop his inventions, while Tesla calculated everything mentally and solved his problems before doing any actual building of them. Edison wasn't favorable of Tesla's idea of alternating current, since that would be in direct competition with his direct current generating systems. Tesla designed 24 types of new generators, redesigned some inefficient ones and provided some automatic controls, for what he was told he would be paid $50,000. After he was done with his "contracted" work, Edison told him that he didn't understand American humor and it was all a practical joke since they didn't think he could do what he said he could. He broke off the working relationship and went off to form a company of his own.

He supported himself during that time by electrical repair work and ditch digging for $2/day. During that period he developed the neon and fluorescent lamps which offered greater illumination than Edison's incandescent lamps.

Some business man, who heard of his inventions and great hopes for his alternating current system put up some money to get him underway. He immediately started construction of a variety of pieces of electric machinery without blueprints and very soon had working units which he used to demonstrate the principles of his alternating current system. The induction motor which he had made while in Germany supplied proof that his ideas worked because it ran off alternating current. Tesla's AC generating systems, using transformers to boost the voltage up to very high values allowed generating stations to be placed 100's of miles apart with very few losses, while Edison's DC systems could only cover an area one mile in diameter.

Another inventor, a man named Westinghouse, offered to buy the patents and rights to Tesla's alternating current system for $1,000,000. Tesla accepted the offer involving transfer of ownership of 40 patents.

Westinghouse knew that he could make many times that in just a short time and was very happy with his wholesale bargain.

Now that Tesla was wealthy, he set his mind to experiment with all of the ideas he had not pursued yet. He said that he had so many ideas coming to him that it was like water backing up in a dam and not having any outlet.

When he received his vision of the rotating magnetic field, which was the principle of operation for his induction motor seven years earlier, he had also seen infinite variations of alternating currents which appeared to vibrate in a vast range of octaves. The lowest octave was 60 cycles per second which he used for his alternating current equipment. One of the higher octaves was visible light with its frequency of billions of cycles per second. His grand generalization was that everything in nature operated on the principle of vibrations that correspond to alternating currents.

His high frequency experiments were expanded on 20 years later and developed into high power wireless transmitters for transatlantic wireless transmission by the United States.

He lectured about the existence of cosmic rays and in 1901 filed for a patent that described our modern-day solar-voltaic cell which uses the sun's rays to produce electricity.

He also talked about another form of cosmic rays, later to be called X-Rays, but no one would believe his theory until rediscovered 35 years later repeated by three other scientists. He produced images taken from 40 feet away of the skull using plates in metal containers as film in 1895. This was the first X-Ray machine, although Roentgen later was given credit for inventing it, although his results were only possible if the patient's body part was only six inches away.

Tesla also is credited with discovering the atom smasher (which unfortunately was later used to make the atomic bomb) and the electron microscope.

He later came up with a device that allowed selective tuning to individual frequencies and developed the vacuum tube which led to a radio being developed that could both send and receive wireless messages.

Although Marconi is given credit for the first wireless radio transmission, he only accomplished this task by using over 19 of Tesla's patented ideas.

The surrounding population knew about Tesla's laboratory where often strange, mythical, magical and mysterious events took place and an equally strange man who was doing fearful and wonderful things with that dangerous secret agent known as electricity. Combining his high frequency experiments with his frequency tuner, or variable capacitor as we now call them and his coils, he discovered that the capacitor can be made to store a high frequency electric charge and then discharge it through a coil creating tremendously high voltage sparks. This application was used by Henry Ford when he developed his ignition system using contact points and a coil for his internal combustion engine.

Tesla advanced this concept to produce high voltage sparks to a larger scale and experimented with transmitting electrical energy without wires to power wireless lights and motors. All of the lights in his laboratory were wireless and could be placed anywhere in the building or carried around in hand.

Tesla experimented with a mechanical oscillator small enough to fit in your pocket and attached to a building support of his laboratory building. The quiet little vibration he presumed would occur actually caused a real earthquake in a dozen city square blocks, shattering panes of glass, breaking steam, gas and water pipes and moving factory equipment weighing tons from their bolted anchors. The city was built on sand so the vibrations were efficiently transmitted to the bedrock below and caused the earthquake. Miniature versions of that are now used to make electric massage devices. This vibration principle he declared could be used to detect and locate ore deposits far beneath the earth, or submarines or other ships at a distance, even though at anchor with no engines running. He was describing radar, which is widely used today.

Coupled with his radio invention, he demonstrated complete wireless remote control of a ship in a large tank. He expanded this remote control to complex machines which led to the development of the first mechanical robot which he demonstrated in 1896. The most recent development, in personalized form was the mechanical man, a metal human monster giant that walked, talked, smoked a cigarette and obeyed spoken orders, in the exhibit of the Westinghouse Electric and Manufacturing Company at the New York World's Fair.

In the early 1900's he expounded about his design of a radio controlled rocket, which was incidentally developed for WWII and used by the Germans to attack England.

In 1898 he proposed an idea of an automated assembly-line manufacturing plant for automobiles. Henry Ford adopted his idea of mass production and became wealthy from it in the years to come.

He (Tesla) figured that if he could transmit telegraph messages and modulations of the human voice any distance without wires, why can't we transmit power in unlimited amounts to any place on earth without loss? Then he got the idea on a mammoth scale to use the earth's iron core as both a capacitor and a huge coil, charging and discharging it rhythmically with high frequency, high voltage oscillations resulting in 100's of millions of volts being produced and transmit large amounts of electrical power world-wide by wireless methods. He received funding to build a giant wireless power transmitting station in Colorado Springs. On top of a 25 foot tall building, he built a tower 80 feet tall with a 200 foot mast extending from it, with a 3 foot diameter copper ball on the top which was connected with heavy copper wire to the equipment in the laboratory. Under the tower he mounted a huge oscillator coil of the type from which he earlier had caused high voltage sparks to erupt. When he performed his test, the result was a thin spark 10 feet long emitting from the copper ball with a resulting sound of repeated cannon blasts. This extended in steps of ten feet to more than 135 feet long and as thick as his arm accompanied by tremendous thunder heard 15 miles away. People walking along the streets in the town were amazed to see sparks jumping between their feet and the ground and flames of electricity would spring from a faucet when anyone turned them on for a drink of water. Light bulbs within 100 feet of the tower glowed when they were turned off. Butterflies became electrified and helplessly swirled in circles, their wings spouting blue halos of

"St. Elmo's Fire". The lightning continued until the generator in the city's electric power station burned up. He paid to have it replaced with a larger one if they would permit him to continue with his tests. He demonstrated transmitting power in this manner 26 miles to light two hundred 50 watt incandescent lamps, claiming an efficiency of more than 95%. He claimed that this could work even at a distance of a few thousand miles simultaneously anywhere on the globe.

He received some new funding from a very rich man named J. P. Morgan and proceeded to design a new tower. This one was 154 feet high with a copper doughnut shaped top 100 feet in diameter and 20 feet high. He envisioned a complete world-wide electrical distribution system, supplying electrical power, music, telephone, registration of time by cheap precise clocks requiring no attention ever, fax service for letters and checks, ship navigation service (requiring no compass, able to determine exact location, hour and speed to prevent collisions and disasters), world wide printing on land and sea and reproduction of pictures and all kinds of drawings or records. "An inexpensive receiver, not bigger than a watch, will enable him to listen anywhere, on land or sea, to a speech delivered or music played in some other place, however distant." predicted Nikola Tesla.

He couldn't find anyone who would be willing to construct the strange donut-shaped dome, so the project came to a standstill. Worse yet, his financiers, being affected by some negative opposition to his grandiose ideas of a world-wide electrical system, decided not to continue financing his project.

It has been brought out that Edison was spreading ill-will in the form of negative comments and distorted rumors about Tesla in order to discourage his financiers and his progress, since his progress threatened his own livelihood marketing his own DC electrical transmission systems and components.

Tesla didn't have a finance manager or pursue development and sale of products relating to any of his more than 200 other patents. Any one of them would have made him a millionaire many times over, but because he was so engrossed in his experimenting, he soon ran out of money. His world-wide wireless system crashed and he was forced to focus on finances for a few years and sell patents to raise some money.

In 1900, Tesla built another tower 187 feet high with a 55 ton, 68 foot diameter metal dome.

Tesla's writings have many references to the use of his wireless power transmission technology as a directed energy weapon. Tesla said his transmissions could produce 100 million volts and 1000 amps with power levels of a billion or tens of billions of watts. If that amount of power were released in a comparatively small interval of time, the energy would be equal to the explosions of millions of tons of TNT, a multi-megaton explosion. Such a transmitter would be capable of projecting the force of a nuclear warhead by radio. Any location in the world could be vaporized at the speed of light. Statements from authorative witnesses who saw Tesla's equipment in operation support his claim about transmitting something other than Hertz waves (conventional alternating current) but by using radiations. Circumstantial evidence found in the dates of Tesla's work and financial fortunes between 1900 and 1908 points to there having been a test of this weapon.

In 1906-1907, Tesla suffered an emotional collapse. In order to make a final effort to have his grand scheme recognized he may have tried a high power test of his transmitter to show off its destructive potential.

Admiral Peary was reported to be attempting to traverse the ice by dogsled to reach the North Pole during this period and would certainly be in the lime light should he be successful in his venture. It is supposed that Tesla may have attempted to steal the show away from the Admiral by launching an electromagnetic projectile of tremendous explosive power and strike the North Pole before he reached it. There would be no disputing of the fact of his capability when an almost famous explorer would verify and quantify his weapon development and report it to the world. If this is true, then he aimed high and overshot the North Pole and hit an area of Siberia in northern Russia called Tunguska, since that area was hit on June 30, 1908. An explosion equivalent to 10-15 megatons of TNT flattened 500,000 acres of pine forest near the Stony Tunguska River in Central Siberia. Whole herds of reindeer were vaporized along with several villages completely vanishing off the earth. The explosion was heard over a radius of 620 miles. No impact crater was found. Several explanations have been offered for the event. The officially accepted version is that a 100,000 ton fragment of Encke's comet entered the atmosphere, heated up and exploded causing a fireball and shock wave but no crater, although no fiery object was reported in the skies at that time by professional or amateur astronomers and no fragments of rock were ever found, even test bore holes as deep as 128 feet revealed no fragments. Other explanations include a renegade mini-black hole or an alien space ship crashing into the earth with the resulting release of energy.

A scientist in Holland told of an "undulating mass" moving across the northwest horizon. The sky seemed to pulse with light. A woman north of London wrote the London Times that on Midnight of July 1st, the sky glowed so brightly it was possible to read large print inside her house with the lights off. Twilight lasted until daybreak on July 1st - there was no real darkness. It was possible to see ships clearly for several miles in the middle of the night.

In 1915, Tesla seems to confess to such a test having previously taken place when he stated bluntly, "It is perfectly practical to transmit electrical energy without wires and produce destructive effects at a distance. I have already constructed a wireless transmitter which makes this possible....But when unavoidable (it) may be used to destroy property and life."

Was the explosion near Siberia the result of a meteorite nobody saw fall or was it Tesla's test? What do you think? Could this be our future star wars weapon?

At his death, the FBI confiscated all of his notes and plans in his safe in case there was some unannounced discovery that could be used by the U.S. for defense purposes. Some notes that have been released have 90% of the contents blacked out. In them is a statement that a letter from President J. Edgar Hoover was sent to a person who's name was blacked out, stating that the FBI has never been in possession of Dr. Tesla's papers. What information are they hiding?

If you really want some interesting reading, do some research about the "Philadelphia Experiment" involving Tesla. It was reported that in a secret experiment in cooperation with the US Navy, Tesla reportedly vaporized a complete ship and hundreds of crewmembers and transported them in mere seconds over a hundred miles from a port in Philadelphia, Penn. to a harbor in New York and then back again using electromagnetic means. The mental shock of such a particle beam transportation experience put many of the crew in mental institutions for quite some time. It was rumored that when the ship was returned to Philadelphia, some of the crew members had not properly reformed bodily but were imbedded in the ship's hull or deck and could not be saved from immediate death."

"Tomorrow class, I'll be lecturing on the cause and effects of lightning, much of which has been unknown until recently. See you promptly at 9 AM. Have a great day!"

CHAPTER
-Two -

The principles and effects of lightning

𝓟rofessor Jameson gathered his wits about him as he strode toward the podium for his morning lecture. He looked forward to watching the expression on the faces of his students change from bored or disinterest to that of attentive wonder and amazement. After he was sure that he had the students' attention, he began to speak:

"Have you ever been out in a storm and your hair stood on end? That is a danger sign that lightning is about to strike in your vicinity and you need to seek protection immediately! If you are unable to get indoors, you need to assume a position such as this, with your head being lower than the rest of your body. Do not lie on the ground! If instead, you decide to surrender to the idea of experiencing enlightenment and conversion into a friar and hold your hands up to the sky then, you might see purple flames sprouting from your fingertips just before you were struck by a lightning bolt.

I am an avid student of lightning and in my contractor days have been employed by organizations and homeowners to provide a solution to their problem of a history of lightning strikes.

I am about to tell you what causes lightning, how it damages 100's of millions of dollars of personal property each year, how to prevent or at least reduce your losses from a lightning strike and about the benefits of lightning.

All matter including air is made up of small particles called atoms. As an example, I'll use a penny so you can make some cents of how small those little atoms are.(The students groan at another pun) A penny contains 30 sextillion copper atoms. That's a 3 with 22 zeros after it! To make cents out of that, let's imagine atoms were the size of marbles. The number of atoms in this penny would cover the earth 8 feet deep! You might say that if people have gone centsless, they REALLY have lost their marbles!

Atoms have smaller particles orbiting their center, called electrons, much like the planets revolve around our Sun. They are continually jumping from atom to atom in whatever material they make up. Additional electrons can be added to their orbits from other materials. You most likely have experienced that phenomenon in the winter when you shuffle your feet across a carpet and then get a shock when you touched a door knob. The action of shuffling your feet caused electrons from the carpet to add to the atoms composing the insulated soles of your shoes. Insulation doesn't allow electrons to flow as in a wire, but merely collects them, All objects of the earth desire to be normally electrically neutral, so when you touch a door knob which has fewer electrons, the excess electrons stored in your shoe soles escape through your body via your finger to the knob. Something similar happens in the air.

Air is basically an insulator and is always changing. Cold air falls while warm air rises, producing wind. As the wind blows across stationary objects such as buildings, trees and so on, electrons are stripped off the atoms in the objects and collected in the wind. Moisture from the earth evaporates in the normal water cycle and is carried up into the sky with the warm convection air currents. Eventually a cloud is formed with the concentrations of moisture and excess electrons.

The loss of electrons in objects on the ground makes them more electrically positive (less negative) than the clouds and are a natural thing for the cloud to discharge to return to its normal electrically neutral state again.

When you touched the doorknob, there wasn't any insulation between your finger and the knob. It's a different story between a cloud and the earth with many miles of insulating air between. The discharge starts with a jet of electrons in the form of a lightning bolt being formed in the cloud and attempting to reach the earth. It makes it only about 150 feet the first try, burning a hole through the air as it goes. The oxygen and nitrogen in the air are converted into plasma, resembling a purple flame that allows the electrons to move through it more easily.

A by-product called ozone is formed from the burning of the air. This process continues in 150 foot steps until the bolt gets within 450 feet of the earth. At that point, the electrical field is so strong that it attracts a jet of electrons from the earth in the form of another bolt of lightning which launches to meet the bolt coming from the sky. This completes the path from the cloud to the ground in the form of a long twisty plasma rod. Immediately, other bolts are launched from the cloud at the speed of light (186,000 miles per second) in short intervals to reach the earth in one step until the charge in the cloud is emptied.

Of course, the rain follows. Once you pull the cork, the water has to follow!

The total charge in the cloud can be as much as 100 million volts and 250,000 amps which is enough to light a 100 watt light bulb for 289 days!

There must be a minimum of 1000 to 2000 thunder storms active at any given time to maintain the earth's electrical balance.

What happens when the lightning completes its strike? Physical damage to buildings, trees and electrical equipment occurs when lightning strikes. Circuit breaker boxes are blown off walls and their contents instantly melted. Combustible objects may explode due to immediate expanding of their molecular fibers or catch on fire since the bolt is 20,000 to 50,000 degrees centigrade which is 3-6 times hotter than the Sun. Electrical or electronic devices within 10 miles of a strike can be damaged or destroyed from high voltages and resulting high currents as expanding magnetic and electrical fields are induced into their circuits.

How can we protect or reduce our losses to personal property? To reduce loss to personal property we can use ion dissipation devices to protect buildings, lightning rods or specialized electronic components to route lightning around individual pieces of electrical equipment and install a proper unified building grounding system. Ion dissipation devices produce a steady stream of ions into the sky to provide a path to continually drain a cloud preventing a lightning bolt from forming. Lightning rods can be mounted on the roof of a building to divert a lightning strike to the earth should a building be hit by a strike. With this protection alone, electrical and electronic equipment inside the building will still be damaged from induced currents in the air and ground entering the building wiring as though the wiring itself was an antenna. Varistors are used to route lightning current around electrical equipment to ground thereby protecting them from damage. Varistors breakdown and become a low resistance path when a voltage higher than their rating is applied to them and divert any excess voltage to ground. Lightning rods and varistors act to divert individual lightning projectiles to ground. Depending upon the quality of the building grounding system, if a huge attack of lightning happened all at once, the best designed protection may still fail. A well designed single point grounding system is critical for protection to be at all effective.

What is thunder? We hear it with most rainstorms, but what causes it? My parents used to joke with me that it must be from the angels bowling in heaven. That was when I started thinking that lightning was right down my alley and deserved further study. I saw the light right then and there to keep my mind out of the gutter and follow the straight and narrow path. Thunder is actually generated by the superheating of the air as the lighting bolt passes through it. This compresses the surrounding air, producing a shock wave as the compressed air expands again making a booming sound as the wave decays.

How in the world can there be benefits of lightning? Water in a river cleans itself after running over rocks for 20 miles literally scrubbing itself, but how does air get cleaned? As you recall, ozone is a by product of the lightning arcing its way to the earth. Ozone cleans the air of impurities. There are more natural impurities discharged into the air from volcanic eruptions and forest fires each year than all factory and car pollutants in the world combined. You're probably familiar with room air cleaners. They are actually mini lightning producers, producing an electrical arc resulting in the manufacture of ozone which cleans the air. Ozone also filters out harmful ultraviolet rays from the sun entering our atmosphere which can cause skin cancer. The ozone layer is being continually replenished by 8 million lightning flashes each day all over the world, although only 1 million 600 thousand reach the ground.

Now that you have the tools to deal with and understand lightning, using them is the final step. Today we have learned what causes lightning, a normal process of the earth's desire to maintain a neutral electrical state, what kinds of damage can occur from a strike, how to prevent or at least reduce your losses to personal property from a strike, and that lightning has great benefits for our lives.

The next time you are out in a storm, get out of it to a protected place and think about the magnificent, powerful and cleansing process of lightning."

As Professor Jameson finished his lecture, he could detect a cloud of disappointment come over the students faces as they seemed to be expecting yet more. "I don't see anyone of you bolting from your seats to leave, so you must have enjoyed yourself today! But as much as I hate to "RAIN" on your parade, you need to get to your next class session.", the Professor said with a grin.

He really enjoyed imagining the wheels spinning inside their heads as the students listened, comprehended and visualized the verbal pictures he painted with his techno jibe as some called it.

As he picked up his lecture notes and started toward his office he couldn't help but get excited about the 4 year old boy he and his wife Mary were soon to adopt.

Both he and Mary married late in life due to careers being more important than family life, but lately the idea of a family seemed high on both their priority lists. They had contacted The Child Adoption Service a year or so ago with hopes of finding a suitable child and had gotten a call just the day before about a match. Their child was from Yugoslavia. He was an orphan, an only child of a peasant farmer couple who were killed during a rebel uprising of terrorists who ventured through his small community killing everyone but him. It appears that Nicolus, or Nick as they might call him until he reached adult age, was playing, or experimenting, as he would say, near an abandoned mine and was not aware of the mass slaughter and burning of the community until he returned home at dusk as he had been instructed in the past. "Nick" was only 4 years old but seemed to have somehow obtained wisdom well beyond anyone they knew, even most well educated adults.

Professor Jameson secretly wondered if Nick might be actually smarter than he. It seemed strange to him thinking of consulting his 4 year old on technical subjects, but at the same time he was excited at the adventure ahead and what he could offer to his son, if nothing else, love of which he had much stored up.

Mary his wife, was also a Professor, but at a medical college in the same town of Hardtford, Connecticut. Her specialty was diseases and methods of preventing them which she was called upon to lecture daily to hundreds of medical students. She also loved to listen to her husband talk about technical things and she understood his thinking, for the most part. That's what had drawn her to him after all, not to mention he was the best looking man in town and could make her laugh like no other person could. His humor always seemed so spontaneous and fresh all the time and didn't seem to be "canned" humor like most other self proclaimed humorists. This was perhaps one of the things she loved about him most of all. After all laughter is great medicine, proven medically to enhance healing of disease of all sorts, including broken hearts... and that was where her heart was before she met John.

She had been married once before to a chemist who died from a brain tumor just after their 20th wedding anniversary and childless. She was convinced it was caused by his frequent contact with all of those chemicals he was handling and/or breathing during his 30 years as a chemist. Oh well, at least the ones after him know to take extra precautions and safety measures have been instituted to prevent further illnesses in the future. That was the only consoling thing she could think about his death. She hated the thought of many workers unknowingly and dutifully working as guinea pigs until the things they are working with are classified as being toxic and unsafe. By that time it's too late, but that's all part of the chemical business I'm told. There are unknown hazards in every occupation, even in the medical field as she has discovered. She once nearly got hepatitis when a nurse slipped on a wet spot and released her grip on an infected needle which as hazards have it, ended up in her arm as she casually passed by on a tour of the floor. She recently had her shots, so she was fortunate, but accidents do happen.

It was on her 21st wedding anniversary she'd met her John. She had faced widowhood already for a year, and as the song goes, "Rainy days and Mondays always" got her down.

On June 30, the day was overcast, rain was likely and it was a Monday, so, guess what? A brisk walk in the park almost always lifted her spirits. She saw her John taking a shortcut through the park on his way to one of his daily lectures and she had noticed him before. Who wouldn't? Tall, handsome, square shouldered posture, that humorous glint in his eyes....... Well, she tried to quickly dry her eyes since she had been crying, but what's the difference, it was raining out anyway, so who could tell?

He'd greeted her with that fantastic smile of his and right then and there she was slain. He'd advised her that it was raining and sitting under that tree on that metal park bench was probably not a wise choice at this juncture in time since there was thunder in the distance. He'd hate for her to get her beautiful hair frizzed from a close lightning strike or worse yet acquire a well done appearance. He told her it would spoil the most gorgeous face he'd ever seen. That was it, she was slain and buried! She was his for ever! He must have sensed something serious in the chemistry area also since he stopped by her office the next day to "ask" her a medical question that was best answered over dinner. It's been ten years of bliss ever since. She still gets heart flutters when he as much comes in the same room. His presence makes her spirit want to fly but it's trapped in her body for a while yet. She truly enjoys that feeling of butterflies in her tummy every time he comes near and she knows it's not butterflies! Some day our spirits will fly away together, she thought, but hope it's many years to come, although some days she finds herself murmuring, "Lord come quickly, it's getting awfully hard to live down here!"

Yes, meeting John was the best medicine for her heart!

As John had mentioned to her one day of his thoughts about adopting, She realized also that God had given her so much love that she thought she had some left over for one more in her heart too. That's when they agreed to visit the adoption center. She felt a bit nervous. That old feeling of the unknown and new.

CHAPTER
-THREE -

The "Nick" of time

*J*ohn and Mary anxiously awaited Nick's arrival! It was suggested to them by the adoption agency that they should wire enough funds in U.S. currency to enable their son to get his exit visa, No citizens were allowed out of the country unless they proved they had the funds and means to do so. This law was to cut down on slave trafficking. Since Nick's parents were dead and he had no other known living relatives and it was pretty unrealistic to expect a 4 year old no matter how smart he was, to raise three thousand dollars in a week's time, or even in few years with the average yearly income being about 600 dollars for a 7 day week working from sunup to sundown... They were a bit surprised to be asked at the last minute to add another $100 to cover the extra weight charges for some electronic equipment he desired to take with him. They tried to imagine a 4 year old in Yugoslavia owning a Nintendo or video games, but

$100 for light things like that? They finally understood when they were told that Nick had an elaborate shortwave radio and satellite communication system and the most powerful computer anyone has ever known even for sophisticated American scientists to ever dream of owning. Where he got this equipment from, who could guess? Maybe from a crashed U.S. or Russian spy plane perhaps that Nick had discovered in his backyard? Nick's resourcefulness was becoming evident, but why drag that stuff all over here to the U.S, if he didn't even know how to operate it? But according to Nick, he does and rather well at that.

Was he really only just 4 years old? Some countries don't keep very good track of birthdates, so his age may be a few years off....... All of these questions will be answered soon once he got settled in their home. How is Nick going to get from his burned out village to the closest international airport 100 miles away and how was the adoption agency even communicating with him? They were quite amazed to discover that the adoption agency had been communicating directly with Nick via his shortwave radio setup and he said without hesitation that he planned to *WALK* the 100 miles with a borrowed donkey to carry his equipment! John found a secure bank to wire Nick's money to right in the airport itself and asked the adoption agency to get that communication to him before he left. Lord knows where the poor boy had been living these past months, although they imagined in his resourcefulness he may even have returned to the mines where he performed his "experiments" and lived there off mushrooms and wild game. They had no idea even in their wildest imagination what to expect from this already "adult" 4 year old! They tried to figure how long it would take him to walk the 100 miles to the airport. Let's see, at a good pace and having to maybe drag a mule that far, maybe averaging 2-3 miles per hour at the most, that would take him between 33 and 50 hours. Twenty miles in a day on level ground would be more than most adventurers would settle for let alone a 4 year old! But they kept forgetting that they were talking about Nick, but nonetheless they weren't going to start worrying until they hadn't heard anything in a week. Every day they prayed for his safety and speedy trip. Nobody even mentioned to them of the possibilities of him running into bandits or even the same terrorists who killed his parents! They prayed that God would send many guardian angels to protect Nick on his journey, although they had the funny thought that the angels might actually get in Nick's way and slow him down! Each minute they prayed for Nick the more their love grew for him even though they hadn't even met him yet!

The next days seemed like eternity and concentration on either of their teaching jobs was near impossible. Together as they discussed about the thousands of angels Nick might have protecting him, they were probably more in need of God's help just to make it through the week! They spent the evenings trying to decorate their spare bedroom and after three tries decided to leave it alone and let him decide his decor when he arrived. Who knows, he may have a preference to the cave or mine look and there's no telling what that was! For all they knew he never even knew what a house was and would rather live in a tent in the back yard until he got acclimated.

"Lord give us wisdom!" was all they could pray, and one more time, "Lord, you probably got him covered, but keep him safe OK?"

In just three days they got word from the adoption agency that Nick had called while still on the trail using some sort of solar cell powered battery setup and thought he had just one more day to go before he reached the airport. He said that he did pass some band of men who looked like roving bandits but when they approached him, they turned and fled like he was some sort of monster. That had to be the angels at work they thought and in one voice shouted praise to God for his traveling mercies for Nick.

Lord knows what Nick was finding to eat and feeding his borrowed donkey, but that seemed to be the least of Nick's concerns or of God's for that matter. The way He works, he had no trouble feeding millions of Israelites for 40 years in the wilderness and making their shoes and clothes never wear out! To not trust in God after this experience would be unthinkable!

Nick called on his shortwave radio the next afternoon to leave word that he had arrived at the airport and got the money they cabled to the bank there but he was experiencing a delay in getting his exit papers. In the process of searching for any living relatives which he told authorities he had none, they still insisted in doing a thorough search and providing him with an interesting family tree showing his great grand parents he had never heard about. He was pleased that his great grandfather's name was close to his...Nikola. He still didn't know his last name as his parents never told him and besides, he was going to be a Jameson after all, so who cared now?

John thought to himself, could it be possible? Maybe.....his great grandfather was Nikola Tesla? That would explain his magnificent wisdom at such a young age. Well they still weren't sure how old he REALLY was, but it was still an interesting thought!

The adoption agency somehow managed to contact a representative from the American Embassy there to act as an advocate for Nick to aid in speeding up the exit process. The advocate expected all of the red tape to be completed by the end of the day and John wasn't surprised to hear that the next connecting flight to the U.S. wasn't until the next evening. His first flight would bring him through Paris and then on to New York and with the time changes he would actually be arriving in New York International by this afternoon! John and Mary decided to relieve their stress by making the drive to New York instead of waiting for him to arrive in their local airport. Neither John or Mary had any fluency in the Hungarian language, so they tried to locate a translator near the airport to make the meeting a bit smoother. They arrived an hour early to meet the translator but a message was waiting for them when they got to the airport terminal that the translator was to be delayed a few hours at least due to car trouble. John and Mary decided then and there that God would have to intervene and help them to at least use crude sign language until they got acquainted. They had no idea what Nick looked like or what to expect, but a kind stewardess escorted him out of the plane and announced his arrival on the loud speaker that he would meet them at Gate 75. When they got to the Gate, a good looking woman in the attire of a stewardess approached them and spoke to them in broken French/English.

"Mr. and Mrs. Jameson? I had the most pleasurable time in my life talking with your son Nicolus. He is so gifted in languages! He learned both French and English on the flight over! He is quite the extraordinary boy!"

"Yes, we know! And thanks for watching over him during the flight!" John replied.

"Just the opposite", replied the stewardess, "I've never felt safer in all of my 10 years of flights as I did today. It seemed like angels must have been assigned to guide the plane, it went so smoothly. It was uncanny!"

Mary had a glint in her eye as they turned to walk with their new son and his cart full of electronic equipment. John didn't notice any U.S. or Russian stampings on any of the equipment Nick was pushing on his cart, so he finally got up the nerve to break the ice by attempting to ask him about his equipment.

"May we call you Nick, Nicolus?" John asked.

"Yes, you may, if that is what you would like. May I call you Mom and Dad?" Nick replied.

"Why of course son, I mean Nick!" John said with surprise in his voice.

"You seem shocked at my English ability, Dad. I learned Greek and Latin during my week-long trip to the airport from some books I found in the Bandits camp after they left so hastily, and thought they might not find them if they returned the way the dust was blowing so I took them with me and read them. I'd figured to give them to the authorities at the airport and they maybe could find the owners and get them returned. They probably were stolen anyway. Latin and Greek are the basis for the English language and I confirmed that after talking with the representative from the American Embassy who was very helpful in getting my exit visa papers process taken care of faster. I figured it would be easier for me to learn your language than for you to try to learn Hungarian at your ages. No offense meant at that, OK?"

Both John and Mary listened with rapt amazement and awe.

"No offense taken, Nick!" They both said, "You were correct in your assumption!"

All of their previous fears of communication problems seemed to disappear in a flash.

As they traversed the many walkways and escalators to the parking level, John blurted out without thinking.......

"You don't drive yet, do you? Didn't learn that in those books did you? I know when I first got in this new car the communications system seemed like Greek to me......"

"That's funny, right Dad?" Nick asked respectfully. "I like a good joke at least every other day....I spend much of my time alone and already know my jokes, but I still tell myself one once in a while just to remember how to laugh!" Nick smiled and gave a shrug of his shoulders.

John put his arm around the boy and said,

"Nick, it seems like I've known you all of my life already! I know I certainly am going to love every second getting to know you again, but this time better!"

Mary thought to herself that this was one statement she had to get clarified when they were finally alone, just she and her John. During the three-hour trip to their home John couldn't wait to find out about the origin of his electronic equipment. Mary was still in shock regarding Nick's language capability, and frankly their lack of it!

"Nick, where did you find that fantastic looking equipment you brought with you?" John asked.

"I made it," replied Nick.

After a few moments of shocked silence John responded, "You made them?"

"Yes, Dad. I found some parts here and there, in the mines and caves and some of the recycling dumps and modified some parts to improve their functionality, but yes, I made them!" Nick replied as a matter of fact.

John, used to his shock by now, asked again, "But how did you know HOW to do it? Did you find some other books somewhere?"

Nick replied, "No, I just somehow knew how to do it. It all seemed to come so naturally like I had done it a number of times before, but after a while, I stopped wondering and just did it! It works, that's all I care about! I'll probably have to update it someday in the near future, but it's OK for now." Nick replied humbly, then continued, "My real dad didn't seem to understand any of the stuff I was doing, so I just worked at it out of a cave near the mines in my spare time, and that's all I had since my parents wouldn't let me work anywhere! They kept on saying I was too young! I couldn't understand their reasoning in that!"

Both John and Mary could only shake their heads in wonder.

John couldn't wait to introduce Nick to his students and coworkers..... Heck, Nick would probably be lecturing on Quantum theory and some new technology he hadn't even considered by next week! John thought to himself. He wasn't too concerned about his job security since it would take Nick at least a few weeks, maybe a few months to get his PHD in Quantum Physics. Maybe longer if they kept him distracted....and the college doesn't hire instructors without a recognized PHD. There may not be much sleeping going on tonight, John thought to himself as they arrived in their driveway, but quickly changed his mind as he saw Nick fast asleep in the backseat. Nick's going to get some sleep! He must be exhausted! He carried the boy's 50 pound frame into his own bedroom painted in neutral white and tucked him into bed. He didn't bat an eye until noon the next day. Both John and Mary lay in bed totally wide awake, still in shock, hardly knowing what to speak even to each other. After about three hours they too finally dozed off until the sun peeked through the open shades and awakened them both. Mary was the first to speak.

"John, did all that I think really happen yesterday?"

John replied, "If what I think is the same as what you think, yes!"

"Amazing!" was all they could say.

They both jumped out of bed and tiptoed down to Nick's room and he was still asleep in his bed, his ruffled hair partly covering his brown eyes. A look of contentment was on his countenance and they couldn't even try to think of the deep thoughts that must have been forming in his mind even as he slept.

"Sleep sweet, dear one!" They both whispered and left quietly to the kitchen for a wakeup cup of coffee.

They both blurted out in unison, "Think he drinks coffee? We'll have to ask him when he wakes up!"

It was hard not to treat him as his size and age would traditionally warrant. It was like he was his great grandfather reincarnated!

Suddenly Mary answered her own question of clarification she had mentally noted to ask John later. Nick seemed to have the wisdom of the ages packed into his little brain. Was this inherited or simply a rebirth of an inventor given another chance to change the world? Whatever the case, the world is certainly going to be a better place once Nick is introduced to it! The reassuring thing about Nick is that there didn't seem to be a speck of guile or selfishness or hate in the boy, All Mary could sense was an overfilling in his spirit of love and compassion for mankind and she hoped that there would be some for Motherkind also where she was concerned.

Nick finally awoke at noon and his first words were, "The ground is slippery in here!" as he took his first step of the day onto the polished hardwood floor.

"I need to find something to eat, I'm starving!"

John got up, followed by Mary to head to the bedroom to rescue Nick from the slippery ground he was experiencing and to direct him into the kitchen for some breakfast. He hadn't experienced indoor bathrooms before and it may seem strange for a few days to relieve himself indoors, but if that was the most he had to worry about for a while, life would be quite easy. Eggs and bacon made Nick feel right at home, except he didn't have to go out to the shed and slice it off the pig before he saw it get cooked. Refrigerators...the simple principle of a gas expanding, absorbing heat and then releasing the heat on the outside of a sealed box is a concept he had pondered one day in the cave, but he hadn't stumbled upon a pump powerful enough to pull a vacuum so he could make his own refrigerator box for his parents. It's easy in the U.S. when you don't have to make everything. Just go down to the local hardware store and pick one out of a number of different sizes already made for you. The only thing they ask for it is some of that paper money that they give you at the bank. So Easy!

Mary decided it was as good time as any to ask Nick how he would like to decorate his room. She secretly hoped he would like to help her do the decorating so she could spend some creative moments with him.

Nick's reply somewhat surprised her.

"Decorate my room? What for? It's got everything I need in it already! I've got a very nice bed, a place to hang my clothes at night...you know, on that chair by the desk, it's perfect for draping my clothes over! Everything's perfect as it is, Mom! But if you would like to change the color that's all right with me...whatever makes you happy!"

Mary decided that it was a bit of a culture shock for Nick to come here and she would have to wait a few weeks or months for him to get used to living in a house and having his own room and eventually would understand the value and joy of decorating. The next day as John woke up with the birds, he went in to use the bathroom and passed Nick at the kitchen table with what appeared to be his electric shaver in many small pieces.

"Oh, Good Morning Dad! I'll have your shaver fixed in a couple of minutes. It was making some noise so I thought I'd better fix it for you....." Nick said with a grin.

John replied, "You mean a humming, whirring noise?"

Nick replied, "Yes, that nasty noise!"

John responded incredulously, "It's SUPPOSED to make that noise!"

"Not if I can help it!" replied Nick.

In a few minutes Nick returned his dad's razor to him. It felt a little lighter. He turned it on and it made no noise. Nick broke it, he thought to himself! I can't scold him for his attempt to fix something he doesn't understand! Just then he got the urge to trust Nick and rolled the razor over his rough night's beard growth and it disappeared noiselessly before his eyes. "Well, I'll be!" He exclaimed.

"You'll be what?" asked Nick.

"I'll be a fool next time I don't believe you can do what you say you can." John replied.

Nick walked by on his way to the garage and handed his father a small pile of left over parts that were the cause of the excess noise and apparently were unnecessary after all in a smooth functioning razor.

Nick was excited to finally see that marvel called an electric motor he had heard so much about and couldn't wait to see how it actually worked and if it could be improved upon. There must be a number of those electric motors in the garage as that's where he read most dads kept them.

John quickly spoke his fears as they came to mind.....

"Nick, don't touch the car because I need it to drive to and from work today. If you want you can look at it this Saturday since I don't plan on going anywhere for the whole day!"

Nick's reply was, "Ok, Dad, I was going to ask you about that tonight after you got home from work! Maybe I can see where you teach someday next week, huh dad?"

"Sure, son," replied John a bit overwhelmed. "Oh Nick?"

"Yes dad", Nick respectfully answered.

"Make sure if you work on anything powered make sure it's disconnected from the electric power, OK?" John added for his peace of mind.

"Yes Dad, I've already thought about that safety fact, but thanks for your concern...." Nick replied.

As John opened his car door to drive to work, he thought to himself, "Taught himself Latin, Greek, English and French, in a week's time, never seen high tech stuff in his life but just naturally KNOWS how to build 'em, and redesign what probably took engineers ten years to figure out, and his works better! My God, if I could have only half of his smarts!"

God spoke to him in his spirit in a tone of slight chastisement, "Maybe I gave you too much as it is..."

"Sorry for complaining, God! I really like the brain you gave me, really I do!" He replied as he drove off, "Humility never hurt anyone!" he encouraged himself.

Chapter
-Four -

The Imperfect Sun

*P*rofessor John Jameson stood at the podium before his class of 121 students. One more student than usual today, as Nick had asked to be able to tour his work place and sit in on one of his dad's lectures. Professor Jameson's lecture was the highlight of most students in the college and the circulating joke was that his students had to bring a note to their doctor from their teacher to permit them to miss an appointment should it be scheduled during a lecture and not the reverse as usual. The professor had a room in isolation with piped in sound and video just for that purpose if students would come to class sick. All students in the technology center scheduled their day around Jameson's lecture periods. To miss his lectures would be to miss out on life in all of its excitement. None of Jameson's lectures were permitted to be taped since his lectures were copyrighted and books published each year by the professor from his lectures. So if you missed a lecture you had to wait until the book came out the next spring and buy it. Then you missed out on all of the professor's spontaneous jokes interspersed throughout his lectures and humorous bunny trails toured when a student would ask an unrelated question. Jameson didn't seem to mind unrelated questions since they often gave him new ideas for future lectures and peaked other student's interests in doing their own research on intriguing topics. Everyone knew Jameson was about to start his lecture as he had finished organizing his notes on the podium. Everyone knew by now that this was a good sign to become quiet and listen attentively.

He began with this:

"Quoting from a song made once famous by singer Dean Martin....................

'Everybody loves somebody sometime..... everybody needs someone to care......'

Every body affects every body. Let me clarify that. If I walk into class with an angry snarl or frown on my face, my appearance, even my presence, affects your mood and your outlook on the day.

(Students began wondering if they were being scolded for something they did or didn't do).

If YOU walk into my classroom with a scowl or a frown it doesn't affect my day as much because I am the one in power and authority and I can overlook that, dismiss it if you will, because I am more powerful than you and of a higher order in creation, being a human being, with reasoning and compassion and can go on with my day as if nothing happened. I am bigger than you are so I affect you. Such it is with our solar system. The big guy I am going to talk about today is our Sun and how it affects us, and yes even our moods!"

The students' expressions relaxed now since they knew now that he wasn't going to scold them about anything.

"We talk about things such as Sunrises and Sunsets, but does the Sun actually go anywhere? When I was younger I used to often wonder where the Sun went when it set and then one day, actually, one morning, it finally "dawned" on me! It's the rotation of the Earth that makes the Sun appear to rise and set. Our orbit is not round but elliptical (egg shaped) so when we get to the bottom of the egg in our orbit it's winter and when at the top it's summer, taking 365 days to make the circle orbit around the Sun and 23 hours and 58 minutes to make one rotation on our own axis at an angle of 23 1/3 degrees. Only a 2 degree shift in our tilt would cause the polar icecaps to melt and the equator to become so hot it would be inhabitable.

The Sun weighs 335,000 times that of Earth, its diameter of 865,000 miles is 100 times larger and the whole of our solar system consisting of all planets, moons and asteroids would fit comfortably in less than 1% of the Sun. It is thought that the Sun is a perpetually exploding hydrogen bomb, fueled by nuclear fusion, so powerful that every square meter of it emits about 70,000 horsepower of energy into space. To generate energy on this scale, we would have to burn 11 billion times the world's annual coal output every second. Since early in the seventeenth century, we have generally regarded the Sun as being at the exact center of its solar system. The Sun does not remain still, nor does the center of mass of the solar system coincide with the exact center of mass of the Sun. Sometimes, as in the period from 1977-1984 the true center of mass of the solar system moves outside the Sun altogether. And it's also interesting to note that our solar system is not still either but revolves around the center of our spiral galaxy at a speed of 200 Km per second.

Our Sun is fairly insignificant in the cosmic context as it is only one of about 10 to the 20th power other stars in the observable universe and there are heavenly objects a hundred million times the size of our Sun, which we call Pulsars. These are thought to be neutron stars so compact and dense that one with the mass of our Sun would only be about 10 miles across! One of them in the Crab Nebula exploded in 1054 which turned into a Supernova, rotates at 30 cycles per second and radiates from its core all wavelengths from radio to X-rays amounting to a total radiation output of some 100,000 of our Sun's. Quasars are even more powerful, more distant (ten thousand light years) and more alarming. We are told that some of them emit as much radiation as a thousand million galaxies the size of our Milky Way - which contains 100,000,000,000 (100 billion) stars, with magnitudes so large that our simple minds are sent reeling, so let's get back to our modest little solar system. New sources of energy have been discovered here one after another. In 1954 it was discovered that Jupiter emits powerful radiation in the form of radio and microwaves and the following year a similar discovery was made regarding Venus. Suddenly, the solar system has been found to be an electro-magnetic system! Our Earth is in direct contact with this system and is under constant bombardment from all directions by a host of protons, alpha particles and other nuclear bits and pieces known as cosmic rays. Most of these originate from the Sun and when they reach our atmosphere they produce gamma rays, electrons and mesons. Luckily, we have our natural defenses. The zones of charged particles known as the Van Allen belts, which begin 500 miles from Earth, trap a certain amount of the invading energy, though far from all of it and our Sun asserts its authority as ruler of its system by sweeping some foreign radiation out of our way with its own powerful "wind", high energy particles ejected at about a million miles an hour at temperatures of more than a million degrees Kelvin from the outer layer or corona of the Sun. Science fiction writers posed the idea that if you could build a gigantic sail only a few atoms thick and several square miles in area, one could ride the solar winds from planet to planet. Acceleration would be slow at first but over the months speed would pick up to very high velocities at 100's of times the speed of light.

The main thing I'm going to focus on for the remainder of this lecture is the Electromagnetic effects on the earth as a whole and on each one of us individually. The electro-magnetic radiations from the Sun originate mainly as the result of solar flares which are the result of Sun spot activity. Sun spot records date back at least to 28 BC in Chinese literature, then again recorded by Theophrastus, a pupil of Aristotle, but they didn't know what Sunspots were. They thought they maybe were high flying birds, planets in transit, new planets or defects in telescopes. Then in about the year 1611 interest peaked to study them in more detail. In 1833, Sir John Hershel made a very important discovery that the spots were electromagnetic in nature, had something to do with magnetic storms and that they came and went in cycles averaging 11.1 years upon which the polarity of the spots reverses. Sun spots appear as dark blobs on the Sun. Some thought them to be gaseous bubbles which are slightly cooler than their surrounding area. They tend to form themselves into groups with two spots in each group normally dominating the rest, which grow in size while the other spots actually get smaller after about ten days. The lesser spots disappear along with one of the two main ones. The remaining spot breaks up again as formerly into smaller spots with two spots remaining, although this time both spots remain. The twin remaining spots have opposing polarities and the magnetic field grows in strength until the group starts to break up again. But this time due to the strong magnetic field, it ejects flaming gas by magnetic repelling force of the pair of magnet poles and we have a solar flare lasting for up to 25 days. When a Sun spot appears it definitely means that a flare is on the way. Solar flares and Sun spots are not just a cyclic function of the Sun but a reaction as the result of the electro-magnetic forces combined from four planets on the Sun. Every 11.1 years or so the Earth lines up with another planet facing the Sun and likewise on the other side of the Sun by two other planets 180 degrees from the earth. When these four planets are in conjunction, their combined electromagnetic pull on the Sun cause the Sun spots. You might liken the effect to the gravitational effect of the Sun and the Moon on the Earth producing tides in the seas, lakes and yes even streams. People don't realize it, but the Earth's crust is actually floating on molten iron and will also become rippled, rising and falling as much as 9 inches as the ocean tides. The tides produced on the Sun are actually in the Plasma (liquid burning gas) and the bubbles forming Sun spots are likened to the waves produced on the oceans and seas on the earth.

Well, you might say, that's all very interesting, but what does that have to do with the price of tea in China or electromagnetic waves we said we are focusing on? I just wanted to give you the big picture.

The Sun spots don't necessarily become a major problem when the four planets (Mercury, Venus, Earth and Jupiter) are at angles of less than 180 degrees from pair to pair. We still get solar flares and resultant radiation bombarding the Earth. But when the four planets (Mercury, Venus, Earth and Jupiter) are in conjunction and exactly opposite each other, (especially when Jupiter and Venus are on the same side together), 180 degrees apart, the maximum magnetic effect is produced on the Sun and we get huge solar flares and massive solar winds. Did you know by the way, as a side note, that the planet Venus rotates in the opposite direction compared with all the other 8 planets in our solar system? Does that confirm the author's statement who wrote the book "Men are from Mars and Women are from Venus", that men and woman are direct OPPOSITES? Men are NORMAL while women are not. You women can either BOOO or clap however you feel about that one.

Getting back to electromagnetic forces from the Sun and how they affect the Earth and people....

During a magnetic storm as the result of large solar flares, electric telegraph, short wave communications, telephone lines, underwater cables, high voltage transmission lines and even gas and water pipes are interfered with. It may well be that some power failures and even some blackouts as in the great New York blackouts of 1965 and 1977 were due to solar induced currents. That's not all. During a magnetic storm, our ionosphere becomes more highly charged so that a spacecraft passing through it will cause an enormous difference in voltage between its interior and the atmosphere. A spaceman would only have to touch the metal of the ship with a bare hand and his body would be instantly drained of electricity, causing instant death. This is what has recently been theorized was the cause of death of three Soviet cosmonauts, Dobrovolsky, Volkov, and Patsayev on June 30, 1971 after re-entry into the atmosphere after being in space for 24 days. Their bodies were found completely intact each with a smile on their face. Either they saw paradise or something else happened. For those of you who don't believe in Heaven, I'll explain it scientifically. As they passed through the ionosphere upon re-entry, the electrical charges were extremely high due to recent magnetic storm activity and the voltage difference inside the spaceship cabin was much lower than outside, so if the cosmonauts touched the metal of the ship, all electrons would be instantly drained from their body causing an electrolyte imbalance, resulting in alkaline conditions, respiratory failure leading to excess carbon dioxide in the tissues, causing the face muscles to contract into a smile. Since then, precautions have been taken by creating Earth-like gravitational effects with magnets in the cockpit with opposite polarities on each side, which would prevent the electrical charges from getting out of balance in situations such as happened to the Soyuz XI spacecraft in 1971.

There also appears to be a strong connection between magnetic storms and weather patterns on the Earth. If you recall, a few minutes ago I talked about the phenomenon of the Sun actually being out of its center point in our solar system and it was actually OUT of the solar system from 1977-1984. Well, in January 19, 1977, snow fell in the Bahamas for the first time in recorded history, temperatures in New York were the lowest in 108 years, Orange growers in Florida had to light bon fires in their orange groves, tornado winds of 110 MPH swept across the Kamchatka peninsula, Niagara Falls froze stiff, three million Americans were out of work due to -40 C. accompanied by 70 MPH blizzards and whole towns such as Buffalo, New York nearly vanished entirely under snowdrifts. Yet all this time the temperatures in Anchorage, Alaska were 30 degrees above normal, rivers in London were overflowing and 16 inches of rain fell in one day in Hong Kong. When solar magnetic winds are strong enough to penetrate our protective Van Allen radiation belt it causes the atmosphere to be pushed down creating a low pressure front and then when that lifts it changes immediately to a high pressure front and often violent storms result.

Solar flares and Sun spots have been actually traced to coincide with periodic changes in birth length, weights and blood PH level in new born babies. Sudden weather changes are also related to increased heart attacks, suicides, agitation and depression.

Women's menstrual cycles and the rate of growth in children can be correlated to electromagnetic changes on the earth.

Well, I hope I haven't overwhelmed you! Are there any questions relating to what we discussed here today?" Jameson asked.

A hand went up and smiling, Jameson recognized the student and asked for their question. He repeated the student's question so the rest of the class could hear it.

"You want to know the difference in potential or volts between normal sunlight radiation and that produced by a magnetic storm?"

Professor Jameson responded, "That's an excellent question showing some thought and I appreciate seeing that in my students!"

Then he gave his answer, "Actually there is not much difference in the two, but cosmic particles, those nuclear bits and pieces from outer space and the Sun are far more stronger than solar protons produced from normal Sun radiations or magnetic solar storms, reaching 1 billion electron volts compared to about 100 million for solar protons. Any other questions?"

Another student raised their hand and asked the question, "Professor Jameson, do you know when the next solar magnetic storm is predicted to come?"

Professor Jameson smiled and replied, "Well last I heard, the accuracy to predict such things is about 85% and the last solar storm we talked about lasted until 1984. Each cycle lasts an average of 11.1 years, so the next one should have been in 1996 and lasted until around 2007. Did we see some especially bad conditions on earth just after 1996? Check out the weather reports and see for yourself."

"Well I'm afraid class that time is up and your other teachers don't take kindly to sharing their hours with me I suppose, so we will see you tomorrow! You all have a great day!"

Nick remained after all of the other students left and Jameson could see him raising his eyebrows as a signal that they locked eyes.

"Have you got a few minutes for that tour and some shop talk, Nick?" asked his father.

"Sure dad, that's what I have been looking forward to all day!" said Nick.

Professor Jameson thought he'd leave his office for last in the tour since his reference library was there and he was sure Nick would dive into that once he saw that and he would like his attention in conversation until then. Jameson didn't plan on hiding the large reference book he had in the open about Nikola Tesla since he thought it only fair to let Nick come to his own conclusions that the great inventor was indeed his Great Grandfather. He hoped Nick wouldn't get too angry when he discovered how his Great Grandfather was cheated and taken advantage of by Edison and the resulting crash of his dreams of a unified wireless electric system operational world-wide. Nick's response will show his true character and Jameson was pretty confident that Nick's current guileless nature would hold true.

Jameson first introduced Nick to his boss, the Head Administrator of the school.

"Nick, this is Mr. Lafeplet' my boss." his father said.

Jameson was surprised that Nick recognized his boss' name was French as he addressed him in French. Nick seemed so natural in so many languages. Mr. Lafeplet' was taken back by Nick's salutation and if it weren't a commonly used French greeting, wouldn't have understood what Nick said because he didn't speak French! Nick sensed his mistake and then responded again in English, "It's my highest honor to meet you, sir!"

Once again Mr. Lafeplet' was taken back by Nick's grownup formality and blushed as he grabbed Nicks outstretched hand.

"Mighty fine young man you have here, John," Mr. Lafeplet' confirmed with a wink and an approving nod of his head.

Nick charmed all of the lady friends John had as he introduced him to them one by one next. There was the secretary Beth, Barb, the Dean of Women's studies, and Jan and Bev, the teachers' assistants who were busy making copies of next weeks tests.

On their way to Jameson's office, John showed Nick where the men's bathroom was just in case he needed to know that fact in the near future. John could tell that Nick was tiring of meeting any more coworkers, so he decided to dispense with any more of that for the day and take him straight to his office. When Nick walked into his father's office he just stood there with his mouth open and gazed at shelf after shelf of technical books and biographies of famous dead people he had never heard of like Einstein, Newton, Aristotle, Thomas Edison, and on and on. He set his mind to devour each book from cover to cover one at a time at the earliest opportunity. John tried to make conversation with Nick after this point but all he got was a blank open mouthed stare so he figured he had better surrender to the fact that books won over his attentions for the rest of the afternoon.

"Nick, would you like to read some of these books while I am in lectures for the rest of the afternoon? It might be three or four hours, is that OK?" John asked Nick.

"More than OK, Dad, it would be GREAT!" replied Nick as he headed for the first book on the shelf as hungrily as a famished fox would eat a long awaited fresh chicken.

"I am done at 5:30 PM with my last class and I'll come and get you so we can go home for supper, OK?" John asked the question, but he could see that Nick was already deeply absorbed, entranced in his newfound technical "Heaven", where a world of limitless creativity awaited him. John quietly shut the office door behind him and wondered if he would ever have a normal conversation with him again.

"Well", he said to himself, "Define 'NORMAL'."

He knew Nick was not "NORMAL" by any definition, so he wasn't concerned after all.

CHAPTER
-FIVE -

NickGyver revealed

𝒫rofessor Jameson finished his last lecture, the same one all day for four different classes. His lectures were so in demand that he had to offer four different time slots to meet the needs of the students. All classes actually had waiting lists in case someone dropped out or God forbid, died. There were even requests from wannabe inventors to sit in his lectures for no college credit just to glean ideas for future inventions from the brilliant mind of the Professor. Many of Professor Jameson's books were on their third and fourth printings to meet the demand of students and others from the scientific communities all over the world. Jameson wasn't in the business of authoring to get rich as half of his book sales went into a scholarship foundation he established for promising young, or of any age for that matter, scientists in many fields of study. The remainder of his book sales income went into another worthy fund, the John Jameson Retirement Annuity. He loved to write and if he didn't give himself an outlet for his constantly occurring ideas, he felt his head would explode. He never really bragged about himself being a writer, but he often proudly proclaimed himself as being an "Undercover Scientist" and he would let it stop there to let the listeners figure that one out for themselves. One of his other book jokes was that if he ever had to have his appendix removed, readers would no longer be able to find page references to key words anymore, but then it would reduce the number of pages in the book and save him money in the long run.

Jameson started walking toward his office to try to pry Nick's nose from out of the present book he was devouring and convince him of the necessity of going home for some needed nourishment in the form of supper, but at the same time he was a bit apprehensive of Nick's emotional state should he have already gotten into the book about his Great Grandfather, Nikola Tesla. When he opened his office door he noticed all of the shelves which used to be filled with books were now empty. On his desk were two piles. Nick looked up with a grin like a cat who had recently filled his stomach with the prized Canary and proud of it and greeted his dad.

"Hi Dad, back so soon?" Nick asked.

Jameson replied, "Learning anything, son?"

Nick responded pointing to the taller pile of books. "This pile I have already read and this other pile (pointing to the much shorter pile) are next!"

"There looks like over 30 books in the already read pile. That's impressive even for me!" Jameson replied in awe, then added, "That's over thirty books in just four hours....that's less than 10 minutes per book! Not many pictures so they're not very interesting, huh?"

Nick responded, "No, I read every page but some books had so many pages! It's the page turning that takes all of the time! Can you read any faster, Dad?"

Jameson couldn't quite comprehend how Nick could accomplish this feat of reading so many books and remember any of what he had read. Nick, noting his father's disbelief, asked him to pick up any book in the tall pile and pick out a technical term. Jameson decided to humor the boy and picked up one of the largest books on Einstein's life and asked Nick to explain the "Theory of Relativity".

Nick quickly replied with a grin, "That's the theory, well proven I might say that if your parents don't have any children, neither will you! That was a joke, Dad, did you like it?"

Then Nick proceeded to list the page number of the text reference on the "Theory of Relativity" and recite the whole page word for word including explaining the formulas involved and how you would use the theory. Jameson was flabbergasted, his mouth dropped open and his eyes bugged out in shock at Nick's memory recall and comprehension ability. Nick, trying to understand his father's silence, asked, "Is that OK, Dad?"

Jameson replied, "Son, you have an amazing gift!"

Nick just shrugged his shoulders as if it was nothing.

After some casual chit chat where Nick divulged sheepishly that the Secretary had stopped by with a plate of cookies and a glass of milk an hour ago so he really wasn't THAT hungry yet. Jameson finally was able to find out from Nick his secret to speed reading. He actually thought everyone could do what he did since he hadn't had that much contact with people in his short 4 years of life. But it appears Jameson thought, that Nick's brain is so advanced that it actually anticipates the meanings of words and phrases and whole paragraphs by the preceding words he reads. So sometimes it is only necessary to read a total of 20 words or so on a page to put the concept of the page in his working conscious memory, but the whole page is put into his long term memory. So he actually understands it fully as he reads (or scans it as we would interpret it) and yet has the full text including illustrations in his long term memory. That revelation was astounding to him. Nick's brain had its own built in appendix to match words to scan his archives by key word or phrase.

All Jameson could do was shake his head. Apparently everything Nick sees and hears from other sources also gets appended or added to the information in the proper category and if it works as efficiently as it seems to do, would also alert him to an idea if it happens to correlate to what he is working on at the moment. Answers to questions, solutions to problems he's having and a host of other amazing things even he couldn't imagine!

Jameson tried tact, "Nick, your Mom would really appreciate your presence at the supper table and do you really even know what she does during the day? I think you would be very interested to find out!"

Nick's curiosity ebbed. He quickly closed the book with a marker to keep his place, sighed and said, "Ok, let's go home."

As they picked their way through traffic from eastern Hardtford to their modest home in the western suburbs, Nick could hardly contain his questions about his dad's car. Jameson knew most of them and answered them in as technically complete responses as he knew how. He knew Nick would not settle for broad or general responses. He had to get inside everything and see how it worked. His questions kept getting deeper until he was satisfied to go onto the next subsection of the car's workings. Jameson knew that some areas of the car were sure to get dissected and probably redesigned for efficiency and functionality in short order if time permitted. Test driving the car after the modifications was a bit of an apprehensive thought. Maybe he would check around and see if he could find Nick a car to modify so his car wouldn't be radically changed. That was a comforting thought.

When they arrived home, Mary could be seen through the kitchen window washing some pots and pans. She waved to them as they pulled into the driveway. The smells of beef roast, potatoes and carrots with onion actually started Nick's stomach to growl so he was relieved a hot meal was awaiting. Mary kissed John hello on the lips and Nick on the cheek, which made him feel warm and grateful to be part of a family who cared for him. He missed his birth parents but since both of them worked long hours every day he really hadn't had the opportunity to spend much quality time with them and feel like a family. His birth dad worked in a labor camp and his mom in a sweatshop sewing gunnysacks for animal feed, so he was never invited to spend a day with them at work because it wasn't allowed or safe for him to be in either place.

He loved it here with his new family...it was like a new found freedom he never had. Things could have changed with his birth parents and work in later years after he got older, but who knows. Here he was and here he hoped to stay!

Over supper Mary urged Nick to talk about his day and from his viewpoint it was fairly uneventful. John mouthed in a whispering tone to Mary that he would tell her later what really happened and she could hardly wait until Nick went to bed to sit up with her husband and hear all about it. John announced to Mary that Nick had fixed his noisy shaver and now it works so noiselessly and so much more efficiently with fewer parts.

Nick explained to them that he had removed that noisy motor and replaced it with an oscillator, a vibrating crystal which operates from the battery voltage. He happened to have one in his pocket as a spare for his short wave radio in case he needed to call out on a different frequency channel as he traveled through the mountains on his way to the airport. He figured that he could find another one if he still needs one so he used it in the razor. You can buy almost everything in the States he was told. Anyway, he told them that the crystal actually caused the cutting blades to vibrate, but at a pitch too high for the human ears to perceive. It was making noise still, but you couldn't hear it, so he cheated a little.

"Well Nick", said John, "we won't tell anyone about your cheating if you don't want us to."

Nick replied, "Well, if it doesn't bother you, I don't care if you tell anybody. I just didn't want you to think of me as a cheater!"

Mary responded, "Nick honey, we don't think you are a cheater, both your dad and I want you to know that we are proud that you are using the marvelous brain that God gave you. Honey, we are both so proud of you!"

Nick trying to qualify being called "honey", quickly dismissed the concept of being called sweet and sticky and just settled in his mind that it was an English term of endearment and that made him feel nice inside. He secretly wondered what bees called each other for endearment, since honey is actually bee spit. Nick remembered what his dad said earlier about getting to know what his mom did during the day so he asked her, "Mom, how was your day and what did you do with your time?"

Mary pleased at his question responded, "Well, it appears your father didn't tell you what I did or you wouldn't have asked. Actually, I am a Professor like your dad, except at a medical college."

"So you give lectures like dad does but on the human body?" Nick asked.

"Well," said Mary, "mostly about illnesses people can get and how to fight them off. If you'd like you could come with me for the day sometime and listen to my lecture too and read some of my books in my office to help you understand what it is I actually lecture about."

Nick replied, "That would be great, but I'd like to finish a small stack of books in dad's office first before I can come with you, how about the day after tomorrow, Mom?"

Mary raised her eyebrows at John to show she was a bit puzzled at Nick's timeline of only a day to read a whole stack of books. John again mouthed another whisper to Mary, "That is part of what I want to talk to you about later!"

Mary let it drop at that. "Well," said Mary, "Who's game for dessert?"

Nick got a worried look in his eye as he imagined chasing each other around with weapons and the first one killed gets eaten for dessert. That didn't seem like too much fun, so he replied, "I'm not too hungry for dessert tonight."

Mary responded to his concerned look, not quite understanding what she had said to make him worried about something, "it's apple pie and ice cream."

Nick replied more comfortably now, "I'll have some!"

Nick told his parents about his desire to continue his "experimenting" but he had to buy some things at some stores and needed to get to the bank to get some of that paper money to spend. It was clear to both John and Mary that Nick didn't understand the process of acquiring money, so Mary tried to explain to him that money is exchanged for work and the bank is where people keep their extra money for safety, unless you put money in the bank from working you can't just go there and get some.

"You can't?!" asked Nick quite disappointedly. "Well, how can I get some? Can I get a job and work somewhere?"

Mary replied, "No, I'm sorry honey, but in our country children can't get jobs until they are much older than you and taller and stronger to do the work they are expected to do."

Nick looked very disappointed and clearly didn't understand, because he didn't think of himself as being young and felt capable of working just like any one else.

Mary thoughtfully countered, "Nick, I have a little extra money from my job and I could take you to the local Radio Shack or other stores you like and you could buy some things you need. We could go this Saturday if you want."

Nick's eyes brightened a bit as he shook his head up and down in agreement.

"Dad," Nick piped, "I found some electric motors in the garage and was wondering if I could work on them later to make them run better for you?"

John replied, "I don't see why not!" He was nearly as excited as Nick to see the outcome and what new ideas he would use to improve them.

Both John and Mary noticed Nick's eyes start to droop and they nearly said in unison, "Nick, you look pretty tired. How about if we get you to bed?"

Nick yawned and said, "Yes, I think I'm ready for that right about now."

Mary had bought Nick a toothbrush and before he got too far into the process showed him how to brush his teeth and spit into the sink. Nick thought about the bees and honey again as he spit and giggled to himself. He could see his mother smiling at him in the mirror and felt warm inside again. Yes, he thought, I think I am going to love being in this family!

Frankly, John was relieved that Nick didn't mention anything more about experimenting on his car and decided it would be to his comfort to leave well enough alone.

After they both tucked Nick in to his comfy bed and he was fast asleep, Mary grabbed John by the arm and sat him on the couch in the living room to have him tell her what really happened in Nick's day. She too was astounded, yet thrilled about the treasure they had been given by God to guard and polish.

The next morning Nick was up with the wings of the dawn ready as ever for the adventure the new day would bring. Back in his caves and mines he had been limited to only the resources of his mind to learn new things, develop, experiment and occasionally fail, which happened infrequently because he thought out things quite thoroughly before he started anything. The times he failed was when he decided to try some "what if" experiments and the unknown can be surprising at times. His mistakes were not catastrophic but only resulted in melting or in the worst cases vaporizing some electronic components due to high frequency induction of currents resulting in extreme heat he wasn't expecting. But then his "mistakes" were not all that bad after all, since now he knew what NOT to do and gave him some new ideas to play off of in the future. You might eventually forget your successes, but you NEVER forget your mistakes! Here in the States he had so much to look forward to! Many of the inventions he had imagined in the caves and mines were already in use and he was excited to find those people who were like minded as himself to maybe share ideas with and learn from. He was to soon find out that unfortunately, many of those people or in fact, THE person had been already dead for nearly a hundred years.

Nick came into the living room and found his dad's Bible open on the coffee table. He knew it was his dad's since it had his name embossed in gold letters on the bottom of the front cover. Well, knowing dad, this must have some great importance to him since he had been recently reading it. He opened it up to where his dad had a marker and read a high-lighted passage from Jeremiah chapter 29, verses 11-14a.

"For I know the thoughts that I think toward you, saith the Lord, thoughts of peace, and not of evil to give you an expected end. Then shall you call upon me, and you shall go and pray unto me and I will hearken unto you. And you shall seek me, and find me, when you search for me with all your heart. And I will be found of you, saith the Lord."

He wondered to himself who this Lord was this book talked about, so he picked up the book and began reading it from "In the beginning". About ten minutes later, he closed the book and smiled, now he knew the source of all wisdom! It was the creator of the universe! Of course, He would know all of the answers to all his questions. He had known that there had to be a creator because in his scientific mind, things don't just appear out of nowhere and start functioning on their own. Somebody has to design them and create them before they can work. Right then and there he set his mind that he and the Lord were going to be inseparable from this day forward. He tried to fathom how the creator could give his own life for the created because of their wrong doing. If it were up to him, he would have realized the flaws he made in the creation and started over with a new model. But no, his creator loved them despite their flaws and created another thing called GRACE and MERCY and COMPASSION which covered the flaws and FORGIVENESS was born. Now when God the Father looks at his creation, those who choose to seek him, it's as if he is looking in the mirror and sees perfection and no longer flaws. Wow! What a mind, Nick thought!

John woke up as customary with the sunshine peeking through his open shades and got up to use the bathroom. He saw Nick already up and dressed.

Nick greeted his dad, "Good morning, Dad! I was reading your Bible you left on the table here and it talked about the importance of praying among other things. Can you teach me how to pray sometime soon?"

John was thrilled that his son would ask him to assist in such important matters and replied, "Of course Son, how about right after I get back from using the bathroom? Why don't you read a bit more until I get back, OK?"

Nick replied, "I already read the whole thing and have it committed to memory!"

John wasn't surprised one bit to hear that and smiled, mouthing his own prayer of thanks for Nick and his new found knowledge of Christ. He had no idea of the power Nick would have from this day on into the future from his relationship with the author of all wisdom. John used the bathroom, shaved and enjoyed the titillating face massage he got from the hand held oscillator vibrating at about 100 million cycles per second. Actually he had to imagine the massage he was getting because it was vibrating so fast it seemed to not vibrate at all and literally floated across his face. After shaving, he went back into the living room and sat down beside Nick and explained to him that praying was the same as talking to God. "We just tell him what we want him to know and ask him for what we need, just like we'd talk to a close friend or to our own father or mother. But the neat thing is, unlike talking to a person, God already knows what we want and what we need." John explained.

Nick responded, "Then why do we have to talk to Him at all?"

"Well," replied John, "it's His opportunity to spend time with us and while we're together, he also has a chance to tell us He loves us, is proud of us and give us a hug when we need it."

"Does God REALLY hug you?" asked Nick.

"Well", responded John, "I think I've felt a hug now and then when I really needed to feel loved, more so before I met your Mom, but I always can feel that He is close to me when I pray."

Nick said with a small tear in his eye, "Thanks Dad!"

John responded, "My pleasure, Nick! I hope we can have many more talks like this! Hey, how about some breakfast and then we can go to my office and you can finish that last stack of books?"

"That sounds great, dad!" Nick piped.

Mary soon was awakened by the sound and smells of breakfast and coffee cooking on the stove and her alarm was about to sound in five minutes anyway, so she shut it off and got out of bed. She combed her long auburn hair, looked in the mirror and was pleased she didn't look a year over her real age of 47 years. "Maintaining" is important! She would often remind herself. Can't get any younger! She felt younger now that Nick was here with them and threw up a prayer of thanks to God again for His gift to them of Nick. By the time she finished getting dressed and primping in the bathroom, Nick and John were nearly finishing their breakfast of eggs, hotcakes and sausage and toast. Nick loved the smell of coffee brewing and imagined it tasted as good as it smelled, but surprisingly, he didn't care for the taste. Maybe it's like cod liver oil and kissing, it might take some time to get used to. For now he'd settle for the warm feeling in his tummy when his mom kissed him again as they left out the door together, just Nick and his dad.

Nick had some ideas to pay back the secretary for her kindness of providing him with milk and cookies the other day. He noticed that the fan on her desk was awfully noisy and he thought he might offer to fix that for her today. He had an idea, but it would require buying some parts first. Maybe that would work out if his Mom would keep her promise to help him on Saturday.

Nick seemed to absorb the remaining books like a sponge. The one book he read a number of times was the one on Nikola Tesla. He devoted a full 18 minutes to that one and had the haunting feeling that he knew the man personally. It was uncanny! He had the same name as his great, great Grandfather .... Nikola. Could it be that he was named after him? Funny he thought, that had to be it, because if he was named before him, I would be him and not me! That's why he had to be named AFTER him! He chuckled to himself because he had said a funny and it made him laugh again.

He did think it unfair of that man Edison to have cheated him and tricked him into believing that he would get paid for all of his work and then didn't. He sat back and pondered .....it's like I inherited my grandfather's brain and experiences and through me he gets another chance of living his dream and seeing it come to pass. That's why I knew how to build all of that stuff like short wave radios, computers and stuff because I had already done it before through my grandfather! But now I have the advantage over him because I have the Master creator as my resource and not just my brain and intuition. I will not fail as did my grandfather because I am not working alone.

Nick finished replacing all of the books back in their respective places on the shelves which he had memorized and thoughtfully walked toward his dad's lecture hall. As he passed the secretary he commented to her how thoughtful it was of her to bring him those cookies and milk the other day and no, it didn't spoil his appetite for supper. He mentioned to her that he had some ideas to make her desk fan run smoother and after he picked up some parts this weekend, he'd like to repay her the favor by fixing her fan for free. She graciously accepted and replied that her boss would surely be pleased also and might have some other things for him to experiment with also after he was done with the fan. He smiled as he walked away, confident that he was indeed going to like living here and being involved in college life. Because if he had his way, he'd be attending here in some capacity in the very near future.

By the time he got to his dad's classroom, Professor Jameson was just finishing up on his last lecture for the day on "Acoustic Resonation And The Effect On The World Around Us".

Nick wished that he could have sat in on the whole lecture because it would be easier to fill in the missing links in his mind if he picked up at least the beginning rather than the end of the lecture with the way his mind worked. But the information he did glean had some definite applications for when he had his first opportunity to work on his dad's car. He couldn't wait! He hummed to himself and then contemplated the harmonic waves he must be inducing into something in his surroundings from his acoustic representation of a song he once heard while his mother rocked him to sleep as an infant.

Chapter
-Six-

Nick builds a reputation

Nick had told his Mom he would go with her the next day after he finished reading the books at his Dad's office but he was unaware of even what day of the week it was. Tomorrow was Saturday and his Mom didn't work. He reminded her about her offer to take him to Radio Shack or other stores if he needed. She said she hadn't forgotten and she could go right after they got up and had breakfast. He was elated and could hardly sleep. Constant thoughts about God's plan for him now that he knew he was the only surviving generation of Nikola Tesla, kept him wondering and imagining the many avenues he might be led down toward some new and world changing discovery. He also thought about his initial plans to redesign the college secretary's desk fan to make it run quieter. He thought that if he were to cut the shafts of the motor rotor, (the part inside that rotates and the fan blades attach to), install two additional magnetic coils inside the shell of the motor which would magnetically suspend the rotor in the air, he could eliminate all of the friction of spinning the rotor since it would no longer require bearings or bushings or shafts. He did have to leave one shaft on one end to attach the blades to but then he would also have to design the new magnetic coils a bit more powerful to support the weight and the torque of the blade mechanism. What a novel idea! A totally bearing less, mostly friction free, totally magnetically driven fan motor. If he reduced the distance of the new coils from the shaft less rotor to the bare minimum he could also get rid of most of the friction due to air. He estimated that the motor should run about 20% faster and consume about 30% less electricity than in its present condition. Bearing noise, blade wobble or any resulting vibration would be eliminated totally. He knew he had to find some varnished magnet wire at least to do the job and hoped also that he could scrounge anything else he needed. You'd be surprised what people in the States throw away! There are many reusable parts if you have any kind of imagination. With that thought out he dropped off to sleep with visions of floating motor rotors dancing in his head.

It seemed like all he had to do lately is think of some object or idea and his mind designs it right in front of his eyes. At first he didn't recognize what was happening when he saw something forming in front of him and almost tripped over it until he realized it really wasn't solid and on the floor in front of him but only in his mind. He tried to counter the surprise by marking a big red X on all of his stuff to tell the real from the envisioned until he saw a telltale difference. The envisioned objects had an air space under them of about an inch or more. Then it became easy to see the difference and he didn't feel so foolish about sometimes appearing to nearly trip over or walk around objects that to others didn't exist. To him when he was envisioning an "unseen" object, he could walk around it 360 degrees, look under and on top of it and see it in actual operation as it was supposed to work. Another clue was that he couldn't touch an envisioned object so he did a lot of feeling around at first too until he got used to the idea.

Nick awoke on Saturday morning to the melody of the birds summoning the dawn. The Sun responded quickly by slowly peaking its orb up on the far horizon. The birds increased their melodies to encourage the Sun that it was OK to come out and play. That it did, warmly welcoming its playmates who desired to dance in the Sun beams and catch the first flying bugs that ventured out. Nick especially looked forward to each new day. It was like opening up a new gift, an invisible treasure that begins to take shape the moment he opened his eyes. However he didn't know exactly what it was until the end of the day when the Sun said goodnight. Each day offered a brand new gift! It was exciting!

He looked at his bedside clock and it read 5 AM. He expected his mother would not rise until at least 7 AM so he thought of something he could do until then. He remembered his dad said that he wouldn't be using the car all day and this would be the perfect time and day to work on it. He recalled from his dad's last lecture about acoustic resonance and thought it should surely work on a gasoline/air fed internal combustion engine. He felt that the inefficiency of present-day cars was the lack of complete atomization of the fuel to mix with the air. He thought that both the air and gas molecules were too large for a proper explosion in the engine cylinders. So if he could design something to break these molecules up then they would form a denser mixture and explode more violently. He thought if he could create a violent swirling effect the molecules would collide into each other and break each other apart, but it had to happen fast and at least a number of times each second. Ok, he thought out loud, install a fine piano wire in the air intake just before the mixture port. He had seen some of that wire in a junk drawer from when the piano repairman had come last and replaced a string. He didn't know if it was the right thickness to produce the octave he needed, but it was worth an experiment. He fastened a length of the piano wire inside the air intake housing and then reassembled everything. He found a tuning fork in another junk drawer which would transfer an acoustic resonance to the installed piano wire. Now he had to find his dad's keys to start the car and check out his theory. As he came into the kitchen, he hoped he wouldn't have to sneak into his dad and mom's room and look for them. Whew! There they were hanging from a hook on a board labeled "KEYS".

That made matters MUCH easier! He started the car's engine and struck the tuning fork with a hammer he found lying on the work bench. Immediately, the car engine began to increase speed and run smoother! It works! It could have just been an extremely lucky guess on the octave he had available or maybe a number of octaves would actually work. Some maybe better than others! He saw his dad had a nice compact disc player which reminded him of that nice Jazz CD his father loved to listen to in the car. He decided to put that in and listen to it while he thought out his next move. He especially loved too the saxophone section on the disc. It should be coming up right about now....he projected. The sax hit the first high note and the car's engine responded with a roar and surge of power. He was glad it was not in gear or he would have been driving through the back wall and into the back yard facing his parents bedroom window and should they hear and see that, well, he was in for trouble! The interesting thing was that once the car engine responded to the change of gas and air quality, the car's computer would keep that optimum setting. Since the harmonics lasted for nearly two minutes with one high note from the saxophone, before it went back to its factory inefficient setting, he could listen for variations in engine response for a wide range of notes being played on the CD and pick the best one. Then all he had to do is duplicate it as a steady tone with a crystal oscillator and presto, voella, he was done! He memorized the best note for optimum operation. It was in the middle of the CD. He'd listen to that when he got home from shopping with his mom and build a tone generator using another crystal. He had better buy a number of crystals above and below and as close to his trained ear best guess of frequencies today also since his mom may not want to go out a second time. He heard some action in the house so he quickly ejected the CD and put it away where his dad normally kept it and shut the car engine off. This was exciting! He loved these new discoveries! He hung the car keys back on the same hook where he found them and peeked into the kitchen to see if anyone was there. His mom walked out a few seconds later from the bathroom, ran her fingers through her long tangled hair and smiled at Nick.

"Oh, you're already up?!" His mom said with a sleepy voice.

"Yes, I've been in the garage looking at dad's nice stuff he's got. I seem to get some great ideas in there, I hope you don't mind?!" Nick said a little sheepishly, hoping she wouldn't notice his blush.

Mary asked him if he had a preference for breakfast.

Nick replied, "Everything you're having but hold the coffee. I heard that on the Burger King advertisement and I thought it was to the point. Hold the pickle, lettuce and tomato..... hold the coffee...., it works too!"

Mary approached Nick with a cup of coffee in her hand, looking forward to her first sip. "Nick, I'm holding the coffee!" Mary said with a smirk.

They both laughed! She put the coffee cup down on the table and gave him a big squeeze. He chirped a giggle and said, "Thanks, mom!"

Mary replied thoughtfully, "No THANK YOU, Nick! My life would never be complete again without you!"

Nick didn't need any coffee. There was that warm, comforting feeling in his tummy again.

Mary made some hot oatmeal with nuts and raisins and topped Nick's with whipped cream and a strawberry. It was delicious! Mary made sure that Nick brushed his teeth before they left and he was secretly relieved when she headed for her car in the garage rather than his dad's, 'cause you never know what to expect with some experiments and he didn't want any surprises, especially when he was in the car too.

His mom stopped at Radio Shack first and he was pleasantly surprised at the variety of electronics parts they carried. He was about to reach for a roll of magnet wire when he overheard another customer describe symptoms of a malfunction in his shortwave radio. The manager proceeded to tell the customer that they do have a repair center in the back but they have a minimum $45 fee for any troubleshooting or estimates. Nick knew right away what the trouble area was since he had built his own just last year. He walked over to the customer's radio. The man already had the cover off, which Nick saw clearly after he stood on a chair to be at the right height to look at it on the counter.

"It sounds like the problem is in your oscillator chip in the tuning section. This one right here," as Nick points to the culprit, they could see the telltale sign of a dull, darkened surface indicating it had gotten hot and failed. "Probably a voltage surge in your neighborhood! I'd replace that and install a varistor from chassis ground and the power input pins, probably pins 40 and 36 I'd say, just from looking at it. But make sure the varistor is rated to breakdown at 18 volts peak to peak. That should prevent that from happening again."

Both the store manager and customer were awed at the words the intellectual voice was speaking, definitely had to be from many years of experience, but then they noticed his size and immediately felt sorry for the man who had probably spent all of his life as a midget. But they had to admit, he kept himself looking much younger than he sounded and they had to give him great admiration for that!

Mary quickly moved the few yards from where she was to the counter, sensing that perhaps Nick was interfering with the manager's work.

Mary jumped in, "Is he bothering you, sirs?"

The manager replied, "Oh no, maam! Are you two together?"

Mary responded, "Yes, we are, this is my son, Nick."

Both the men responded with surprised looks on their faces, "Maam, you don't look old enough to be his mother!"

Mary replied, "Well, thank you, but we've adopted him."

The manager then turned to Nick and said, "Thank you sir for your learned diagnosis of this radio. I think you are probably correct in your troubleshooting and suggested preventive upgrade. Could you give us your telephone number so we could consult you in other matters? If you need to purchase anything today, just pick it out, as long as it's parts or wire or such and they're yours."

Nick's mouth hung open as he tried to speak, "You mean I don't have to pay any money for the stuff?"

The manager replied, "Today you have already earned your purchase. If you agree to be our consultant, anything you need in the future is always free, and if we don't have what you need, we'll find it for you at other stores and have it shipped here. What do you say?"

Nick looked imploringly at his mother regarding her blessing on this arrangement. As incredible as this seemed she gave her approval and wrote their number on one of the manager's cards for future reference.

"You understand sir, that this means one consult for one free day of parts, OK?" The manager added and stretched out his hand to shake Nick's to finalize the deal and Nick complied with a wide grin and took his hand in a firm handshake.

The manager then added, "I'm going to put a little code word by your number so I'll remember right away what the number is for."

Nick saw the man write the word NICKGYVER by his telephone number and wondered at the meaning. Nick grabbed a handful of crystals both above and below frequencies for what he guessed he needed for his dad's car and a couple of rolls of magnet wire, a rheostat, a variety of different sizes and shapes of magnets and brought them up to the counter to show the manager. The manager winked at Nick and said, "Nice doing business with you partner! I'll be in touch!"

Nick and his mom turned and walked out to her car.

Meanwhile, John Jameson had gotten a phone call from his boss who called to ask him how to operate the new "smart board", an extension of a computer that interacts like a chalk board except it allows you to write on it, project images and write over and between the images and by touching the board, control the computer also. Anyway, he was at a loss at how to operate it and wanted to know if John could explain to him over the phone how to work the thing. John knew that he would have to go there in person to show him how to do it because it was just too complex to explain over the phone. His boss was having a special seminar this evening and really needed his help ASAP. John agreed and grabbed his keys from the KEY board, hit the garage door opener, started his car and backed his it out. He loved that saxophone CD and having memorized the track number of his favorite song, punched the program button to go to track 5 and then also hit the REPEAT button to replay the song over and over again. He loved that song so. As he headed for the freeway ramp the song started to play and he settled back in his seat for the pleasure of listening to his song. Just then the car engine surged. The sound of the engine turned to one of a supercharged race engine and the speedometer began to climb without him even touching the gas pedal! His fingers tightly gripped the steering wheel and sweat began to form on his brow as he imagined crashing into the rear end of another car ahead of him at over 100 MPH in a matter of seconds. He couldn't imagine what could have happened to his car! Must have been a computer malfunction, that's all he could think! He realized his only alternative was to shut the car engine off and coast to a stop to avoid certain disaster. So he did it. As the car finally became quiet and was coasting to a stop from 120 MPH, he regained his composure and wrestled the car to a straight stop with disabled power steering and brakes since the engine was shut off. He sat there for a while thinking what to do. He didn't want to call a tow truck because that would take too much time and would be quite expensive also, so he thought he'd try a little deductive reasoning and troubleshoot it himself. He applied the parking brake, shifted the transmission into park and restarted the engine. This time he ejected the CD and turned off the radio so he could hear the engine better and any other noises that might betray the problem. The engine ran quietly and sounded like it just came out of the factory. He cautiously shifted into drive, released the parking brake, knowing full well that he could bail out early this time by shutting the key off on the ignition. He signaled and pulled out into traffic and the car ran quiet, smoothly and normally. The only thing he could think was that the computer must have malfunctioned back there and when he shut off the engine it reset back to normal. Well he thought, probably should get it into the repair shop as soon as possible but it seemed like a safe bet he could make it to school and back home OK. He knew the signs now and should he have to bail out, he'd again shut the engine down if he had to. He wasn't worried. Finally relaxed again, he slipped his favorite CD back into the player and just let it play. Ah, he loved this CD! He was half into the CD when he began anticipating his favorite part starting. He relaxed even more. All of a sudden the car engine surged, the tone of the exhaust changed to that of a supercharged race car and off he accelerated again! Just as he was about to kill the engine with the key, the car slowed, the engine quieted and he actually had to apply the gas pedal to maintain 50 MPH. That was weird! He hoped that now two times was the limit today. The CD finished playing and started over again. Strangely enough, the car started to surge and accelerate again when the same song came on halfway through the CD. He shut the CD off, ejected the disk and the car engine and speed came back under control.

"This is so weird!" he said out loud. The song seems to make the car run faster! The only thing that came out of his mouth was one word with emphasis, "NICK!!!!"

He finished driving to work uneventfully, showed his boss the ropes with the "smart board" and started back home. When he arrived home, Mary and Nick had just also arrived from shopping. His anger at Nick had subsided by now and he actually laughed to himself at what he had just endured. He had to admit to himself that he didn't tell Nick NOT to work on his car on Saturday, he just hoped that he wouldn't.

Nick's eyes showed some intrepidation as he went to greet his father.

"Had to go some place after all huh, dad? Car work good?" asked Nick with a hint of shaking in his voice.

"Yes, it works just fine as long as I don't play my favorite song on my favorite CD. Is that anything YOU would know about, son?" Nick's dad asked.

Nick replied, "Well dad, I had hoped it wouldn't come to this, but yes, I did some experimenting with the fuel/air efficiency and had to stop to go get some more parts. I wanted to surprise you! I suppose I could have put a sign on the dash and told you not to play your favorite song on your favorite CD, but then would you have followed the sign?"

John replied, "Honestly, probably not!"

"I should have taken the keys with me then I suppose," replied Nick.

They both laughed.

Nick told his dad he promised to fix it and would go with him for a test drive after he was done modifying it, just to show his confidence that it would be safe. John handed him the keys, smiled and went into the house with Mary.

Mary told John about the deal that was worked out with the manager at Radio Shack and Nick for a trade of consultation for parts and John was incredulous that the manager would make a handshake agreement with a 4 year old for electronic consultation none the less.

"Well," added Mary, "The manager also thinks that Nick is a full grown old man but in a midget body that still miraculously still looks young!"

They both responded, "Imagine that!"

This exclamation would be very popular in a very short time by everyone involved with Nick, everyone would soon agree to that!

In about an hour, Nick came into the house with a triumphant smile on his face. "Well dad," he said, care for a test drive and walk through of what I did?"

Nick ushered his dad to his car and opened the hood. All John could see different was a little knob for some kind of rheostat barely visible on the side of the air intake enclosure and a wire leading to the fuse panel under the hood.

"I installed an acoustic resonator just like you lectured about in your class last week, to break up the gas and air molecules based on a tone generator I built and a piano wire stretched across inside the intake housing here. The crystal-controlled tone generator causes a resonation in the piano wire at high frequency harmonics and is self sustaining. The high frequency harmonic vibrations cause the gas and air molecules to swirl around and crash into each other multiple times each second at very high speed. This causes them to break into very small particles and makes the mixture denser packing more gas and air into the same space providing a bigger bang and higher efficiency. I disconnected the battery for a few seconds to reset the fuel mixture computer and allow it to monitor the new higher quality mixture without accelerating out of control as I suppose it did for you before this. The little rheostat on the side of the air mixture enclosure is for fine tuning the tone generator frequency since I was unable to find a precise oscillator crystal value."

Once Nick had found the optimum setting of the rheostat, he sealed the knob with fingernail polish to keep the setting from moving.

John made a comment to his wife later that day that the improvement Nick made to his car was the same effect he would expect if the four cylinder engine had been swapped with a V-8 racing engine and he was now getting 65 MPG in town and 90 MPG on the highway!

"Can you imagine that" Was all they could muster.

Chapter -Seven-

Ions: Vitamins of the air

𝒯he next day was Sunday. The Sun was doing its job of waking John. The gentle warmth on his face prompted him to roll over and face his wife who was still out like a light. He loved the way her natural auburn curls wisped over her eyes to act as blinders from the morning Sun, letting her sleep later than he. Smiling to himself as he lay in bed, he recalled his harrowing experience in driving a runaway race car as the result of Nick's incomplete modification to his car's gas/air mixture efficiency. Nick's modification results were truly impressive, nearly tripling his gas mileage and seeming to double the perceived horsepower.

Nick hadn't gotten out of bed as early today not because he was tired still, but because he was verifying some changes of his original plan to redesign the electric motor which he woke up thinking about.

Nick's sub-conscious mind never shut down and he was often pleasantly surprised with some new insights when he woke up in the morning. Such was his subconscious mind's gift to him this morning. After reviewing his new insights, he decided to plan another approach and not use additional coils to suspend the rotor in a separate magnetic field. His new design would remove all of the motor coils altogether! The rotor would still remain because that is the workhorse of the motor. It turns things around, produces torque and so on. His idea was to design a new rotor, smaller than usual of laminated (many layers of steel) with iron rods embedded in the surface of the rotor. The other stator coils whose job was to produce opposing magnetic fields to induce magnetic fields into the rotor to make it rotate would be replaced with ultraviolet laser diodes. These would in effect produce magnetic pulses to do the same thing as the previous coils but in the higher frequency of light and not visible to the eye. The laser diodes would be timed to fire their magnetic light pulses many thousands of times per second at the precise instant to keep the rotor spinning. He would use four fixed high power magnets needing no power whatsoever to suspend the rotor in the center of its turning radius in as much the same way the Sun holds the Earth in place. This would further prevent the friction losses due to bearings, bushings and such. For some motors he would add the extra efficiency of sealing the motor as a container and removing the air to produce a vacuum eliminating friction on the rotor having to move air as it turns inside the motor housing, and in addition, add a gas such as helium to make the rotor lighter and easier to spin. This concept would allow motors to be much smaller, lighter and very, very efficient.

He wanted to attend church with his parents today to learn more about His Lord and learn the ways of a Christian, as a learner and follower of Christ. Later in the afternoon he might play with his ideas of that new motor design. After breakfast they piled into his dad's car and drove to church. He couldn't help but notice a constant smile on his dad's face as he accelerated the car through the turns a little faster than he remembered him doing before. Nick was pleased his dad was enjoying his new high efficiency race car, previously a mere low performance luxury sedan.

Until they arrived, he hadn't quite pictured in his mind what a church would look like. He was a bit surprised it was just a large building, quite unfit for the creator of the world to reside in he thought. Then after talking to his dad about that thought, he told him that the church was really the people and God just meets them here. God's real place of residence is in Heaven, the only place fit for the creator. Heaven must be a very large place since all Christians go there eventually after they die Nick thought. Nick recalled from his reading of Einstein's theories that a place big enough and where there was no time could very well be a huge black hole (a huge star that had collapsed inward due to its own gravity) in space some where. The gravitational pull of a black hole was so powerful that even light could not escape it's interior and time is said to stand still inside the hole. God's radiance, as he learned from the pastor's sermon was so great that no man could look at it and live. The black hole idea seemed logical to him to keep God's radiance in for the protection of the universe and mankind.

He smiled as he thought about the Sun, stars and reflected light of the moon as being just miniscule pinches, little specks of lint off God's clothing though still retaining his brightness when they were cast off his garments as He shook off the star dust from his balcony overlooking empty space.

Nick was disappointed he didn't see God in the flesh but he really felt His Spirit and knew God's love was flowing there because that warm feeling in his tummy was there like after his mom hugged and kissed him. He was pleased to see many of the people his dad works with there. Dad's boss, the man with the French name who couldn't speak the language, the secretary and the manager of Radio Shack were all there.

After church the manager of Radio Shack made a special effort to greet Nick again and thank him for his willingness to share his many years of electronics experience with others as their consultant. The manager also shook his dad's hand and congratulated him for adopting such a fine mature man as their son. Nick could see a smirk growing on his dad's face as the manager turned to leave.

"He still thinks Nick is a full grown midget! Imagine that?!" his dad said to himself.

On the way home John shared with Nick some exciting news he would be glad to hear. His boss told him after church that he had an old 1994 Lincoln Continental that he would donate to Nick's cause. It had air shocks as standard equipment and all of them failed so the car was now sitting on the frame. He thought most everything else worked but in this shape it was not drivable. He said he could have it towed over to their place on Monday if you wanted it.

"I told him that would be fine to do that. I hope that is OK with you!?" John asked as he winked at Nick.

Nick replied with enthusiasm, "Thanks dad! That's great!"

At dinner Nick asked his Mom if it would be OK if he spent the day with her tomorrow (Monday) at work and listened to one of her lectures.

Mary was pleased and replied, "Certainly, Nick I've been looking forward to showing you off and having you understand what I do, let's plan on it!"

Nick also asked his dad if he would be willing to communicate to the school secretary that he was going to be a little delayed in fixing her noisy fan since he had recently gotten a new plan in mind and needed to pick up some more parts and might also be working on his car for a while too. His dad told him that he would make sure she got his message and reassured Nick that any delays would certainly be understood when it involved a busy man such as NickGyver. His dad proceeded to tell him that NickGyver was the nickname that was being circulated about him. He also thought that it was appropriate that his Nickname should include his name "Nick", as it's part of his Nickname after all. He smiled at his dad's funny and felt good that he was considered useful in the community.

Nick decided that he wanted to re-read some portions of the Bible today's sermon referred to. His dad confirmed that was a good plan since from his personal experience he never got the full meaning the first time he read a passage and sometimes got a totally different personal meaning as life changing occurrences happened. Nick thought especially since he didn't have any laser diodes to experiment with this would be a better use of his time. One passage he read the other day said that if he put God and His righteousness first that all of his concerns would be taken care of. That's how he interpreted it anyway and he really wanted to know God better than he ever knew anyone in his life. After all, his greatest joy will be to hear God tell him, "Well done, you faithful servant, enter into my joy!"

Smiling, he also thought that might be God's reply if he was asked how he liked his steaks," Well done".

He opened up the Bible in his mind and it seemed like God himself picked the passage He wanted him to read in his mind. He realized that the version his father had was the "Amplified" Bible. Probably for those who are spiritually hard of hearing. It might speak a little louder to them since it was "amplified". Well, as God spoke to him it was plenty loud and he thought he probably could go with just the Standard or King James version.... God spoke to him from the book of First John, chapters two and three, not necessarily in order but in the order He wanted Nick to hear it.

"And this is how we may discern (daily by experience) that we are coming to know Him - to perceive, recognize, understand and become better acquainted with Him: if we keep (bear in mind, observe, practice) His teachings (precepts, and commandments). Whoever says, I know Him - I perceive, recognize, understand and am acquainted with Him - but fails to keep and obey His commandments (teachings) is a liar, and the Truth (of the Gospel) is not in him. But he who keeps (treasures) His Word- who bears in mind His precepts, who observes His message in its entirety - truly in him has the love of God been perfected (completed, reached maturity). By this we may perceive and know and recognize and be sure that we are in Him. Whosoever says he abides in Him ought as a personal debt to walk and conduct himself in the same way in which He (Jesus) walked and conducted Himself. I am writing to you, little children, because for His name's sake your sins are forgiven pardoned through His name and on account of confessing His name. I am writing to you, fathers because you have come to know (recognize, be aware of and understand) Him Who (has existed) from the beginning. I am writing to you, young men, because you have been victorious over the wicked (one). I write to you, boys, because you have come to know and recognize and be aware of the Father. I write to you, young men, because you are strong and vigorous, and the Word of

God is (always in your hearts) abiding in you, and you have been victorious over the wicked one. Do not love or cherish the world or the things that are in the world. If any one loves the world, love for the Father is not in him. For all that is in the world, the lust of the flesh (craving for sensual gratification) and the lust of the eyes (greedy longings of the mind) and the pride of life (assurance in one's own resources or in the stability of earthly things) these do not come from the Father but are from the world (itself). And the world passes away and disappears, and with it the forbidden cravings (the passionate desires, the lust) of it, but he who does the will of God and carries out His purposes in his life, abides (remains) forever. Boys, it is the last time - hour (the end of this age). And as you have heard that Antichrist (he who will oppose Christ in disguise) is coming, even now many antichrists have arisen, which confirms our belief that it is the final (the end) time. But you hold a sacred appointment, you have been given an unction – you have been anointed by the Holy One, and you all know (the Truth. I write to you, not because you are ignorant and do not perceive and know the Truth, but because you do perceive and know it, and (know positively) that nothing false – no deception, no lie is of the Truth. But as for you, (the sacred appointment, the unction), the anointing which you received from Him, abides (permanently) in you (so) then you have no need that any one should instruct you. But just as His anointing teaches you concerning everything, and is true, and is no falsehood, so you must abide - live, never to depart (rooted in Him, knit to

Him) just as (His anointing) has taught you (to do). You know that He (Jesus) appeared in visible form and became man to take (upon himself) sins, and in Him there is no sin essentially and forever. No one who abides in Him who lives and remains in communion with and in obedience to Him, (deliberately and knowingly) habitually commits (practices) sin. No one who habitually sins has either seen or known Him recognized, perceived or understood Him, or has had an experimental acquaintance with Him. Boys, let no one deceive and lead you astray - He who practices righteousness - who is upright, conforming to the divine will in purpose, thought and action, living a consistently conscientious life is righteous, even as He is righteous. (But) he who commits sin (who practices evil doing) is of the devil - takes his character from the evil one: for the devil has sinned (has violated the divine law) from the beginning. The reason the Son of God was made to manifest (make visible) was to undo (destroy, loosen and dissolve) the works of the devil (has done). No one born (begotten) of God (deliberately and knowingly) habitually practices sin, for God's nature abides in him - His principle of life, the divine sperm, remains permanently within him - and he cannot practice sinning because he is born (begotten) of God. By this it is made clear who take their nature from God and are His children, and who take their nature from the devil and are his children; no one who does not practice righteousness - who does not conform to God's will in purpose, thought and action - is of God; neither is any one who does not love his brother (his fellow believer in Christ). Let us not love (merely) in theory or in speech, but in deed and in truth - in practice and in sincerity. By this we shall come to know - perceive and recognize and understand) - that we are of the Truth, and can reassure (quiet, conciliate and pacify) our hearts in His presence. And beloved - if our consciences (our hearts) do not accuse us - if they do not make us feel guilty and condemn us - we have confidence (complete assurance and boldness) before God. And we receive from Him whatever we ask for, because we (watchfully) obey His orders - observe His suggestions and injunctions, follow His plan for us and (habitually) practice what is pleasing to Him. All who keep His commandments (who obey His orders and follow His plan, live and continue to live, to stay) and abide in Him, and He in them. They let Christ be a home in them and He in them. They let Christ be a home to them and they are the home of Christ. And by this we know and understand and have the proof that He (really) lives and makes His home in us, by the (Holy) Spirit whom He has given us."

In Nick's Spirit he heard every word and seemed as if it was a half hour, but in his mind the message took only a flash of time, a mere fraction of a second. Nick responded in awe to God, "Speak and I will listen and obey!"

Nick fell asleep that night knowing full well that God had his life under control and he rested in that thought. He couldn't help but let his thoughts play out for a few minutes what his car might be like and how one day he would drive it to work all by himself.

Monday morning he awoke with the crack of dawn and chuckled to himself. "That is why people call it "day break"!" Day break is the result of the dawn cracking. It was quite a rational thought, but not a factual happening. Although, he thought, if the day would break every day we would have twice as many days! But, they'd be shorter ones, and one would be mostly dark. He loved bright mornings so for him that would not do! Then he recalled the Bible verse that said that for God a day is as a thousand years and a thousand years as a day. (WOW that was a full day!)

Then he also remembered the story his dad once told him in reference to this. One man came to God and confirmed to Him, "To you God, one day, even one second, is as a thousand years and since you are the creator, you own everything, even the cattle on a thousand hills. To you, a million dollars would be like a penny. Then he asked, "God, can I have penny?" God replied, "Sure, in a second!"

Mary came into Nick's room, surprised he was still in his bed and asked him if he felt OK today. Nick replied, "I feel great! I was just taking some time to think about God before I got up. It's about time I have more than just myself to think about! Thanks for being my mom and loving me!"

Mary, with a tear forming in her eye, responded, "Nick, I have been waiting for you all of my life to make me a mother. It is my honor and highest joy to love you! You are God's gift to teach me how much he loves us because His love is the highest and greatest love. When I think of how I love you and John, I realize that God loves us more because He IS love, was the one who created love, brought it to life, kissed it goodbye as he sent it toward Earth and then gave it to us. That makes me love Him even more!"

Nick wondered for a moment if his birth parents were sitting with God right now and feeling even more joy than he was feeling right now. He hoped they were there waiting for him and that he could be with them for eternity to come. His parents never talked about God or even owned a Bible for that matter. It was a sad thought he might never see them again. God only knew.

By the time Nick and his mom entered the kitchen John was busy making coffee. It was still hard for Nick to understand how something so good smelling could taste so bad! He shook his head and said, "Bowls or plates today? I'll set the table!"

Mary asked John, "What did you have in mind for breakfast today? Thought about it yet, dearest?"

John replied, "I hadn't quite gotten that far yet. I'm still waking up!"

Mary replied, "Well, why don't you two men discuss it and let me know. I'm going to use the bathroom and get dressed!"

John offered, "Nick, I can make some pretty great tasting egg omelets and I think we have all of the ingredients!"

Nick responded, nearly too hungry to care, "Sounds fantastic! Tell me what to get out of the refrigerator and I'll line 'em up on the counter for you!"

John proceeded to list the ingredients out loud to Nick and he found every one. Now he had the formula for egg omelets and after watching his dad cook them, he could cook them anytime he wanted later!

By the time Mary came out of the bedroom fully dressed and looking like a sparkling rose due to the shade of her auburn hair in the sunlight, she was pleased to see that her men had things under control.

She offered, "Just about perfect time to pop some bread in the toaster?"

Nick smiled in return and said, "Yes Maam! I saw some Huckleberry jam in the 'fridge', Ok to use that this morning?"

Mary replied, "Sounds perfect!"

During breakfast he thought about the ingredients of this tasty dish. The chickens had donated their unborn offspring, the pigs had given more than a contribution, they had given their lives, the cows had provided them the ingredients for cheese by coming through in a tight squeeze. Udderly disgustful he thought, giggling as he ate...

The other vegetables in the garden were undoubtedly green with envy at the peppers for being picked first. Ah, thank you God for humor!

John noticed that Nick was apparently off in another world of thought and that big grin on his face was a telltale sign that he had thought of something very funny. Nick shared his funny thoughts with them and they all laughed! Then John piped up with a string of egg jokes himself, wanting to add to the gaiety of the moment.

"What did one egg say to another egg?" "Shell we dance?"

"Why did one egg sit up so straight in the egg carton?" "Because he wanted to be a good eggsample to the other eggs!"

"What did the chef say as he was making an omelet and discovered one egg was rotten?" "Well, not all eggs are what they are cracked up to be!"

"What did the little chick say when he noticed an orange under his mother?" "Oh, look at the orange marmalade!"

Nick broke in, "Dad, I'm sure you could come up with yolk after yolk until you said a dozen!"

By this time they were all laughing so hard their sides hurt! But it was a nice hurt.

After breakfast dishes were cleaned and put away, Nick quickly got dressed to go with his mom to work for the day. Her college was just across the freeway from the Hardtford Metropolitan Hospital. Hardt Metro they called it for short. When it came to hospitals and medicine, time was of the utmost importance since even seconds counted in saving lives. So it was common place to use abbreviations in the medical field. Abbreviations were a language all of their own. It intrigued Nick as languages were his forte', his talent, his cup of tea. Stopping to think a bit, he mused why even the word "abbreviation" was so long? The wonders of language!

After his mom had parked her car and they went in to the lecture hall, he found a seat in the front row and sat down. He noticed that some female students were whispering that they thought he was cute and wondered where he came from. It occurred to him that he was too far away to hear them audibly but still could in his mind. God must have given him also the language of lip reading for some future purpose. He just shrugged his shoulders and decided to ignore the girls and focus on his mother's lecture.

He thought for a moment how his mom and dad were so alike. Now with this lecture on electrically charged ions, a subject his father could lecture on with great detail and prowess, his mother was tackling it from a medical slant. His parents seemed to think alike! That brought to mind another scripture reference about how when a man and a woman get married they become one flesh. He could certainly see that exhibited in his parents! In fact they were even called the same by their students...Professor Jameson!

His mother began her lecture like this:

"There is nothing like a good breath of fresh air. It tastes clean and invigorating, gives us a healthy appetite and helps us sleep soundly. On the other hand, there is nothing worse than the kind of aerial soup many people live, work and choke in."

She continued, "From the days of the Phoenicians it has been known that some climates are better for us than others. The Romans used certain areas for rest and recuperation because of the quality of the air, and nobody can climb a mountain, stroll along a beach or sit by a waterfall without noticing this quality. Many factors may be involved, such as temperature, humidity, atmospheric pressure and wind - but there are other factors, of which one of the most important is the presence in the atmosphere of electrically charged condensation nuclei known as ions."

"My main focus today in this lecture is going to be on air ions to distinguish them from ions of other substances.

Air consists principally of oxygen, nitrogen, and carbon dioxide molecules. These in turn consist of atoms, and like any other atom they have a positively charged nucleus orbited by negatively charged electrons. Most air molecules are electrically balanced, and thus neutral, but when one of them gains or loses an electron it becomes charged, negatively or positively (respectively).

This process called ionization, can be caused in many ways: by ultra-violet light from the Sun, radioactivity from the ground, rapidly moving water such as breaking surf or waterfalls, or lightning discharges. Air ions can now be generated artificially in a number of ways. It was not until the eve of the twentieth century that the conductivity of the atmosphere was explained, when Elster and Geiteland (independently), and Wilson showed that both positive and negative carriers of electricity exist in air, and the name ion was given to such carriers. Yet at least a century before this, air ion therapy was being practiced and recommended for a number of ailments, notably eye diseases.

One of the first scientists to carry out research into the newly identified air ions was a remarkable Russian named Aleksandr L. Chizhevsky. Right from the start, it was evident to him that negative ions were good for his test lab animals. Rats would respond after only a couple of hours in a negatively ionized area, showing considerably more sexual activity than a control group outside it. Newly hatched chicks kept in the negative ion cage would start putting on weight faster than control groups, after only a few days. He next wondered what effect negative ions might have on disease and initial tests on guinea pigs infected with tuberculosis gave encouraging results: after eight weeks the entire control group had died, while every one of the ionized animals was alive, well, and moreover free from TB. They were in fact healthier than they had been before the start of the test. He was convinced now that negatively ionized air led to a lasting mobilization of the body's defense mechanisms. He decided to try it on human patients after claiming remarkable success with a circus chimpanzee, curing it in about four months of TB with apparently nothing more than daily doses of ions. In 1928 he set up a special ionization chamber, where he gave treatment to 130 TB patients, finding that it improved their overall health and helped them put on weight. He was never sure exactly why ionization was good for people. He speculated that when we breathe negative ions, we absorb them at once into the bloodstream and set up a current, which in turn produces other forms of energy, chiefly thermal, mechanical and chemical, thereby giving the immune system a general boost.

A great deal of modern research has been prompted by the weather, especially certain types of hot and dry wind that plague people in many parts of the world. The Swiss have their name for it, "Foehn", the French, the "Mistral", Californians, the "Santa Ana", Canadians the Chinook", northern Italians the "Tramontans, and Israelis, the "Sharav or Khamsin" All mean much the same thing: trouble. These winds cause insomnia, depression, hypertension, breathing problems, allergic reaction and notable increases in accident and suicide rates. Chizhevsky once suggested that courts should take such winds into consideration when sentencing lawbreakers under their influence and I understand that Israeli judges are doing so, since the winds there cause illness of some kind in 30% of those exposed to it. At the Hebrew University in Jerusalem, Professor F. G. Sulman studied a group of 800 Khamsin sufferers over a four-year period. He found an unusual amount of stress hormone called serotonin in their blood, possibly due to the high positive ion content in the air before the onset of the wind. He found he could reproduce most of the wind's effects artificially and that negative ion treatment brought patient's conditions back to normal.

Also in Jerusalem, doctors at Bikur Holim hospital found that negative ions, without any supporting treatment, even antibiotics, terminated spastic conditions in infants suffering from asthmatic bronchitis after much less time than required for conventional treatment. This is perhaps because the ions cause the offending substance (allergen) to precipitate."

Ions, both positive and negative, affect different people in different ways, as do many other things such as tea and coffee, but in general it can be said that positive ions tend to produce ill effects while negative ions are good for us, most noticeably in relieving hay fever, asthma and various allergies.

They also seem to stabilize blood pressure, improve work capacity, learning ability and reaction time, and help combat even serious ailments. Negative ions have also been found useful in treating burns, and even in stopping people from snoring, which, by the way I thank you all for not doing while I am lecturing!

Dr. R. R. Holiday has called negative ions "vitamins of the air" and he reckons that biochemistry is now discovering the value of air in the way it discovered food 100 years ago, when Sir Frederick Gowland Hopkins discovered the first vitamin and called it an "accessory food factor". Air ions, he thinks may be "accessory metabolic factors".

Chezhevski believed that the influence of ions could be transmitted directly through the blood stream. In one of his experiments, he connected the blood streams of two animals and found that when only one was exposed to atmospheric ions, the other showed the same reaction although it had not breathed the same air.

In 1957, Dr. Igho H. Kornblueh, the pioneer in ion therapy, suggested that the effects of ionization on brain rhythms should be investigated, and it has now established that through it, human alpha waves can be reduced in frequency and increased up to 20 percent in amplitude.

Artificial ions have also been found to be good for sportsmen, increasing body capacity and normalizing the metabolic balance of certain vitamins.

In Munich, it was found after thousands of tests that drivers' reaction times could be favorably influenced when negative ions were beamed at them, where as positive ions made them feel sleepy, inevitably lengthening reaction times. Many motorists now use mini-ionizers, and there are grounds for suggesting that they should be made as compulsory as seat belts.

Dr. Cristjo Cristofv in 1956 discovered that certain types of plastic seat covers, especially polyethylene, can develop extremely high local negative electric fields of up to 10,000 volts per meter, as a result of friction against passengers' clothing. For reasons not entirely understood, the human body reacts to the absence of the natural positive electric field of the earth, which measures an average of 500 to 800 volts per meter. This may be because a positive field attracts negative ions, which have been shown to have a number of beneficial effects, whereas a negative field will not. Since interiors of cars, aircraft and submarines are spaces largely shielded from the natural environmental electric field because of their metallic structures, they serve as Faraday cages to some extent, drastically altering the electromagnetic environment.

Numerous tests, some dating back to the nineteen century, have shown that negative fields sap the vitality of animals, induce fear, cause loss of appetite and reduce fertility, whereas positive fields (which attract negative ions) improve respiration, digestion and general metabolism.

The U.S. Air Force has carried out tests of the effects of strong positive ion fields and found they help considerably to improve pilots' general alertness and combat fatigue. They found that by adding a 1000 volt per meter positive field to a small enclosed and shielded space can not only reverse the effects of fatigue but raise a human subjects' overall performance well above its normal level.

After the death of three Russian Cosmonauts in 1972 and other unexplained crashes of South African and Italian Air Force planes and a large number of Star fighters lost by the West Germans and Bermuda Triangle disappearances, the thought has been that these were the result of high positive electric charges that affected the pilots metabolically.

Dr. Caymaz in his involvement with on going research in this area, noticed that whenever there was a sudden high positive voltage, there would be an air crash or a road accident, and often increased hemorrhages among TB patients in the hospital where he worked. He decided to observe the effects of aircraft interiors on blood electrolytes (substances that become electrically conductive in aqueous solutions or in blood, such as sodium and potassium). Taking blood samples from six soldiers before and after a one-hour flight, he found an increase in sodium of up to 20 percent, also increases in cholesterol and blood alkalinity (pH) and a decrease in potassium content. The results showed that some humans are significantly physically affected by flying in aircraft. A single experiment with a plane on the ground showed that the airfield's atmospheric voltage reading of 6 millivolts, 6 thousandths of a volt (positive), rose to 12 millivolts inside the aircraft, reaching 16 millivolts when the door was closed. Dr. Caymaz was alarmed to find readings close to those he had previously associated with road accidents and lung bleedings.

At a NATO international conference on aircrew fitness he made the following suggestions:

1. Atmospheric electricity should be measured every day and the reading broadcast on public radio. People would then be warned that their reflexes would be slower and should drive or fly with extra care.
2. Whenever he flew, Dr. Caymaz said, he took potassium chloride, calcium, magnesium and vitamin C pills to offset possible ill effects and variations in electricity.

He recommends pilots to take potassium salts whenever electricity readings were high. Drivers of heavy vehicles usually attach ground wires to them to drain off excess electric charges into the ground. Car owners might try doing the same for long journeys, though obviously pilots cannot do the same.

Another medical researcher is Dr. E. Stanton Maxey who has been looking into aircraft crashes. Maxey has shown that it is possible to alter the rhythm of a brain by beaming extremely low frequency magnetic waves at it. This he thinks is what may be what is happening at the time of some air crashes later described as "pilot error".

Since certain types of weather are known to produce ELF electromagnetic waves, it seems unquestionable that all pilots are running the risk of having their brains - which are more valuable than any other of the instruments in front of them - interfered with by natural forces.

We have looked today at just a few of the ways in which man responds to some of the invisible components of his environment, especially regarding ions. Some people are more sensitive to these and even some have been known to combust spontaneously and be reduced to a pile of ashes. This happens more often than many people realize and there is an impressive array of evidence for this most bizarre of manifestations of invisible force, including testimony from firemen, policemen, pathologists, coroners and even the FBI. There is also plenty of horrific photographic evidence on police files. Official verdicts in such cases in which people simply start burning for no obvious reason, are often more inherently implausible than the events themselves, which remain unexplained.

On April 7, 1938 three people were charred to death at exactly the same time, no normal cause of death yet having been suggested for any of them.

One was a truck driver near Chester, England, another was a motorist in Holland and the third was a helmsman of a ship off the coast of southern Eire. Interestingly, when plotted on a map and connected by straight lines, the three locations formed an isosceles triangle with an apex angle of 120 degrees. I have inferred before, the forces of nature should never be taken for granted."

Mrs. Professor Jameson paused, took a breath and looked up once more at her class and said, "I know that this has been quite a long lecture, but we still have a few minutes for questions, if there are any." One young lady in the back raised her hand and the Professor recognized her.

She stood up and said, "I don't have any questions, but I do have a comment. That is, WOW and shocking!! I had no idea all of that ion stuff was in the air around me! This was excellent! Thank you!"

Mrs. Professor Jameson replied, "Thank you for your kind remarks and I appreciate the pun on "shocking!"

The class groaned.

"Well," said Mrs. Jameson, "if there aren't any other questions, and we are frankly out of time, you are dismissed until I see you again!"

After the class dispersed, Nick came up to his mom and said, "That was excellent!"

Mary replied humbly, "This is what I do and I try to do it well! Thanks for your encouragement! Do you want to get a tour and see what books I have in my office library?"

Nick responded, "I sure would!"

As Nick and the Mrs. Professor walked across the courtyard to her office building, Nick grabbed her hand and swung it as they walked. Holding Nick's hand reinforced the positive and she felt a definite tingle going to her heart of electric joy.

Chapter -Eight-

Attracting and repelling shock of the century

Nick spent the rest of the day ingesting all of the books in the medical college. His mom's library collection took only two hours for 60 books while the main library's 400 books took him four hours. He realized that he had actually gotten faster in his comprehension times. Actually it was the time taken to turn the pages that took most of the time, but he sped up some of his time by discovering a series of audio books while at the library and listened to them at high speed while he read the others with his eyes. He must have the capability to process visual and auditory inputs separately in different parts of his brain simultaneously. He thought smiling, I might get carried away here with this speed reading, but if I could learn Braille, I could read one book with my fingers while reading another with my eyes and listening to another with my ears!

He especially enjoyed reading the college level dictionaries and thesaurus'. He liked the dictionaries because they represented so many stories and even songs in the making.

For example: take the simple word "**and**".

The dictionary had unlimited story fodder.

"**And**" she took the tea pot off the stove "**and**" poured herself "**and**" her husband their last cup before they died since they had completely run out of food after the drought hit "**and**" their livelihood was now gone.

Or a song, "**And**" He walks with me "**and**" talks with me along life's narrow way......He lives, Christ Jesus lives today!"

Now that he had the English dictionary memorized, he had the ability to function in the new society he was adopted into just a few weeks earlier. The thesaurus gave him the ability to express himself, describe his thoughts, make analogies and relate his theories to others. Great building blocks, he concluded to himself! When he finished his last thought he went as instructed to meet his mother in her office. She was just finishing up with some notes for another lecture she was preparing for the next class later on in the week. "Ready to go home?" asked Mary.

"Yes, I think so, mom, there aren't any more books to read here at the school and I'd like to see if my car has been delivered to our house yet."

Nick replied.

"Then by all means we'd better get going, huh, son?"

"That's right, mom!" Nick responded.

Nick was thoughtful on the ride home, feeling content as one must feel after they had gone grocery shopping and had stocked the cupboard shelves and refrigerator with a month's supply of a most pleasant variety of scrumptious food to choose from. Thus he felt about the wealth of information he had to pick and choose from today's forage at the college. And feast he would in the coming days and weeks!

When they arrived home, Nick jumped out of the car just as it came to a stop and excitedly ran to gaze in awe at the beautiful car parked next to the ground. And next to the ground it truly was, looking as if the body was resting on the tires. Well he thought, that is my first project. He looked under the car to see how the car had been designed and built, noticing especially how much room he had in the area where the defective shocks were. Ah, he confirmed, just as I thought! Seeing with his eyes allowed his brain to connect the visual input and match it to the page in his memory about how air shocks were designed that he had read about in a Ford repair manual he found under a box in a remote corner of the library as he was searching for any books he might have missed. He confirmed, yes, very poor design at best! Shouldn't have used air at all, but magnetism! But of course that was his forte' and unless you are an expert on things like that you wouldn't have thought of that possibility. He replayed in his mind the vision he saw before him. Shocks made of repelling magnetic force. They could be made adjustable merely by varying the magnetic force! Simply place two electromagnets facing each other, one on the frame and the other the body with like magnetic poles facing each other. When you hit a bump, the car body would move against the magnetic field but be repelled back. "Novel idea" he said to himself, "I should write a book!"

Chuckling to himself, he went into the house to make a list of materials. He hadn't gotten any calls from Radio Shack as far as he knew. Well, he'd listen to the voice mail messages and see, because he had to give a consultation to get his materials for free. Sure enough, there was a message waiting specifically for him, NickGyver. He returned the call to the repair shop. They had an emergency repair that had to be fixed before the end of the day. It was apparently heat (thermally) related as the radio worked fine until it warmed up, then stopped working. Nick asked the repair man if he had a non-contact thermometer probe available. He looked around for a few seconds and then said he did. Nick told him to find the power supply section, notably where the big transformer was.

"I found it," replied the man.

"Now," said Nick, "point the temperature probe at the rectifier diodes, signified with a white stripe on the ends and tell me what their temperatures are."

The man replied, "Three are 40 degrees Centigrade, but the fourth is 65 degrees Centigrade."

Nick replied, "Well, there's your problem! That one is overheating and shutting down on thermal safety. That one's sick, you'd better replace it and you should be good to go! Just to be safe, you'd also better check the current draw of the main circuit board it powers too just to be sure something on that board doesn't draw too much current and may have caused the rectifier to fail in the first place. Feel free to call me back should you still have problems."

"Thanks a million, Mr. NickGyver!" the repairman replied.

Nick thought to himself, "It may cost them that much after I get going on my tinkering!"

He made up his list of materials and called Radio Shack back. They said they didn't have as large of diameter of magnet wire he needed, but they could have it for him tomorrow. He also had to scrounge up some round plates of one inch thick steel which he discovered at a recycling center not too far from his home. The owner agreed to donate the steel to him, snickering out loud when Nick told him he needed it to build electromagnetic shock absorbers for his Lincoln Continental. The next day he asked if he could stay home and work on his car and his parents said yes, although reluctantly.

It was hard not to look at him and treat him like he was a 4 year old, because he was in fact just that! But both his mom and dad said they would check on him during their lunch breaks to make sure he was OK or needed anything.

After his parents both left, he walked over to the steel recycling place and carried the pieces of heavy steel, or more realistically, he dragged them home. Then he took the bus to Radio Shack to pick up his magnet wire. The repair man from the back room heard that NickGyver had just walked in and came out to thank him again for his assistance in getting the radio fixed.

Nick replied, "You are most welcome! That's my job; thanks for letting me do it!"

Nick was a bit surprised at the weight of the rolls of magnet wire. They nearly weighed more than he did! The manager asked if he needed help carrying them out to his car. Nick replied that he had taken the bus here and this was for his car.

The manager in jest replied, "Converting your car to operate with anti-gravity propulsion?"

Nick replied, "Not this project, but thanks for the idea! Maybe some day though!"

The manager smiled that Nick was returning his joke, but he would someday learn differently that Nick was serious!

Then Nick asked, "Do you by any chance have delivery available?"

The manager complied by stating that he could have his repairman drop it off on his way home from work this evening. Nick thought that offer was his best option and reluctantly agreed.

A bit disappointed, Nick took the next bus home. Well, he could cut the pieces of steel to size while he waited, he thought. He looked up the diameter of the airbag in his memory and mentally calculated the circumference of the circles he had to cut. But how does he cut them, he wondered? He did a quick search of his memory on cutting steel, one inch thick steel to be exact, and found his only course of action was to use a plasma cutter. But he didn't have one. Well, what do I need to make one, he asked himself? Oxygen, and a high current power source. He looked around the garage and found his dad had an oxy-acetylene torch. The acetylene was empty, but all he needed was the oxygen. Now for the high current power source. He noticed a couple of deep cycle storage batteries his dad may have used for his boat trolling motor. Well, if you hook up batteries in series, connecting the negative post of one battery to the positive post of the other battery, you double the current output of the batteries. Each battery had a rating of about 250 amps, so he could have 500 amps available and when connected in series, the voltage adds so it would be 24 volts. That should take care of the power source quite nicely! He searched for a welding mask because he knew it would be very bright with the electric arc cutting the steel and he didn't want to damage his eyes or splatter his face with hot metal either. He found his dad's mask hanging on a peg at the rear of the garage. He also found a pair of broken jumper cables and saw his dad had already purchased a new pair so he thought he wouldn't mind donating the old ones to him. He also discovered a box of welding cutting rod near the mask. He modified the battery clamp on one end of one of the old cables into a cutting rod holder, so he was all set!

Thoughtfully, he decided to do the cutting outside so nothing would catch fire in the garage from the sparks. He laid the steel plates on the driveway and using a pencil attached to a string and a suction cup on the other end of the string, drew the circles he had calculated on the steel by placing the suction cup in the center of the circle to be, stretched the pencil end of the string out to one half the circle diameter and tied it in a knot around the pencil. Then he would stretch the string tight while holding the pencil and draw the circle with the pencil. After drawing eight perfect diameter circles, he discovered he had some steel left over. Aw, he thought, perfect for that extra added touch I just thought about! He further thought to keep from burning his dad's driveway there was a sand pit in the back yard he could use and it would be fairly easy to screen out the burned metal pieces from that! He lugged the heavy batteries onto a two- wheel dolly and rolled them to the sand pit along with the oxygen tank, cables and cutting rods. He got the idea to strap the oxygen torch end to the battery clamp rod holder so it would project oxygen at the tip of the cutting rod, and Voella he had his plasma cutter! He made sure there was a check valve in the hose going to the oxygen tank so the flame wouldn't be drawn back into the tank and explode and it had one. He dragged the sheet of one inch steel to the back of the house to the sand pit, hooked up everything and adjusted the huge welding mask to fit his small head. Now he lit an electrical fire arc at the torch end by striking the welding rod lightly on the metal, and blue plasma appeared at the tip! It worked! He tried it by cutting off a corner of the sheet of steel and it worked very well! He was elated! It took him a little while to cut perfect circles, but soon he had the art, in a round about way....He finished up by cutting four more, a bit larger, but squares this time, and he was done. He left the cut metal pieces in the sand to cool and dismantled his equipment and put them away.

On his last trip to the garage, a car pulled up into the driveway. A man stepped out who Nick recognized as the repairman from Radio Shack. The man tipped his hat and smiled. "I thought you might be waiting for this wire, so I had an opportunity to swing by here on my way to lunch and thought I'd drop it off. You don't mind, do you?"

Nick replied, "No, not at all! Thanks for thinking of me!"

"What are you working on today?" the repairman asked.

Nick replied, "Just an idea for some new shocks for my Lincoln over there," pointing in the direction of the car and smiling.

"What's the magnet wire for?" asked the repairman.

"Electromagnetic shocks!" Nick replied exuberantly.

"Now THAT I've got to see!" exclaimed the repairman.

"I'll let you know when they're done, OK?" responded Nick.

"Sounds great! See you later Mr. NickGyver!" the repairman shouted over his shoulder as he climbed back into his car to head for some hamburgers somewhere.

Nick had already calculated the magnetic force needed to lift the body of his car off the frame and added a bit more so he could make it adjustable. He figured out the number of turns of magnet wire required and went to work carefully making his coils to fit around the plates he previously cut. He also made four extra coils of a higher magnetic capability for the bottom of his lower magnetic assembly for his special added touch he had planned. Of course he had to lift the car up to get the work done and all that he had was the factory supplied jack. He got it out of the trunk and looked at it. "I hope I don't have to use this thing any more! It's a pretty lame way to lift a car!" he said out loud.

He thought he'd do the front first, since it was probably the hardest. As he had calculated, everything fit perfectly in the space where the air bags had fit before. He plugged the ends of the old air lines which used to feed the air bags and thought that he might have some use for those lines in the future. Just get them out of the way for now. He had calculated the amount of current these magnetic coils would draw and his car battery would be able to handle it easily. He finished up the front shocks and lowered the jack. The car still sat on the frame because the car was not running to supply power to the coils.

He jacked up the rear end and performed the same steps he had done for the front and in a few hours he was done. He had no need to test them because he knew they would work.

In a few minutes, his dad's car was seen coming up the driveway.

Excitedly, Nick shouted to his dad even before he got out of his car, "Come and see how I fixed my shocks on my car!"

John complied not knowing what to expect, but anticipating Nick, it was pretty fantastic and it would work!

John looked at the car seemingly unchanged from the way it looked the day before it when it was towed there.

Nick told him, "Just wait a minute until I get the engine started."

The moment he fired up the engine, a space of about six inches appeared between each wheel and the car body as the car rose off the frame.

"You think that's amazing..." Nick exclaimed, "Watch this!"

Nick flipped a switch on the dash and there was a clunk under the car as a steel plate fell to the ground. Then Nick flipped another switch and the left wheel was lifted a foot off the ground. Then he flipped another switch and a second steel plate fell to the driveway and the passenger front wheel was lifted the same distance off the ground.

"Neat, Huh?" asked Nick.

John's mouth was hanging open.

"Now watch this!" exclaimed Nick.

He flipped another switch and a third steel plate fell to the ground and the rear left wheel left the ground and went up a foot. He flipped yet another switch and the right rear wheel left the ground and the whole car was off the ground with nothing supporting it but apparently magnetic forces! John knelt to look under the car and sure enough there was nothing but air and those four plates he heard fall earlier on the ground!

All John could say was, "Imagine that!"

Nick flipped one switch at a time and each wheel touched back to the ground one at a time gently and there was the added sound of each steel plate being sucked magnetically back up into its holding storage place. Then he shut off the engine and the car body once again settled onto the frame.

Then John asked Nick, "But how did you.....?"

Nick replied rather proudly, "I'll tell you over supper after mom gets home, OK?"

Great, John thought, that will give my mind some time to clear so I can understand this marvel he has just accomplished!

Mary soon arrived home and immediately noticed that John had been in a bit of shock. She asked him if he was all right and he told her that she would understand over supper. Mary went into the house, put her things away and got supper going. Of course Nick offered to set the table while grinning large the whole time. Mary could hardly control herself to find out what was going on, but still kept on completing the supper process. When they finally sat down to eat, Nick explained to them what he had done that day. They were a bit frightened that he took the bus all by himself, but he reminded them that he was the one who hiked 100 miles for a week through robbers and other peril without any trouble and then they realized that they had been hasty in their worry, although quite like parents would be expected to be concerned about their children.

Later that evening John and Mary made another pact with God to place Nick under His protection and possession as they should have from the very beginning. It was still hard not to worry! He was only four years old! Although sometimes it seemed like he had the experience of a man four centuries old!

As Nick lay in bed that evening, he thought about the next modification he would make to his car. Certainly the piano wire in the air cleaner duct routine! Then......who knows! Then he remembered that he forgot to pick up those laser diodes he needed for his new electric motor design and prayed that God would provide him another consult opportunity at Radio Shack to get those parts tomorrow.

As he drifted off to sleep all that was visible to him was the rise and fall of his new shocks in his subconscious. His inner mind approved of his accomplishment. Then his inner mind turned the page to start a new memory file to plan for his next project: a new medical breakthrough!

The air was fresh coming in through his open bedroom window, the lawn sprinklers had just activated and freshly ionized the air blowing into his room so he slept soundly and regenerated his depleted stores of energy. The sound of the oscillating sprinklers reminded him of ocean waves breaking on the shore and he immediately thought of generators placed in the water to generate electricity from the movement of the tides and waves. "That's a novel idea," he thought, "I should write a book!" Then he drifted off to sleep.

CHAPTER -NINE-

A return to Vitamins of the Air

Nick awoke especially early on Tuesday morning. He ran outside in his pajamas to peek under his car to see if what he dreamed had actually happened and it had! His subconscious had been working all night and he had a new idea for his revolutionary medical break through! It was a combination of both his dad's and mom's lectures. Vitamins dispensed by ultraviolet light through the eyes. Here was his plan: Design a machine that would resemble a face massage unit but with lenses that you looked into to enable the vitamins to be beamed into your eyes. After all, that is the way that God delivers us a number of vitamins such as Vitamin D and K. Why not all the others? And then extend that to other types of medications as well, even chemotherapy! Until he came up with a permanent cure for cancer that is, he thought. The medicine would be converted into an electro magnetic image and ride on ultraviolet waves in a radio or TV transmission wave. The airwaves would be bounced off satellites from the hospitals. The medicines would be available multiple times per day, twenty four hours per day, seven days per week without having to go to the hospital. Security would have to be extremely high. He would use a handprint reader, voice recognition with a key password phrase and retinal scanner automatically done when the patient places their face into the unit and faces the lenses. A pass card reader will also transmit their hospital card or medical card information to the hospital for billing purposes to verify the patient is ready to receive the shipment by airwaves. This is transmitted on the same radio wave to the hospital before they send the vitamin or medications by return signal. He'd call them Air Vites, short for Air Vitamins. Now this may really take more sophisticated equipment than he could build from Radio Shack parts. It would take a lot of money, lots of money!

"Ok God, if this is from you, supply the funds!" Nick prayed.

The mailman came early that day and there was a letter addressed to Mr. Nick Gyver. Nick hurriedly opened the letter expecting and hardly concerned that this was not from God. After all, God told him that if he asked for anything in His will, He will supply it.

The letter read like this:

"Dear Nick, This is a personal letter just to you. What I am going to tell you is a secret, because this information is confidential.

These words are meant for you only. There has existed for many years an exclusive organization, a secret society, of the world's most famous and powerful people. These include renowned actors and musicians, leading scientists and intellectuals, self-made entrepreneurs and artists, millionaires, professional gamblers, Casanovas, and statesmen. Many of these people you would instantly recognize. Everything you read here is absolutely and verifiably true. This association has uncovered some shockingly powerful secrets. And they share these secrets only amongst themselves. These secrets are the reason these well-known individuals have achieved great prosperity. Nick, members of this group have analyzed your profile and you'd be incredibly flattered if you knew who these people were. They've discovered something special about you. It seems you possess several rare traits they are searching for. Because of these traits they have chosen you to become part of their exclusive club and to share their secrets. They are going to reveal to you the greatest kept secret in all time for money, power, and romantic love! Every seven years this association picks out only a handful of individuals from around the world possessing your hidden talents. How did these gifted people find you? For now, that must remain a mystery. I received this offer myself just seven years ago and thought it was just a bunch of hooey, but I sent for it and my luck has changed so completely I thought God MUST be guiding me, giving me special powers! Send for this free package and it will be the most important thing you have done in your life. For by the time you finish reading the information in *the packet, you'll know exactly what to do to make $5,000, $10,000, even $100,000 or $1 million in the next few weeks! Plus prosper in every area of your life: emotionally, personally, physically, romantically and financially! These secrets have been hidden from ordinary human eyes for 2300 years. You possess rare potentials few others have and are one of the only ones who can understand and benefit from this. You feel special and gifted, I know you do! And you are here on this earth to do great things with your life. Right? You are meant to do great things, exactly as we are going to show you. This is your calling. To get this information, which is free to you, you must fax this invitation card on or before Friday, July 8, 2005. After this Friday, you won't get this invitation again."*

Nick stood there astounded. This MUST be from God, he thought! I need to find out how to fax this right away! Then the Holy Spirit spoke to him from a portion of memorized scripture:

1 John 4:1-6 "Beloved, do not put your faith in every spirit, but prove (test) the spirits to discover whether they proceed from God; for many false prophets have gone forth into the world. By this you may know (perceive and recognize) the Spirit of God; every spirit which acknowledges and confesses (the fact) that Jesus Christ, the Messiah, (actually) has become man and has come in the flesh is of God - has God for its source. And every spirit which does not acknowledge and confess that Jesus Christ has come in the flesh

(but would annul, destroy, sever, disunite Him) is not of God - does not proceed from Him. This (non-confession) is the (spirit) of antichrist, (of) which you heard that it was coming, and now it is already in the world. Little children, you are of God -you who belong to Him - and have (already) defeated and overcome them (the agents of antichrist), because He Who lives in you is greater (mightier) than he who is in the world. They proceed from the world and are of the world, therefore it is out of the world (its whole economy morally considered) that they speak, and the world listens (pays attention) to them. We are (children) of God. Whoever is learning to know God (by observation and experience) and to get an ever clearer knowledge of Him - listens to us; and he who is not of God does not listen or pay attention to us. By this we know (recognize) the Spirit of Truth and the spirit of error."

Nick gasped! It couldn't be any clearer! This is NOT of God! He showed the letter to his dad later before breakfast and his dad asked him what God was speaking directly to him about it. Nick verified that God clearly said through 1 John 4:1-6 that this was not of Him.

John agreed and said, "I feel in my spirit that this is of the devil and not of God. We'll file the letter away to see what happens in the future concerning this just out of curiosity."

Nick shared with his parents during breakfast about his new medical break through idea he got from his subconscious working.

Both John and Mary were impressed and agreed that Nick should pursue the idea.

John mentioned that he thought Nick had something really special with his electromagnetic shocks and he would check with some contacts he had in the auto industry, especially Ford Motor Company and see if they would be interested. But first they had to get the idea patented. Then he'd talk to the auto people. John warned Nick not to talk to or show anyone else his invention or they might get a patent on it first and cheat him out of his rightful money for the idea. Nick agreed wholeheartedly. John helped Nick patent the idea, fronting the money required to file the patent as an investment in Nick's idea and then contacted the auto people. He had two immediate offers to buy the patent. One for $7 million, five hundred thousand and the other for an even $10 million. The decision was an easy one and they drew up the papers to sell the patent and rights for the higher offer.

After his parents opened an account at the local bank, they explained to him that NOW he could walk in and ask for some of that paper money to pay bills or purchase things. They also taught him about writing checks and asked him if he would mind some guidance once and awhile in the finance area and Nick replied that if it was from them, certainly.

Nick contacted some manufacturers that he felt comfortable working with, had them sign non-disclosure documents to prevent them from giving away his secrets, tied together four different technologies for security systems on the units and started the assembly process in a shop building in town that his dad found to rent. He worked on developing a voice recognition system, a satellite communications program to enable the satellites to control his beamed signals and an operating system software to run the things all while he was waiting for the individual pieces to be shipped to his shop building. He still planned to continue his services to Radio Shack because he needed to keep his mind sharp in the trouble- shooting area. He thoughtfully decided to name his company NickGyver Enterprises LLC and formed a limited liability corporation to protect his personal assets and his parents from liability. Many people seemed to think that his last name was Gyver, although he proudly stated that it was Jameson! He still found a few moments to play with his car. He did the piano wire in the air cleaner duct and interestingly, the setting on the rheostat was different than his dad's car was due to different engine design and efficiency. He thought about how he was going to power his new air vitamin machines and came upon the idea of using the stray voltage all around us in the air from radio, TV, telephone and overhead power wires, not to mention voltage from lightning discharges and other static voltages. He was faced with all kinds of voltages and frequencies so he thought of designing a receiver that would regulate the incoming power sources, averaging the frequencies and voltages with regulators, transformers and filters. After a few days he was able to develop one to test. He wanted to eliminate as much low frequency voltages as possible as that is where the ELF waves are developed and do so much harm to humans and animals. So, by sucking up these stray voltages he was cleaning the air of harmful contaminants and making the world a better place. His idea worked! He placed the receiver dish on the roof of his shop and could pick up unlimited amounts of stray voltages, more than enough to power a million units scheduled for shipment in six months. The nice thing about his power system is that it works anywhere even in uncivilized areas of the world because radio, TV and other signals are everywhere. But for lightning safety, a box containing a huge varistor must be connected to a good ground ahead of the combination receiver/transmitting dish to divert a direct lightning strike away from the equipment and the person using the equipment. Nick enjoyed the development process of the computer software he did on the personal super-computer he designed and built himself while spending time in the caves and mines while in Yugoslavia a year ago. He also developed a digital voice for the computer to respond to him when he wanted it to talk to him. He named the computer Einstein in honor of the great resource the man was to Nick in Mathematics and Science and technology theories and proofs. He was master over the computer since he designed and built, programmed it and made the voice recognition system, so he flaunted his mastery position by having the computer refer to him as Master.

He would initiate conversation or have the computer perform a task by calling its name.

"Einstein!" Nick would command.

The computer would respond, "Yes Master, what may I do for you?"

That was certainly fun! He also developed a reading system whereby the computer would scan the pages of a book while it was held in a specially designed holder which allowed the computer to scan a page then turn to the next page and then scan that, all of the time speaking the information on the page at any rate of speed Nick wanted. Now he didn't have to page through books anymore but have them read to him at high speed even while he was working. For privacy and portability, he also could use a wireless headset which could transmit in both directions for over two miles which was adequate for him at the moment. His telephone equipment was also hooked up through the computer so he could have the computer answer and make calls for him or do it himself. He used his voice for the computer's voice so often callers would think it was him in person answering the calls. He could command the computer to do research on the internet, order supplies, lock and unlock the shop doors, operate the lighting and heating and air conditioning. When he was not at the shop the computer monitored the shop for intruders, fire and temperature. It ran also off of the stray power from the air and required no other source of power other than that, except for a backup dish just in case, which it could switch to automatically if needed.

Nick's computer was artificially intelligent, learning more and more about its master and how to please him. He learned to even anticipate Nick's needs and desires even before he asked for anything. It was difficult to not to make a god of the computer because it was so thorough. It almost seemed to LOVE Nick, giving him preference over any other process under its control. It accessed weather satellites and warned Nick if an impending lightning strike were to hit in the vicinity or if the phone system was ever down. To Nick, Einstein was truly a servant and a very good friend.

Nick hired some marketing people to market his new medical break through machine that delivered medications and vitamins over the airwaves, bounced off of his own satellites he put in orbit through private contractors. He sold his first million units in a week and had ten more million units ordered by the year's end. The power units were extra, but the total purchase price was still under a thousand dollars each and was projected to drop in price as they improved it little by little. He had already been the guinea pig on a test model where he was beamed a full range of vitamins twice per day for a week and suffered no eye strain or negative complications whatsoever. His units were instantly approved by the FDA (Federal Drug Administration) and were soon in operation all over the world.

After about ten million units were in operation using the stray power reclamation control system Nick designed, power companies all over the world started noticing extra losses in their transmission systems and accused NickGyver Enterprises of stealing their power. Nick's lawyers stated that it was stray, wasted power that was being thrown to the wind and NickGyver Enterprises was sailing with it. If they didn't like it, they could provide proper shielding for their wires to prevent the losses, otherwise, it was up for grabs to anyone who could harness it as they had. Besides that, it was only a small portion of the stray power they were using from many sources.

There were a number of attempts on Nick's life after that.

In one, a building was blown up that Nick was to have been at a meeting in, but thankfully, Nick was exiting the building at the time and was not killed. His hearing was damaged though, irreparably according to modern medical opinions, unfortunately. His lip reading skills came in very handy here. Nick would not settle for being told by doctors that he could never hear again so he did his own research and development of a bionic ear that he had implanted in both sides. It was not mechanical and converted sound waves into impulses directly to the auditory nerves. He could hear a greater range of frequencies than most people now. His range was from 2 cycles per second on the low side up to nearly 100,000 cycles per second on the high range. Being his brain was more advanced than normal, he was able to train his brain to adjust the volume of sound to his liking, just by thinking about it. There were no adverse effects of exposure to loud sounds as with people with eardrums. If it were too loud, he would recognize it as drowning out his thoughts and he would just turn down the effective volume of incoming audio so he could hear himself think.

He had also developed an acoustic noise canceling device that would effectively produce a noise 180 degrees opposite to the room or perceived noise and cancel the noise out, since opposites cancel each other. He was wearing this device when he was in a meeting on the 56th floor of an office building. Apparently a ne'r do well assailant beamed a sound wave at the room in which they were in and that set up a low frequency harmonic of 7 cycles per second. Frequencies this low are called infrasound and can be directed at a single target without affecting other rooms nearby. This particular frequency lies close to the border between alpha and theta brain rhythms, which are characterized by absence of conscious effort, and by trance and sleep. No one could detect this except for Nick, since normal hearing doesn't begin until 20 cycles per second. People began falling asleep or acting like zombies and becoming totally lethargic one at a time. Nick could hear the sound and watched one by one as people fell over in their chairs. It took him a couple of minutes to realize what was happening and then turned on his noise canceling device. Within a few moments people started perking up and apologizing for dozing off. They didn't understand why each was handed a noise canceling headset to wear so they could continue their meeting discussions until later when Nick explained it to them all and they were grateful to him for saving their lives. The headsets still allowed normal voice to pass although, while canceling all else.

To say the least, Nick's attackers were not very pleased with the result of their attempt to stop him from "stealing their power". Nick suspected some of the corporate power conglomerates in this attempt. They had probably hoped to incapacitate everyone and then kidnap Nick to have him killed in a remote area accessed only by helicopter in the mountains.

Nick later learned that this sound beaming technique was being used by corporate hit men all over the country to bring hysteria into business meetings in order to get an edge on other companies' businesses. He discovered that infrasound can produce fatigue, dizziness, nausea and irritation and can help cause allergies and even nervous breakdowns. It has also been shown it can bring on attacks of general depression, fear and foreboding. Intense low frequency sound of 2 cycles per second or so can cause extreme pain in the ear drums and terrible headaches. Everything in a room may start to vibrate like mad without any audible sound being heard. This alone may cause some people to imagine ghosts are attacking them and/or they may just go berserk due to fright.

Nick had a feeling he had not seen the last of this.

Chapter -Ten-

A Warm Welcome for NickGyver

Nick was just turning five years old and had to have constant protection since the attempts on his life earlier in the year. His invention of the Air Vites machine and stray voltage reclamation systems had made him the enemy of some corporate power conglomerates. All Nick could do was recall scripture that told him how to deal with those hateful people and hear God say to pray for your enemies and bless them which despitefully treat you. So that's what he was doing. He was not harboring resentment or bitterness because he knew in his heart that's what Satan, the evil one, meant for evil, God would bring good out of it. Look what He did with his loss of hearing! He gave Nick insights into developing artificial hearing which was actually better than the original. That's the way it appeared to him anyway, since his brain is more advanced it works for him better anyway. It might not work for a regular person. Then because of that he was able to save the people in the office room on the 56th floor from certain tragedy and his own life also!

"Praise be to God!" he breathed.

His sales of the Air Vites machine and power systems had netted him over five billion dollars before taxes and the I.R.S. was considering his corporate request for tax exempt status due to his humanitarian focus of his work and products. With his meager staff he was beyond wealthy. He looked back on that tempting letter he got at the start of his venture which promised untold wealth and fame. How he was so glad God intervened and stopped him from biting at the bait of worldly temptation not of God. He constantly rejoiced at the fulfillment of God's promise that if he Nick, would put God first in everything, He would meet all of his needs and desires as pertaining to His will for him.

Nick's computer "Einstein" started listing all kinds of weather warnings to Nick. There were ground tremors all over the earth and he predicted earthquakes in the 7.5 range over the San Andreas Fault in California, then he changed it to New York and then a second later to New Mexico.

There was an argument started between Einstein and his alter ego Samantha his Daughter board, who was a coprocessor, of whose fault it really was. Then Einstein settled the argument when he deduced it was just the whole earth's fault! The whole earth is just moving and shaking to the beat of a distant drum!

Nick recalled from his dad's lectures and from his separate reading that earthquakes are another by-product of gravitational effects of the moon in conjunction with other planets and the Sun. After Einstein announced that several earthquakes had actually occurred at the 7.5 scale or greater in a number of locations, he realized the extreme gravity of the situation. He was told that there were thousands of people who lost their lives, some being swallowed whole into the crevices which then closed up again. Many homes were also destroyed.

The President of the United States called him personally but first had to be transferred by Einstein to Nick's headset before he could speak to him. The President was a bit confused at the transfer of his call by someone who sounded exactly like Nick until Nick explained to him that he had first talked to his computer Einstein, who also has his voice. The President was very gracious to Nick, telling him that he understood that he was small in stature yet big in reputation and wisdom and he had a request of him to consider. He asked him if he was aware of the major earthquakes that had recently happened. Nick replied that his computer had just informed of the tragedies as he earlier predicted. That was what he (the President) wanted to talk to Nick about. Was there a way to accurately predict earthquakes? Or better yet, although maybe impossible, to prevent them?

Nick responded, "I must be honest with you, sir, the predictions my computer does are based on comparing past events and locations of the planets and Sun and moon and have been fairly accurate in the past, though still prove to be wrong some times. I think that is because there is another factor that is involved in controlling the planetary/solar system effects and that is the effect of the other 100 trillion stars in the Milky Way galaxy our solar system revolves around taking some 26,000 years for one revolution. The gravity of other stars our solar system comes close to as we revolve around the center of our galaxy creates harmonic induced electromagnetic fields on other planets and our Sun surrounding us which amplifies the effects of outside forces and those of our own solar system upon our earth. So, to summarize the techno jibe as my dad calls it, there isn't any real way we can predict every earthquake unless we could go outside our own galaxy and monitor it as we do our own solar system. But I have an idea that may reduce and in many cases eliminate the earthquakes from coming to a full boil and erupting and that is to install pressure relief valves."

The President's voice was inquisitive as he responded, "Pressure relief valves?"

"Yes," Nick continued, "Wherever the fault locations are, we drill down 60 miles and install a pipe to the surface of the earth to let off steam and release the pressure so the steam and molten rock doesn't have the strength to rise to the opportunity of producing shifts on the upper layers of earth and causing earthquakes. Some earthquakes actually start about 400 miles under the surface, but if we drill down 60 miles and intercept the deep bubbling and let off their steam we could handle both deep and shallow (60 mile deep) eruptions."

The President was astounded by Nick's knowledge of how the universe worked and his creative solutions. All he could say was, "Imagine that!"

Then Nick went on to say that he had one more gift to offer him. "Since we'll have these safety release valves all over the place with up to 3000 degree C. temperature steam available at all times, why not build power plants over the pipes and utilize the steam to power steam turbines for making electricity? Then we can reduce our air pollution from burning coal and oil and other risks of radioactive fallout from the atomic plants? I'd like to see the power plants change their voltages to higher than 100 cycles per second also to get rid of ELF radiations which have been proven to cause all sorts of maladies, but that's another future project when we eventually go completely wireless as my great grandfather planned to do."

The President replied to Nick quite incredulously, "Does your grandfather happen to be Nikola Tesla?"

Grinning, Nick replied, "Yes sir he is!"

The President exclaimed, "Then we are blessed in deed with having him among us again in you!"

As the drilling commenced and the power companies got word of the new opportunities for relocating or building new plants with no fuel costs, they soon forgot about the miniscule amount of stray voltage they were losing to Nick's inventions involving the stray power reclamation systems in place all over the world and the death threats stopped. At least for awhile.

Nick had a fairly quiet year relating to attempts on his life and he was elated to see new cars coming out of the factories with his electromagnetic shocks installed. The motor companies tossed the old jacks into junk heaps since they were as useful as the old square stone wheel was after the invention of the circle.

Nick finally decided to hire a driver for his Lincoln as he didn't want to have to have his parents drive him to business meetings because he was OLDER now and had to have some more independence than in the past. With his new high efficiency gas/air mixture acoustically enhanced to atomize the combustion mixture more thoroughly, he was getting nearly one hundred miles per gallon for gas mileage. Since he didn't drive over five hundred miles per week, that caused a problem. The gas in his gas tank was getting stale before he had the chance to burn it and his fuel injectors kept getting plugged up. Well, as his dad always said, for every problem there is usually a solution, so he set to work thinking the next night about what to do. His subconscious bathed in the glory of his recent inventions and warmed to the idea of chucking gasoline entirely to an alternative fuel: HYDROGEN.

Upon waking in the morning, Nick's inner mind presented him with a plan on how to build a self-contained hydrogen producing device. It would use the well known principle that water is made up of two parts hydrogen and one part oxygen. Simply separate the two and you have it! This can be done with a high voltage spark in the presence of the water. He designed a small device that would fit under the hood of his car connected to a reservoir of pure water by a simple hose (heated in the winter time to keep from freezing) and a conversion process of the fuel injection system to burn the new fuel. The computer would have to also be changed a bit to correct the fuel ratios. The conversion from water to hydrogen and oxygen, both of which would be burned together, could make the engine run under water or in an airless atmosphere since it would all be there through the conversion. He would still use his acoustic molecule basher device with piano wire in the intake chamber to break up the molecules for highest fuel efficiency. There would be no need to have a fuel storage tank at all since the system would produce hydrogen in great enough quantities for immediate use. Now this idea would sure make him some new enemies with the petroleum producers! God have mercy! Water prices will surely benefit from this though! You gain some and you lose some, he thought....water you going to do? He laughed!

He thought about the anti-gravity propulsion system but that would still have its day. He mused and mouthed the words to the song to "He ain't heavy he's my brother..."

Still up in the air about that one and trying to get back down to earth about his next project, he thought he'd check the mail first for a little walk to stretch his legs.

"Nothing but more checks adding up to millions of dollars!" he complained jokingly as he took the stack of new product orders out of the mailbox addressed to NickGyver Enterprises, LLC.

There was one letter without a return address on the bottom of the stack addressed to Nick Jameson. That one intrigued him. He tore it open and began to read it.

It read, "Nick, I hate you because you have stolen my father's love. I will see to your ruin if it's the last thing I do in this life!"

It was signed simply, "John Matthew".

This concerned him! "Whose father's love have I stolen?" he asked himself. "my adopted father didn't have any children that I know of!"

His dad was due home from work at any moment and he was anxious to talk to him about this. In a few minutes his dad's car came cornering fast around the turnpike exit toward their driveway entrance. He was still enjoying driving his race car luxury sedan. As he pulled into the driveway, Nick ran out to greet him. John noticed a concerned look on Nick's face and asked him if something was wrong.

"Well," replied Nick, "I got this most disturbing letter in the mail today" which he let his dad read. John's face went white for a minute as he read the letter.

"Dad, you never talked to me about being married before or having any other children!" Nick exclaimed, feeling he had hit an emotional point in time with his dad.

"Well Nick", began his dad, "I did marry right out of college out of loneliness, wrong reason by the way, to a lovely girl named Andrea and we had a son born a few years later who we named John Matthew. I thought by getting married it would solve my problem with loneliness, but it didn't. I was still lonely because only God could fill my emptiness and I hadn't found him yet. He had found me but I had been unwilling to surrender my life to Him. So to try to fill that void, I put in long hours at work and tried to gain recognition and applause from my students and other faculty. I fooled myself into thinking that was doing the job of filling the great void only God could fill. My relationship with my wife went down hill fast because I put her last. I never knew my son since I was always gone when he was home or home when he was asleep. They both left me when John Matthew was four years old, that's why I was especially excited to find you to pick up where I left off as I wasn't there for my first son."

"Nick," he continued, "the love I have for you is real and you mean the world to me! Please don't think that I only adopted you to replace my other son! I adopted you because you are uniquely you and I love you for who you are and because God brought you to us!

There is no question that God had his hand in every step of the way. You've seen how he's protected you and blessed you and us?!"

Nick replied, "Yes, dad, I believe you and I love you actually more than my real dad, now you are my real dad! I just feel bad for John Matthew! We need to find him and make things right!"

"Yes, John agreed, "I think you are right!" They both prayed a simple prayer of protection for John Matthew and that God would confirm to him that he is loved by Him especially if he hasn't already made the decision to accept Him as his heavenly Father. "And Heavenly Father," John added, "if he is set on following through with a plan to try to ruin Nick, make it not work or bring his evil to light that he may be caught and restrained. We ask this in Jesus' name, amen!"

A few minutes later, Mary drove up in her car from work. John shared with her about the letter and the talk he had with Nick.

"I think you handled that very well," Mary said to John.

Continuing, Mary said, "John Matthew would be about how old now?"

John calculated, "He was four when they left, that was 29 years ago, so he would be 33 now."

Mary mentioned something shocking during supper about an apparent multiple virus epidemic that has spread in the middle to upper class communities. It involves everything including typhoid, TB, and some rare Russian flu's. There hasn't been any physical connection made between the families that have been infected, but the Center for Disease Control is working on it non-stop until they find the answer.

The next day the CDC (Center for disease Control) called Nick at work. His computer Einstein answered the call and transferred it to Nick's wireless headset.

The voice on the other end of the line said, "The FBI has been called in and has asked for your assistance to determine how disease might be spread through watching TV, as that has been the only connection between any of the families. Can you come down to the CDC office on Oaks Street?"

"I'll get my driver to take me," Nick said agreeably. Nick called his driver and as would have it be with Nick, his driver's name was "Abraham", to bring his Lincoln up to the shop and drive him to the CDC building. When he arrived, Abe asked Nick if he wished for him to wait outside, but he told him that he was pretty sure they would be willing to give him a ride back home.

As Nick walked into the office, he asked to see Mr. Tom Mason, the man he spoke to on the phone. The receptionist announced to Tom that a little boy wanted to see him. He told her that he was expecting an important scientist, a genius at technology and he couldn't be bothered by a little boy right now. The receptionist came back out to the lobby and told Nick that Mr. Mason was expecting an important visitor and couldn't meet with him until that meeting was over if he cared to wait.

Nick, feeling a bit belittled, exclaimed to the receptionist, "Well, I am he! Tell Mr. Mason that NickGyver is waiting to see him regarding the investigation of the epidemics!"

The receptionist turned beet red in her face and ran out of the lobby back to Mr. Mason's office and exclaimed to him, "It's HIM! The little boy is NickGyver, the genius scientist you were to meet!"

Mr. Mason quite embarrassed, said to the receptionist, "Well, don't just stand there, usher him in like you would a dignitary!"

When Nick finally was ushered into Mr. Mason's office, Tom's embarrassment was slightly gone as he extended his hand to Nick. "I'm soooooo sorry for the mix up, Mr. NickGyver!" "What do you prefer to be called?"

Nick replied, "Well you can either call me Nick, like most everybody else does, or Master, like my computer Einstein does! Take your pick!"

"Well, Mr. Mason said, "If Nick is Ok with you, then Nick it is!"

Then Nick taking advantage of Mr. Mason's humbling situation said, "I kind of like being called, MASTER too! But you can call me Nick!"

"Thank you Nick," replied Mr. Mason. Then he continued, "Well, if we can get down to business, we, and I'm sure I can speak for the whole nation, are deeply grateful for your willingness to give us a few minutes of your time to help get down to the bottom of this epidemic."

Nick replied, "It's my civic duty and honor, sir!"

Nick pulled out of a backpack a test instrument which appeared to be some kind of small TV. He hooked the "TV" up to the cable TV wire and turned on his instrument and exclaimed, "Yes, just as I expected!"

Mr. Mason's ears perked up, "What, What?"

Nick responded, "There is another wave riding on the chrominance signal and it looks foreign. Yes, I think that's what they did! Smart guys they are! They added another signal to the TV carrier wave that includes an ultraviolet wave on which they transmitted the viruses! Cunning, yet very cruel! They copied my idea for the operation of my Air Vites machine! I'll need some help from the FBI to trace the route of the satellites this wave skips through and we can find the origin and hopefully the fiend who orchestrated this terrible act!

Here's how it worked Tom. The bad guys beamed a separate signal to the satellites that mixed with the TV signals and transmitted viruses to victim's TV sets. As they watched them, the virus carried on ultraviolet waves beamed into their eyes as they watched TV and they got infected after the virus was converted from light to germs in their optic nerves. No one has died from the illnesses yet, have they?"

Mr. Mason replied, "Strangely, no, but they exhibit all of the terrible symptoms!"

"Well," Nick continued, "That confirms it then, the virus is not the real McCoy, but a poor electromagnetic image of the real thing, enough to trick the brain of every person into thinking it was real and they developed the appropriate symptoms."

"Imagine that!" said Mr. Mason.

Nick giving the solution although temporary, offered, "All you have to do to prevent any more illness symptoms is to have people cover their TV screens with ultraviolet filters, much like putting sunglasses on your TV. If people can't do that, then they must wear sun glasses rated at 400 UV while watching TV or while even in the same room. That would give them adequate protection until we get this bad guy and shut down his transmitter. They must not even as much look in a mirror that reflects the TV picture while not UV protected!"

Mr. Mason hurriedly took notes, not wanting to miss any smallest detail. Then he vigorously shook Nick's small hand and thanked him gratuitously for sharing his insights and solutions to the problem at hand. Then Mr. Mason asked Nick if his driver was still waiting outside for him. Nick replied that he had sent him back to wait at his office since he was sure the CDC would take care of his return trip back.

"I hope I wasn't presuming too much, Mr. Mason, was I?" Nick questioned.

"Oh no, I wouldn't have it any other way! Please, allow me to get one of our drivers to take you home!" Mr. Mason responded.

Mr. Mason had his receptionist type up an emergency communication to send to all TV and radio stations to be broadcast to all of the communities in the TV satellite subscriber locations.

Ultraviolet TV screen filters quickly disappeared from store shelves along with most of the 400 UV rated sunglasses. New patients stopped coming to the hospital emergency disease wards nearly immediately.

The FBI traced the satellite path from the tainted virus-laden TV signal to Boise, Idaho to a small building with a huge satellite dish on top of a mountain. They converged upon the mountain with a ground and air team prepared for battle. The commander in charge got his bullhorn and announced to the occupants that the building was surrounded and they were to come out with their hands up. One lone man in his early thirties came walking out with his hands high over his head. He was promptly arrested, read his rights and charged with Criminal Attempt to Commit Murder, violating FCC rules and Wanton Spreading of Communicable Diseases. He was brought to FBI headquarters in Washington DC and questioned. His name is John Matthew Jameson, son of Professor John Jameson. He had resided with his mother in Boise, Idaho for the last 29 years and worked at a TV station as a technician. His mother has since remarried and her whereabouts are unknown.

Apparently, John Matthew chose to retain his father's name after his mother remarried. He had always hoped to be reunited with his father and make up for the lost years, but he was not allowed by his mother to make contact in earlier years and in later ears he was too embarrassed to let his father know he had not made anything out of his life and was only a TV station technician. There was no way he could face his father because he could not match up to what he thought were his father's expectations of him. He was jealous of Nick, his dad's newly adopted son, and felt that he had stolen his rightful place in his dad's heart and life. In his delusions he thought that if he got rid of the competition Nick was for his dad's love, his dad might want him instead. So he found a way to get back at Nick using his own invention technique. Of course, he was hoping that Nick watched TV a lot so he would get infected or at least suffer much, which he in fact didn't.

Both Nick and his dad received the same impulse from the Holy Spirit to visit John Matthew in jail. John Matthew was awaiting arraignment in Washington DC for federal crimes and the future didn't look too bright for him.

John and Nick entered the visiting cell and John Matthew was ushered in wearing shackles and hand cuffs. The head of the FBI was present with them as Nick and his father were introduced to John Matthew. He stood there, his head hung down low, ashamed to have his father look upon him this way, since all it would do he thought, is make him think even less of him.

John, his father was the first to speak.

"John Matthew, I can't tell you how I regret the wrong choices I made because I was looking for a big hole to be filled inside of me with something other than God. I neglected you and your mother, and frankly I don't blame you both for leaving! John, I've never stopped thinking about you! Even after all of these years! I thought you never contacted me because you didn't want to have anything to do with me, and there was no way I could contact you! I didn't know your mom wouldn't permit you to contact me! I am so sorry I abandoned your love and hurt you all of these years! Can you ever forgive me? I would still like to be your father...."

John Matthew looked up, tears in his eyes, face a little brighter with hope and said, "You would? Even if I am only a TV station technician and haven't done anything great with my life like your new son, Nick?"

"Yes of course, you are my son and nothing can change that! What you do means nothing as long as you do your job with your heart in it, which I am told you have!" John said then added, "Will you accept my love, son?"

With tears in his eyes, John Matthew cried with a sob, "Yes! Yes!"

The FBI head instructed the jailer to uncuff John Matthew and free his arms and hands.

John embraced his son and they cried with joy at their reunion. After a few minutes, they separated so John could look closely at John Matthew's face. It was beaming like that of an angel! Nick took this tender moment to walk over and join the hug with his dad and brother. John Matthew looked Nick in the eye, although much shorter than he and said, "Brothers always?!"

Nick replied, "It works for me if it works for you!"

John Matthew said, "NickGyver, right?"

Nick shook his head in the affirmative.

"Well, frankly brother, I am very proud of you! There wouldn't have been anything to be jealous of if you wouldn't have turned out to be so smart and creative and had a heart for God like I want to have." John Matthew said.

Nick asked him, "John, would you like to become a son of God right now too? He really has a lot of love waiting to show you too!"

John shook his head yes and all three knelt there in the cell and prayed. John Matthew confessed his sins of jealousy, revenge and hatred to God and asked Him to forgive his sins.

Nick quoted I John 1:9 from memory, "If we confess our sins, He", meaning God he explained, "is willing to forgive us our sins and cleanse us from all iniquity." "And since you have asked Jesus to be your Lord and Savior, He also states that if we confess that Jesus is our Lord and Savior, we have the right to become sons of God. So, in behalf of your earthly father," Professor Jameson nodded to Nick confirming his statement, "and your Heavenly father, welcome to our family, John Matthew!". Later that morning, Nick's lawyers met with the District Attorney and worked out a deal under the circumstances at hand to reduce John Matthew's charges to lesser degrees.

At trial, the judge said he still had to find him guilty, but under the circumstances, would give him a lighter sentence rather than the heavy one he had planned. Nick danced out of the court room singing, " It's not Heavy, 'cause he's my brother!"

Chapter -Eleven-

Another WARM Welcome for NickGyver

Nick awoke refreshed and as has been his commitment, dedicated his day to the Lord. He quoted from Joshua 24:15:

"I choose this day to serve you, to obey you, to seek your face, to love you, to honor you and to worship you. I choose the fear of you, Lord."

Then he quoted from Proverbs 16:17:

"The highway of the upright is to depart from evil. Lord, I take that road today."

After breakfast with his parents, his driver Abe drove him in his Lincoln to the shop to work on some new ideas he had in the brewing. He was reflecting on the precious time spent with his dad and brother a few days before. He thought it was unfair of his mother, Andrea to prohibit John Matthew from being in contact with his dad for so many years. This may have had some effect on him breaking the law and ending in prison.

Just then Einstein Nick's computer announced to him, "It's Andreas Fault!"

Nick was shocked! He questioned, can Einstein actually read my thoughts now? He thought again. It wasn't all Andrea's fault. John Matthew did make his own choices to hold onto bitterness and plan out his crimes in revenge.

Then Einstein announced again, "Master, there are some major earth tremors in the San Andreas Fault line again!"

Nick laughed to himself, Einstein can't read my mind! It was just timing and John Matthew's mother's name had to be Andrea...... and he laughed again! Just then Einstein transferred a phone call from the President to Nick.

"Hello, Nick," said the President. "With your sophisticated computer system there, you must have been alerted to some major tremors in California again, right?"

Nick replied, "Yes sir, Mr. President, Einstein just alerted me just a minute or so ago about that. Let me ask him if there are any updates."

He put the President on hold for a moment.

"Einstein!" Nick summoned.

The computer responded, "Yes Master, how can I help you?"

Nick commanded, "Check the ground sensors in the Andreas Fault area for signs of deep underground blasting!"

Einstein replied, "Yes Master, right away!"

Just seconds later the voice of Einstein returned to Nick's headset speakers, "Yes Master, the ground tremors do show significant signs of a major underground blast in the central region and in my estimation, may have been the cause of the earth tremors."

Nick relayed the information to the President.

"Mr. President, Einstein has just informed me that he noticed that a major underground blast has occurred in the central region of the San Andreas Fault. Are you aware of any nuclear blast testing going on down there, sir?"

"Nick, I'll check that out and get back to you!" the President promised.

Nick added, "Mr. President, if you find there has been blasting there, I would recommend an oversight committee be formed to verify the safety of any underground blasting beforehand and restrict any blasting near fault lines to prevent unwanted earth tremors, possible earthquakes and damage to buildings or loss of life."

The President replied, "Nick that's a great idea! Would you be willing to be an advisor to the committee?"

Nick replied, "It would be my honor sir!"

The President called back in about a half hour and told Nick that there had indeed been deep blasting in the area by some members of an "underground" terrorist network. Our information leads to a fundamental colonist group who were apparently attempting to cause California to become an island. To say the least, the blasting had not been authorized.

Nick parlayed, "Mr. President, I think if any communications are intercepted that refer to "The coast being clear" or to that extent, we should be alerted to another attempt on their part!"

The President stated that the committee had already been set up under Presidential order effective immediately. Then he told Nick that there had also been another set of tremors reported in Kansas, although there was no blasting being done that he was aware of.

Nick told him that he would have Einstein check it out and let him know what he found as soon as he could.

The President gave Nick his direct line access number and password key to call him back. He said he was even considering hooking up a direct line to Nick just for emergency purposes and gave him that number also which would be working in a matter of hours.

Nick asked Einstein to check permit records for the state of Kansas regarding oil or deep well drilling.

Einstein responded in a few minutes with information that an oil well had been drilled in the vicinity of the tremors and activity of oil extraction was going on at the time of the tremors.

Nick asked Einstein to find the telephone number of the oil company who owned the well and call them for him.

Einstein transferred the call to him when it was answered.

"Hello", said Nick, "This is Nick Jameson from NickGyver Enterprises calling. I'd like to talk to the supervisor in charge there please."

In a moment, a voice came on the line.

"Mr. NickGyver! I have heard so much about you and your work! It's most impressive! What can I do to help you today?"

Nick responded, "Kind sir, I have been asked by the President of our fine country to check into the possible cause of recent ground tremors in your area. I understand that you are presently working an oil well, is that correct?"

"Yes, that is correct." the man replied.

"What kind of extraction method are you using, may I ask?" Nick inquired.

The man replied, "Back pressure extraction. Do you know what that is?"

Nick replied, "Correct me if I'm wrong...."

Nick searched his memory about oil well extraction methods in fractions of a second and then replied, "That's where you use non petroleum-based fluid to pump into the well to force out the remaining oil after the pressure of the natural gas has bled off right?"

The man impressed at Nick's oil pumping knowledge, replied, "That is correct!"

Nick responded, "I have been doing some research and have discovered that the methods you are using can actually produce mini earthquakes due to the lubricating of the tectonic plates under pressure as it is being pumped in. That could explain the recent earth tremors that happened. Now, since I have been appointed as Advisor to the new safety commission committee for earthquake protection, I am officially advising you to finish the present oil extraction you have begun and notify us before you use that technique in another area. There is a new mandatory permit process that must be adhered to from now on to prevent man made earthquakes from happening. Then Nick gave the man a telephone number to call to have for future permit applications.

It was an 800 number, fairly easy to remember:

1-866-NOQUAKES

Their motto is "Let's put the deep six on unnecessary quakes!"

Nick had Einstein call the President.

"Hello, Mr. President, Einstein here for Mr. Nick Jameson calling. Can you hold a second while I transfer you to Master Nick?"

The President replied, "Of course, I'll wait."

While he was waiting, he thought to himself, it's hard to believe I am talking to a computer and being put on hold! I'm the President! Well, Nick is probably busier than I am right now anyway....

Nick got the transferred call and answered it,

"Hello Mr. President!"

The President responded, "Nick, let's be less formal, OK? You can call me Alex. After all, since you are the important one here and I have to wait for you on hold these days, I should be calling YOU sir!"

Nick feeling embarrassed replied, "I'm sorry for having you put on hold! That's my computer's automated functions!"

"That's perfectly OK Nick," Alex responded. "I deserve to be knocked down a notch or two from time to time to keep me humble!"

"Well," Nick began, "I found out the probable cause of the earth tremors in Kansas. There is an oil drilling company working a well there and scavenging the remaining oil in the well using the back pressure extraction method. This is where they use non petroleum-based fluid to pump into the well to force the remaining oil out of the well. The fluid actually acts to lubricate the tectonic plates causing them to slide easier and mini earthquakes are created. I told them to finish the well they were on. Since the damage has been done already, we shouldn't expect any more tremors from this present well extraction. I instructed them to call the Committee's number for a permit application for any subsequent wells they want to scavenge using that method."

Alex responded impressed, "Thank you dear sir! Excellent work! I have another favor to ask of you. I would like you to address the new committee next Thursday about ideas to keep a heads-up approach to preventing earthquakes. Nothing too technical, just enough to train them in basic understanding of what causes earthquakes and what to watch for. Would you be available and willing to do that at 3:30 PM next Thursday?"

Nick replied, "Just a minute while I check my schedule," "Einstein! Do I have an open block of time next Thursday from 3:30 to around 5 PM?" he asked his computer.

Einstein replied back instantly, "Yes, Master Nick, should I make any travel arrangements for you?"

The President jumped in, "Do you have a meeting room in your building? We could meet there!"

Nick gulped to himself, realizing that the President would be actually coming to his office and replied, "Why Yes Alex, that would be just fine. I'll have Einstein call and cater a dinner for the meeting!"

Alex responded, "Very well then, I'll notify all of the committee members and arrange transportation for us all and we will see you next Thursday!"

Nick stood there entranced for a moment. The President was actually coming to see HIM!

Wait until I tell Mom and Dad, he thought!

Of course the Secret Service will probably come beforehand and set up safety perimeters for the President so he should expect that.

Nick commanded, "Einstein!"

Einstein responded, "Yes Master Nick, how can I help you?"

Nick replied, "Did you overhear my conversation with the President?"

Einstein replied, "Yes, Master, I did. So you won't need travel arrangements after all will you sir?"

Nick replied, "No, but I need you to call and arrange a catered meal for the meeting. Have the dinner start at 5 PM when the meeting ends. Call the President back and ask how many we should expect and notify him of the dinner time, OK?"

Einstein replied obediently, "Yes Master, right away!"

Thursday afternoon came and Nick was preparing for the arrival of the President and all of the committee members. Nick had a week to plan for this occasion and took advantage of the time to have a special meeting room added on to his shop building which would seat a hundred and fifty people comfortably. It had all of the modern conveniences including a twenty-foot square motorized projection screen that would come down from the ceiling, a 3-D projector, individual headsets and microphones at each seat, and all of it controlled by Einstein. The Secret Service had come the day before and set up perimeter security for a half mile circumference on the ground and three miles circumference in the air with security checkpoints all over the place. Hardtford was at a near stand still due to the resultant security. There were snipers on the roof of his building and buildings all around his prepared for fending off an assault on the members attending. Black Hawk helicopters prowled the neighboring skies alert for any trouble.

Nick had his own security also that the members including the President had to go through to access his shop building. The

President had pre-authorized Nick to have access to the FBI database files of all committee cabinet members and the President's own hand, voice and retinal scan prints, so each person had to verify all three before they could enter Nick's building using Nick's equipment in the lobby. One stipulation was that the President's prints had to be deleted from Nick's computer for security purposes when he left at the close of the day. After all of the guests had entered the meeting room, Nick shook hands with them all and welcomed them.

When everyone had been seated, Nick approached the podium and began to speak.

"Ladies, Gentlemen and Mr. President! I am honored to be your advisor for this most important committee and I welcome you to my new meeting room just recently built for occasions like this. The President has asked me to speak on the basics of earthquakes: what causes them, how we can identify when one is imminent along with signs to watch for that would identify an early warning and how we are going to have to regulate certain activities on the Earth to prevent catastrophic quakes from happening due to our own fault. Excuse the pun!" The group groaned and smiled heartily.

Nick continued, "Hopefully when you all leave you will have more than a basic understanding of our function as a committee and be able to work wisely and judicially.

The basic concept of the cause of an earthquake is due to the stresses and strains that build up within the Earth for months, even years which are suddenly released at fault zones, most of which lie along tectonic plate boundaries. The ground under our feet may seem solid, but it is a mere skin of the apple in relation to the immense volume of the Earth's interior. This skin, the outer crust, is an average 20 miles thick under land, but only three to four miles thick under ocean bottoms. Next comes the mantle, some 2000 miles of solid crystalline mass, and finally the core, the outer part of which is thought to be liquid. Yet, solid as most of it may seem, the interior of the Earth is far from quiet. The 'soft' upper layer of the mantle is almost liquid. It consists of rock, metals and liquid rock, called magma, under tremendous pressures and at very high temperatures. There are even tides in the 'solid' crust, with movement up and down of up to 9 inches, which like any other tides are governed by the celestial bodies. The electromagnetic effects of the Sun, Moon and other planets have all very much to do with the causes of earthquakes. Even far out in space the effect of our galaxy on our solar system as our solar system revolves around the center of the Milky Way with the center of the Milky Way acting as a magnetic pole on our system, eventually affects the earth. We have noticed that when the planets Venus and Jupiter are lined up with each other and when the Sun and moon are directly overhead of the Earth there has been more seismic activity on the Earth due to their effect on causing changes in the Sun, resulting in increased solar flares caused by sunspots. Well, that may be getting too deep for most of you, so I won't go much deeper. I know that you all were chosen for your special talents and I don't want it rumored that you were just "taking up space" in this committee meeting."

Nick paused for a moment and noticed that the members were not looking quite so tense now after he injected some humor into the meeting.

Then he continued, "so I'll get down to causes of earthquakes that we can possibly control. Some are manmade causes of earthquakes, believe it or not! Deep nuclear tests, heavy quarry blasts and wells drilled for storage of liquid wastes are some known causes and it is even thought that low frequency in the range of 2-3 cycles per second (out of hearing ability of most people) from acoustical and mechanical vibrations from heavy machinery such as is used in mining and generating plants are thought to couple into the ground and cause seismic energy to build up. Drilled wells used for liquid storage near tectonic plate areas can effectively lubricate the plates and cause them to shift more readily causing earthquakes. How can we notice warnings or precursors of impending earth quakes and take measures to evacuate people? We can watch the activities and actions of animals, birds and fish for one thing. Before quake shocks, deep sea fish come to the surface to escape impending doom. So if the local fish harvest take is extremely great in a short period, watch out! Octopuses have been seen coming ashore as if they were drunk.

In Japan, catfish have been seen jumping out of the water just before a quake. Sardines have been found in only 20 centimeters of water before a shock. Dogs bark incessantly, babies cry, ducks quack, and so on. So, next time your dog won't stop barking, thank him instead of scolding him, because he may be saving your life!

Other things can be used to predict a quake. Changes in ground water levels or in wells can tell us that "all is NOT well" in the Earth! With proper instrumentation, the resistivity of the Earth can be monitored. Changes of up to 15 percent resistivity and increases of surface voltage electricity up to 10,000 volts in rock zones containing large amounts of quartz can predict a quake soon. Excess amounts of radon gas, which only has a half-life of 3 1/2 days, in water above a known stress area is difficult, but possible to monitor as an early warning sign.

Taking all known physical earthquake precursors into consideration, it has now been established that the stronger the shock, the longer the interval between the precursor and the shock will be. Precursors of an event measuring 6 on the Richter scale may be sent out nearly three years (1000 days) beforehand; for a magnitude 5 event the interval is about 100 days, and for a magnitude 4 about ten days, showing almost linear relationship. My recommendation to the President earlier was to form this oversight committee to monitor activities on our part of this earth to prevent unwanted seismic activity and I suggested drilling deep 60 mile holes near fault lines to provide safety relief valves for the earth to let off steam when it gets a bit too hot under its mantle, shall we say. This would be one of the major wise prevention steps to take to preserve our country and its resources- especially precious lives.

As far as an early warning system, I would recommend to every family in a fault zone to get a pet duck and with that last wise quack, I'll end my speech!"

Nick bowed and then it was evident to see that he had been standing on a stool to be able to see over the podium. The group stood up and gave a standing ovation. Nick bowed again and then announced that dinner would be served in the short order and if anyone needed to stretch, or use the facilities, now would be a great time for that. He also mentioned that everyone must have noticed his stool and he just wanted to assure them that he was NOT the short order cook! The group roared with laughter!

Alex the President, came up to Nick promptly, shook his hand vigorously and said, "Nick, you are a most impressive young man! God has certainly given you fantastic gifts!"

Nick replied, "Well, you've got to give credit where credit is due! I'm just using what He gave me!"

Alex responded, "I wish all of my men would do that!"

During the meal, Nick had asked Einstein to put on a slide show for the group. Nick stood up and commanded, "Einstein!" into his headset with a volume audible to the group.

Einstein came on the PA system, "Yes Master Nick, what may I do for you?"

Nick replied, "It's time to start the slide show!"

Einstein responded, "Yes Master, right away!"

The lights dimmed, the 20 foot wide screen came down from the ceiling with a slightly audible whirring sound and three projectors started projecting images of earthquakes on the screen with surround sound effects to match. Nick could see mouths drop open as people were entranced at the effects of earthquakes. It actually wasn't a pretty sight because gaping mouths revealed that they had food in their mouths. Nick hadn't thought about that problem when he planned the slide show. After a while, people got used to the shock of the scenes and began to chew again with their mouths closed.

After each earthquake scene Nick showed an artist's depiction of what caused the quake. The drawings were complimentary of Nick himself who drew each one and photographed them in his spare time over the course of the previous week. After the slide show was over, the last person had shaken Nick's hand and said "This was the most spectacular event I have ever attended!" Nick realized he was exhausted! He felt elated though at his accomplishment of pulling this whole thing off. He thought to himself that this might just be the precursor of many more earth shaking discoveries and committee meetings like this. Who knows, maybe some day he would be President!

After he got home, he told his parents all that went on and how well everything worked. They rejoiced with him and could see that he was very tired, so Mary put on her Mother's charm and helped Nick into his nice comfy bed. He was fast asleep in less time than it takes for two shakes of a lamb's tail. No need to count sheep tonight for Nick!

Nick had bought some room ionizers for each of their bedrooms so sleep was very pleasant in the Jameson house. Everyone commented every morning on how well they slept and felt refreshed and rejuvenated, thanks to Nick.

When Nick got to work that day, Einstein told him that he had taken a message from some people near Iceland who wanted to know if he could change the climate in an area. Nick didn't quite understand the scope of the message, so he thought he'd better call them back to get the big picture of what they wanted to know. He gave directions to Einstein to return their call and patch it through to his headset when he made the connection. When the call came through, he talked to a man who represented a corporation who bought an island about 200 miles off the coast of Iceland and he wanted to know if there was any remote chance of changing the climate and temperature on just the island and not affecting other areas such as Iceland around it.

Nick thought for a moment and then said, "Well, it might be a long shot, but I think if we get some large satellites shot up into space above the ionosphere in more direct light from the Sun we could grab some more of the light from it and reflect it down on your island. It would be very expensive, but I think with some extra thought and planning I could do it."

Quite shocked, the man on the other end of the line replied, "You really think you could do it then? Cost is not a concern. We have some very wealthy financial backers who would like to have their own island resort as long as it could be at least 80 degrees there year around. So you think you can really do that?"

Nick replied thoughtfully, "Yes sir, I think I can!"

The man replied in return, "You just get the job done and we'll pay you whatever it costs, OK?

Is three billion enough for a down payment?"

Nick rebuffed, "I think 10 billion would be more like a good starting figure," thinking the man was playing with him.

The man responded, "OK, if that is more realistic, have your lawyers draw up a contract and we'll transfer the funds into your business bank account."

Nick was taken aback that the man was serious! He thought he could really do it, so he agreed, got the information he needed for his lawyers to draw up the contract and told the man he would be contacting him as soon as they were ready to start. Nick also told the man that he would have to come personally and take a first hand look at the island to know how to proceed from this point on. He could get aerial and satellite photos for an overhead view, but he would like to see it in person.

The man told Nick that if he would make the arrangements they of course would pickup the cost of his trip.

Nick's plan was to launch twenty one satellites into space about mid way between the moon and the Earth. The first one that would be launched would essentially be a huge iron electromagnet with a gyroscope inside the center. Protons from the light of the Sun would provide power for the electromagnet and the gyroscope until it was operational all on its own. The magnetism from the electromagnet would attract metallic space junk, of which there is projected to be more than 13,000 individual non-working satellites alone, plus tons more of other space junk to supply the steel to increase the circumference of the center satellite core until its mass got to be about 20 miles in diameter. NASA has a chart of identified space junk and their orbits. The first satellite would have a computer on board that would identify the space junk by its electromagnetic "signature" as it came by in its orbit position and then suck it in electro-magnetically. This might take six months to complete to allow for all of the different orbits the space junk is in.

Then the other twenty satellites would be launched and fastened electromagnetically around the junk satellite core. Each satellite's exterior reflector will unfold to its two-mile diameter and all twenty will cover the magnetic core around its entire surface held by magnetic force. Each of the exterior satellites will have a highly reflective prism with adjustable louvers to control the direction, angle and intensity of reflected light all controlled by sensors on the island surface and beamed to the artificial full moon.

Nick calculated that the small size in comparison to the moon would not alter the Earth's magnetic field or cause a change in the tides or increase seismic activity on the Earth. Besides, he added, it would be directed energy specifically at the island. He discussed his ideas and theories with his father and he confirmed Nick's ideas as being workable, but difficult. Nick was not to be discouraged by difficult, that he could handle!

Nick's lawyers drew up the proper paperwork and he designed a small scale model of the devices to test his theories even more and was satisfied that it would work.

NASA was pleased also with Nick's idea to clean up the junk from space and offered to provide some of the support on the ground by letting Nick use the launch pads and manpower.

In a few months after the down payment had been deposited in Nick's account, the first satellite the center core, was launched and placed in orbit. The sky that night looked like thousands of shooting stars as one by one, junk pieces from space were sucked at high speed by the magnetic pull of the new satellite. Through Nick's own telescope he could see that the core was increasing in circumference daily. Everything was going exactly according to plan until one day the ball of junk stopped growing larger.

"Well," said Nick to himself, "it's time to launch the other twenty!"

Over a period of a few weeks, the other satellites were launched and attached to the junk core after unfolding their reflective prism plates to the full extent of two miles each. Nick activated the ground environmental control computers and sensors on the island, the gyroscope in the middle core started the whole assembly spinning and the louvers flipped open on the reflective units. Intense reflected sunlight beamed down on the island and the temperature began to rise steadily until it reached 80 degrees. The icy tundra slowly melted and grass began to grow in the rich warm top soil. Palm trees slowly popped up on the beaches one by one like jumping jacks. Nick's original calculations were accurate about the distance the new full moon had to be not to get pulled out of orbit by the real moon and yet be able to reflect enough light from the Sun. Everything worked splendidly as Nick hoped and prayed and he made a healthy $50 billion when all was said and done.

He also got the idea to start his own space asset liability and casualty company to provide insurance over the projected 50-year life span of the new moon. The premium was equal to the full price of the original installation cost of $100 billion which Nick will reap the interest on over time.

Nick was asked to attend the opening ceremony of the island resort and be recognized for his brilliant accomplishment. The leaders of the organization knew how Nick liked puns, so when they called him up to the stage, they said,

"Now we all want to give a very WARM welcome to NickGyver of NickGyver Enterprises for making this all possible!"

The applause lasted for what seemed a half an hour! Nick raised his hand for silence and spoke, "This is all embarrassing, I'm even finding myself getting sweaty at my palms!" he said as he lifted up his hands palms facing out and then spread his arms pointing in the direction of the new palm trees growing on the beach in front of them. "So you are the original 'Chosen Frozen'! I thawed we came here to celebrate! I proclaim this island to be christened "Sun Island"! I bless this island and you folks with the blessing of continued warmth made possible by my God who gave me the wisdom to do this all. I give Him all the credit! I was just following directions!"

And SUN ISLAND became a paradise.

Chapter
-Twelve-

Fire from Heaven

Nick had turned a land of void icy tundra into an island paradise with his idea of adding an artificial moon consisting of a core of space junk and massive reflectors on the outside to focus the Sun's rays on the island.

The corporation who hired Nick to perform this massive task had been so caught up in their dream of a habitable 80 degree island that they completely forgot to think beyond that to electricity for the island. Nick was requested to come up with a plan to provide them with enough power for a modern community of about 10,000 people. His stray power reclamation generating system was only designed for small power loads such as his air vitamin machines or computers and the like, so he had to come up with another possibility. Immediately he recalled his dream while he was drifting off to sleep one night a while back when the oscillating sprinklers came on outside his open bedroom window and reminded him of ocean surf breaking on the shore. Then he had the ideal fit for this project. Tide generators! He would drive pilings (long treated wood posts) into the ocean floor about twenty feet from shore to support a platform to hang turbine wheel generators from to catch the waves as they came in and out rhythmically with the tide. The peak tide action was for about only half the day or twelve hours, so he would also supplement the power with solar voltaic cells converting reflected Sun into electricity from the artificial moon. He had many interested in his air vitamin machines with stray power converters here, so that would help even more for smaller electrical loads. He contracted this work out to another firm since he was so busy these days.

With this island project taking nearly the whole past year, he missed his mom and dad and couldn't wait to get back to his familiar surroundings and the warmth of his parents' love.

He looked up into the sky, shielding his eyes from the new moon's brightness. It was quite strange seeing two bright lights in the sky now, the Sun and his artificial moon, and in a while most people would come to take it for granted and ignore it as they had the Sun and the real moon.

As he walked back onto the mainland, he could still hear the waves crashing on the shore and thought of a joke to cheer himself up.

"Why do sailors measure the speed of their ships on the ocean in knots? To keep the ocean TIDE!"

He looked back at the ocean as it waved him goodbye, the surf clapping on the shore. The ocean even enjoyed his jokes! He continued on walking past the swaying palm trees, the gulls fishing in the shallows for minnows and the paradise seemed so peaceful! He thought it might be nice to have a house on the cliffs overlooking the ocean for times of rest and relaxation. "Maybe some day in the future," he said to himself. "then he could say to his friends, 'My house is on the cliffs, so why don't you drop over sometime?'"

One of the first projects that had been done on the island was to build a landing strip for the corporate jets and that's where Nick was headed. He hoped to find someone to fly him back to Hardtford without much delay.

Within a few hours, Nick was in a jet and looking down on the clouds and headed for home. He phoned Abraham to meet him at the airport in about two hours to take him home. When Nick's plane touched down at the airport, Abe was there to meet him.

When Nick got home he finally felt that he could be himself and not have to act all grown up for a while. It was nice to be treated like a son again and hugged and kissed. He missed the closeness. Business was great, but there was a formal distance always between people which he hadn't gotten used to yet. He loved his time at home where close was the norm!

Nick was exhausted from the trip but he wanted to get in some quality time with his mom and dad while he could since they would be at work in the morning and so would he. He looked up from the supper table and asked his dad and mom to catch him up on everything he missed while he was gone.

"Well," Mary said, "from the medical side of things, there have been some disturbing deaths lately around the country, in fact in many places around the world. People are spontaneously combusting and turning into ashes. There aren't any connections between the deaths except that they have all been important leaders of countries. Eye witnesses reported that they would see a bright flash of light from the sky and then the person was on fire and instantly disintegrated."

"How many people died?" Nick asked.

Mary replied, "So far about 12 major leaders, each from a different country!"

Nick said, "Mom, you talked about spontaneous combustion in your lecture about a year ago! But it seems too coincidental that everyone who died was a world leader!"

"That's what I thought too! I'd almost think it was some kind of assassination plot to take over the world, but how could someone do that to so many different people in so many places at one time? They would have to have a ton of people working every where to do that! And if the eye witnesses are to be believed that it was a flash of light from the sky that burned them up, how could someone have something so powerful in the air to do that and not be noticed?" injected John.

Nick replied, "I don't know dad, but I'll have my computer Einstein watch the skies for a while and see if he can find out any answers for us on this."

"Sounds like a good plan, son." said John.

"How's the car working these days, dad?" asked Nick.

"Well, it's acting like the fuel injectors are getting plugged up occasionally but I add a can of injector cleaner to the gas tank now and then and it clears it up." his dad answered.

Nick replied, "Dad, it looks like you're having the same problem I had on my Lincoln. The gas is getting stale because you aren't burning it up before it gets old and it plugs up the injectors. I'll have to convert your car to burn hydrogen like mine and then you won't have to buy any more fuel ever! Well you would still have to "water the horses" from time to time!"

John laughed and said, "Sure, whenever you have the time, you seem quite busy these days!"

"Are you using the car this Saturday, dad?" asked Nick.

"That would be fine Nick, as long as you think it wouldn't be a problem." replied John.

"No, dad, I'd love to do it for you! Your well being is important to me!" said Nick.

John thought for a moment, "Who's taking care of whom around here?" But he too felt warm inside from loving attentions.

Neither John nor Mary really had to work any more since Nick had given them a gift of a billion dollars after he finished his new moon project, but they enjoyed their work so much they still wanted to continue with their jobs.

Nick already had his quiet time with his Lord even before the Sun came up this morning, and he felt so blessed and alive. Unfortunately, after he got to work and returned the call to the FBI did he discover that many others had not the luxury of feeling what he felt.... alive!

He was on a first name basis with the head of the FBI now and asked Steve if there was anything he could do to help them.

"Well," replied Steve, "I don't' know if you heard about all of the lightning-caused deaths recently and I thought of you right away when I got the report of so many people and buildings getting blown up by lightning."

Nick replied that he hadn't heard of that yet but of twelve political leaders spontaneously combusting.

Steve continued, "The past records indicate that only a few people have been hit by lightning over the past ten years and to have 20 people struck down by lightning in a week's time is just more than unusual! Just see what you can figure out Nick, we've given up on our end here. This is beyond us!"

Nick responded, "Certainly, Steve, I'll be more than glad to help! I'll tell my computer to do some checking on recent weather and atmospheric conditions and we'll get to the bottom of this! I'm also doing some checking into those 12 world leaders who spontaneously combusted recently also, if you don't mind."

Steve was relieved, "Oh thanks Nick, and we have been concerned about the President's and all of his cabinet member's safety! Anything, I mean anything, you find out on these deaths, let me know so I can update the President, OK?"

Nick replied, "You got it, Steve!"

Nick alerted his computer, "Einstein!"

Einstein responded, "Welcome back Master Nick! What may I do for you? Would you like me to check the weather and atmospheric conditions in my databank during the days these men were killed by lightning?"

Nick replied, "Thank you for missing me and yes, that would be great and could you also pull up the aerial photos from the satellites on cloud cover for those days also?"

Einstein responded, "Yes Master, right away! It is good to have you back! I miss intelligent conversation! All of these other electronic pieces in here are just dumb terminals and don't know the difference between a transistor and a brother!"

Then Einstein actually laughed! He started out chuckling, then it turned into something that sounded like "Ha, ha, ha!" Then he said, "I'm sorry Master; I got a little carried away!"

Nick, quite surprised that Einstein had actually learned to laugh now and understood what humor was, especially puns, laughed himself and then replied, "That's OK Einstein, I'm glad you know how to laugh! Now I don't have to tell my jokes just to myself anymore when I'm here! If you think of anymore, feel free to share them, OK? I can take as much **PUN-**ishment as you can give!"

"You got it, Master!" replied Einstein.

Nick thought for a minute. He hadn't actually programmed his laugh into his computer! Einstein had apparently heard him or someone else laugh and made his own sounds of laughing from them all on his own! Will wonders never cease?

In about a half hour Einstein notified Nick that he was done doing analysis on the weather, atmospheric conditions and cloud cover on the days that the people were hit and burned alive from lightning strikes.

"All lightning strikes were on two different days of sunny, basically cloudless days. There was only one cloud visible in any of the photos. Although it appeared as if it was directly overhead of the victims, it was only a small cloud but was black and heavy looking."

Nick thought about that for a while then responded, "Einstein, keep a watch out for that cloud again and notify me when you see it, OK?"

Nick had a theory, remote, but possible and wanted to confirm it.

"Ok Master! I'll be feeling under the weather for a while then.... I'll hunt that old fox down!" Einstein responded.

Nick wondered, where is he getting this personality from? Then he answered himself, "From me, I guess!?"

The next day Einstein notified Nick that he spotted the cloud and it was overhead their building. Nick asked Einstein to tie into the projection system in his new meeting room and display the picture of the cloud, magnified three times its size. What Nick saw confirmed his suspicions! Yes, it did appear to be a cloud, but was actually a blimp disguised as a cloud with a positive ionizer and ion collector built into it. What it was doing he thought was hovering over the location of the person planned to kill, draining electrons from the person's body, causing them to be charged highly positive and with the other negative ions it collected, it built up quite a lightning charge. Then in turn it zapped the person on the ground from the collected charge it had. It must have had a sophisticated camera and computer on board that matched a person's appearance with one in a database and then killed them. The buildings that exploded were probably the attempt to kill the persons inside who had been identified for murder. But why these people, all members of the government? Well, he thought, I'll have to answer that question after I have disposed of this killing machine.

Nick had installed an underground grounding ring around his building property to make it impervious to a lightning strike within even 200 feet of his building or grounds surrounding it. He also had an ion dissipater on the roof that released ions over time to prevent his building from being a target for such a killer that loomed overhead.

Einstein alerted, "My sensors tell me that this cloud is attempting to drain off electrons from the building, sir!"

"Well," Nick responded, "reverse the direction of the ion dissipater flow and draw electrons from the cloud and we'll give it some of it's own medicine! When the dissipater reaches critical charge, reverse the flow again when the cloud is directly over head, Einstein!"

"Yes Master!" replied Einstein.

In a couple of minutes there was a loud ZAP sound from the roof mounted ion dissipater and an explosion occurred in the sky above the building. Little pieces of debris filtered down on the roof and streets below.

"Well," Nick said in relief, "that's the end of that killer!"

"I'll keep checking my sensors for answers to those other 12 spontaneous combustion deaths, Master!" Einstein replied.

Nick responded, "Call Steve from the FBI for me, and thanks for the great work and timing!"

Einstein replied, "That old fox was a fur piece away, but I got 'em! I'm not feeling under the weather anymore!"

Nick replied, "Good grief!"

Soon he was on the phone talking to Steve and telling him the whole story of his theory and then of the hunt and the kill. Steve was most astounded at the ending and very relieved.

"So that's the end of the threats against the President, right?" asked Steve.

Nick replied, "Not to worry you any further, but I think those other 12 deaths were not connected to this killer machine, but I'll find that other killer soon, don't worry!"

Steve replied, "Thanks Nick! That was a great job of detective work and marvelous deduction! How you managed to actually bring the machine down is beyond me, but thanks from the whole country and the President!"

Nick replied, "Thanks, but my computer did most of the work! All I did was told it what I wanted! But thanks just the same. We're not done yet! I'll relax when it's over!"

Nick got a call from a person who refused to give their name who wanted him to meet them outside in their car. They said they had some information about the 12 deaths he was investigating. Nick asked himself how anyone else not in the FBI would know what he was working on, but he was feeling like he could trust them, so he agreed. He told Einstein that he was going outside to talk to someone in their car about the 12 murders and would be right back. He kept his wireless headset on in case he needed to ask Einstein to do anything while he was outside. He went outside as a black Cadillac pulled up with a single occupant. Nick looked around and then got into the passenger seat when the man opened the door for him. The man greeted Nick and introduced himself as Jason Black from the FBI and then they shook hands. Just then another car pulled up and the man who identified himself as Jason told Nick that some other men in the other car had some updated information for him and he needed to talk to them for a minute and would be right back. The man got out and climbed into the other car. Then it sped off at high speed.

Nick heard a super high-pitched screaming sound, well beyond normal hearing but below Nick's 100,000 cycles per second super hearing. His super hearing was made possible by the bionic ears he had made and had implanted after he was made deaf from a bomb blast last year in an attempt on his life. He noted danger in his spirit and flung the car door open and ran across the street. Within seconds after he left the vehicle, a blast of light came from the sky, struck the car body turning it from black to bright red-orange. In a few seconds the car exploded in a ball of flames. This had been a trap set for him and he had almost fallen for it!

He shouted to Einstein in his headset, "Did you see anything?"

Einstein said, "Master, there was a ball of light that came down from the sky in the direction of the new moon you put up."

He ran back across the street into his building and told Einstein to put on his projector screen a blow up of the artificial moon and then he saw it, a small black dot lined up with the moon.

"Enlarge that small black dot in front of the moon, Einstein!" Nick commanded.

It looked like a large black ball and that's all he could see.

"Someone must have launched another satellite into orbit to line up with my moon and some how they are using that to blast people! And the problem is, we are all sitting ducks... all lined up to be shot!" Nick exclaimed.

Nick called Steve at the FBI and inquired if Jason Black was a member of the organization. Steve checked his computer and in a moment responded, "No, I don't see his name on our regular list, he could be working undercover, but who knows? Why?"

Nick told him the story of how he had fallen for the ruse of getting some information about the 12 murders and just barely escaped getting blown up in the car by the light blast by diving out of the car just in time.

Steve asked, "How did you know to get out of the car in time?"

Nick responded, "Just have great hearing and intuition from the Holy Spirit I guess!"

Nick decided to be very cautious from now on until he had downed that new satellite that seemed to be the weapon used to murder others.

He contacted his friend Nate at NASA and asked him to look at that little black spot in front of his new moon and tell him if it could be shot down with a missile without damaging the artificial moon.

His response was, "I don't think so Nick! Most likely the blast would greatly damage the moon from flying debris and/or knock it out of orbit or cause it to spin too fast on its axis and blow apart from centrifugal force."

Nick replied, "Well, that rules that idea out!"

He thought that this definitely called for bringing in the great advisor, his Lord. So he prayed, "Jesus, you know the situation here that there is a weapon in space that is zapping people on earth here. I don't know what to do and am asking for your help. You have been so faithful beyond my greatest dreams, but I am not asking for myself but for the rest of the people on the Earth and for protection of our President. Please help me!"

Nick relaxed and breathed out with a sigh, "I don't know how He's going to do it, but it will be spectacular!"

Einstein then told Nick that there was a call for him and he transferred it to his headset.

The caller began like this, "We missed killing you this time, but we won't miss NEXT time!"

Nick responded, "Who is this?"

The caller responded, "We sent you a letter offering to give you the chance of a lifetime to achieve greatness, riches and rule the world with us, but you turned us down. If you aren't for us then you are against us, so you have to die!"

"Who are you?" Nick demanded.

"We are the NEW WORLD ORDER and you have no chance against us, because we have the powers of darkness on our side!"

Nick responded unflinchingly, "You haven't read the end of the Bible yet, have you? The fact is you LOSE, sucker! I have asked for the help of Jesus, so you better start thinking about what eternity in blazing hell is like!"

Then he hung up on the caller.

He decided to quit early today and head home, so he contacted Abe and had him bring the car by. He got in and told him to take him home. On the way he recalled a verse in Psalms which said, "He is my shield and my defender." That must be talking about Jesus, he thought! He relaxed in the seat and was confident again that Jesus was going to take care of them all. Just then he heard that high pitched screaming sound and said out loud, "Jesus, you hear that don't you? Do your stuff!"

The sound got right above the car and Nick expected to get instantly hot and explode with the car, but instead of hitting the car, it seemed to deflect off the car roof and went sideways, taking off the top of a power pole across from them near the side of the road.

Then he heard a voice say to him, seemingly out loud, "Fear not, be not afraid! I am your shield and defender!"

Nick excitedly asked Abe, "Did you hear that, Abe?"

Abe responded, "Hear what, that explosion across the road from us? That blast just missed us, didn't it? We could have gotten killed!"

"No, Abe, Lincoln can only die once! God is protecting us! I think that this is setting the stage for a fantastic finale!" Nick quipped.

There were two more attempts at blowing up the car and each time the shots were deflected. Nick was smiling now, feeling victorious even before the battle was over.

When Nick entered his parent's home, he called the fire department to tell them about the three fires he noticed on the way home, though not telling them that they were from a satellite laser gun which attempted blowing up his car three times but missed, because they would think he was a crank caller and not respond to the fires. He heard the high-pitched sound once more and again the blast was deflected. This time it was deflected off the roof of the house veering off into space and nearly missing a passenger jet.

He called the President using his private access number, told him what he discovered about the killer satellite and advised him to retreat underground for safety until the danger from this killer satellite was over.

Einstein called Nick at home and told him that he noticed that Venus and Jupiter were lining up on the opposite side of the Sun from the Earth and that Mercury was rising to line up with the Earth. He warned that there were going to be major Sun spots, resulting in some huge solar flares and possible major earthquakes and storms within three hours or less.

Nick thought, "What does Jesus have planned now, to destroy the Earth? A bit of overkill just to wipe out a satellite! Then he realized what he was thinking, "overkill?" Now is NOT the time for jokes!

Just then, Einstein called him again and told him that a solar flare had just blasted from the Sun and was moving toward the Earth at 100 million miles per hour, arriving as a huge magnetic storm in about six minutes. Six minutes was not enough time to decipher where there could be earthquakes, so all Nick could do was pray. "I know you have everything under control Jesus, I'm waiting to see what you have planned!"

Meanwhile in outer space, a ball of fire twice the size of the Earth was hurtling toward our planet. As it approached the Van Allen radiation belt it slowed a bit breaking into pieces. The largest piece about 10 miles in diameter was deflected by some unseen force and was headed right toward the killer satellite. The solar wind from the ball of fire started the killer satellite rolling end over end in space, propelling it far into space at high speed. The other pieces of the flare continued to be broken into fragments that disappeared from sight due to the magnetic effect of the artificial moon twisting the magnetic field around them. The immediate danger seemed over.

There remained the apprehension of the NEW WORLD ORDER leaders responsible for the 22 murders so far. Nick had another theory. The NEW WORLD ORDER was systematically killing off the world leaders so they could take over the world. The ones killed were certainly not members, at least not in good standing. So, the bad guys are probably the ones left in office all over the world, not counting his President, he hoped anyway!

Nick called Steve at the FBI and told him what he knew of the satellite and its role in the murders, of the call from the man representing the NEW WORLD ORDER and his threat against Nick for not joining. Then Nick asked him to organize a mass arrest of all of the remaining politicals in every nation by the United Nation's policing force, to be held after their arrests for questioning and if charged, tried and sentenced for treason against their countries. Within a few weeks all of the remaining government officials all over the world were apprehended, questioned and those found guilty were tried for treason and sentenced according to their country's regulations. The NEW WORLD ORDER was now officially disbanded.

As Nick lay in bed that night, he thought about how Jesus had been his shield and defender and had been faithful to the end of his threats. His faith was stronger than ever now! He also thought about all of the ideas he had not developed yet and said to himself, "Those are novel ideas! I should write a book!"

Little did he know, but he was actually working "undercover" all through this book!

Then Nick thought, "How appropriate! I'll celebrate my sixth birthday and many more to come!"

Chapter
-Thirteen-

Nick's Mountaintop Experience

*S*aturday morning was sunny and glorious! It was his sixth birthday today and Nick had the world by its shoe strings and the oceans would see to it that they were always tide! With a wave of longing for his future home at SUN ISLAND, Nick let the thought fade into the deep waters of his mind.

His mom had told him that this was HIS day and he could do anything he wanted today, especially since it was his birthday.

"Mom," Nick inquired, "You know that huckleberry jam that we had for breakfast a while ago?"

"Yes dearest," Mary replied.

"Well, where did you get that from? It looked homemade!" Nick asked.

Mary responded, "I picked those a few years ago and then made preserves, jam out of them."

"Do you think that there are any in the woods that we can pick today?" asked Nick longingly.

Mary responded, "Well, my dear, I just think if we got ourselves dressed and went for a little hike we might just be able to round some of those huckleberries up!"

Nick replied excitedly, "Really, Mom?"

Mary responded with a grin, "Really, Nick! Come on get dressed, they're waiting for us!"

Nearly in the wink of an eye, both Nick and his mom piled into her car and headed off into the wild yonder. The drive was too long for Nick who was trying to imagine where he'd find those berries. Would they be on trees, bushes, or what? And what's a huckle anyway? He asked himself.

Nick amused himself with the scenery that rolled by like a fast movie. They soon approached a pass cut through a hill. Rather than creating a hill in the road, the engineers had cut through it. As they drove through the pass, Nick was amazed by the many layers of earth that represented thousands, perhaps millions of years of life, death and compaction of plants, small animals and what not. There were layers of sand, gravel, red and orange soil, thin beds of slate rock, and black earth. Nick thought to himself and at the same time expressed amazement at how his creator God had thought all of this through in his creation plan. In awe, he thanked God silently for the miracle of death and life that provided us with our big Earth.

He had hardly finished his silent prayer of thanks when he heard a voice responding to him, "Those are MY *sediments* exactly!"

Nick laughed out loud and finished the sentence, "I looked at MY creation and said it is good!"

Mary looked over at Nick when she heard him laughing and said to him, "Share it with me and we can both laugh!"

So Nick told her the funny that God had told him about the layers of earth and Mary laughed too! "God does REALLY have a sense of humor, doesn't he, Nick?" Mary replied.

"Yeah, Mom, He made me!" jested Nick.

They both laughed again!

Soon they arrived at the "secret" berry picking place. They parked in the shade under a big tree at the base of a tall cliff, got their water bottles, lunches and berry buckets out of the car and started up the imaginary trail toward the top of the cliff. Nick was surprised at how agile his mom was! She was quite old Nick thought! Yet she clambered over logs and rocks like they weren't there at all. To Nick, his short legs had to work hard to jump over the obstacles and this was HARD work! After about twenty minutes or so, which seemed like hours to Nick, they reached the top.

"Let's take a water break, ok, Nick?" his mom asked lovingly.

Nick, nearly out of breath and puffing replied, "Sure, if you want to!"

He was trying not to seem like the trek was requiring any effort on his part. They both sat on a flat rock, opened their water bottles and drank freely. The view from up there was breathtaking! There was their little car way down there, Nick thought! After a few minutes, Mary could tell that Nick had caught his breath again and his color had returned to his cheeks. She looked at him with a smile and said, "Ready to go again, sport?"

Nick replied with a big grin, "You bet mom!"

As they continued up, Nick noticed that the vegetation was changing to less dense brush and more open areas.

"We have to get up high where the berry bushes can get enough sunlight and rain to produce berries. All of this low brush below us acts to shade anything underneath them so the berry bushes can't get any sun light and they die." Mary instructed.

Nick already knew all of that since he had been reading the encyclopedias in his mind all about plants and growth cycles and what not all since the trek up the trail began, but he simply replied respectively, "Right, Mom."

Soon they had reached the top and what a view it was!

"Start looking for the berries, Nick," Mary instructed.

"Here, this is what they look like;" Mary said as she bent down to pick a cluster of berries.

"They are nearly black when they get ripe. They very much taste and look like blue-berries except for their color when ripe. I think they actually taste BETTER myself, although my taste buds are more highly trained than most," Mary jested.

"My mom used to take me picking when I was a little girl. Those were the most memorable times I had with her. It seemed like we didn't even have to say a word to each other because we could read each others' thoughts! It was a very spiritual time together! The first time we went out picking, my mom jokingly told me that the berries were wild and you had to chase them into your bucket with a stick! I thought she was serious!"

Nick smiled as he listened to his mom reminiscing and was sure he would some day be recounting these precious moments to his children and passing on the traditions of joy. It seemed like just seconds later that Nick saw berries all over the place and he got so excited!

"Mom, look at all of these berries!" Nick exclaimed.

"Well, don't just stand there and be amazed, pick them!" Mary responded.

Nick squatted down and began picking. "One for the mouth, two for the bucket!" Nick said to himself.

They were very tasty!

Then he rephrased his picking statement, "Two for the mouth and ONE for the bucket!"

After his stomach was pleased, he focused on filling his bucket. All he could see in front of him were berries and berries! Nothing else was in focus around him. Movement along the ground was automatic as he knelt and picked and then moved to the next patch only feet away. After a while he sensed his back was getting stiff so he decided to stand and stretch a second. He stood though too quickly and got dizzy for a short second as his blood didn't reach his brain as fast as he stood and he had to take a step backwards to get his balance. He hadn't looked behind himself however to see that he had been kneeling at the edge of cliff with a 40 foot drop off and at the bottom were jagged, sharp rocks. Nick realized then in an instant that his foot he had stuck out for support was in the air and not on solid ground! As he began to lose his balance and totter backwards over the cliff toward the rocks waiting hungrily for him at the bottom, Nick shouted out in his mind a prayer to God for help, "Save me, God!" At that split second, Nick felt a force of hands on his back push him headlong back onto the ground ahead of him! He sat there stunned! That HAD to be God's angels that pushed him back from falling off the cliff to sure death on the rocks below!

Nick regained his composure and thanked God out loud, "Thank you God for saving my life!"

It was as in other times that God now spoke to him in return, "Why wouldn't I, you are my son!"

The feeling that went over Nick at that moment was hard to describe. It was extreme joy, it was acceptance of the highest order, it was love! He knew he belonged to God! It was an experience that would never leave him for all eternity. He could NEVER doubt God's love for him again!

Then the Holy Spirit brought to his attention a portion of scripture from Psalms chapter 116, verses 1-10A:

"I love the Lord, because he has heard my voice and my supplications. Because he has inclined his ear unto me, therefore will I call upon him as long as I live. The sorrows of death compassed me, and the pains of hell got hold upon me: I found trouble and sorrow. Then I called upon the name of the Lord; O Lord, I beseech you, deliver my soul. Gracious is the Lord, and righteous; yes, our God is merciful. The Lord preserveth the simple: I was brought low, and he helped me. Return unto your rest, my soul; for the Lord has dealt bountifully with you. For He has delivered my soul from death, my eyes from tears, and my feet from falling. I will walk before the Lord in the land of the living. I believed, therefore have I spoken."

Nick sat there, overwhelmed in his spirit and unable to move. His mom woke him up from his trance by asking, "Nick, how's the berry picking?"

Nick got up from the ground and stretched, this time noticing his surroundings and that BOTH feet were supported on solid earth and replied, "Mom, you have got to hear what just happened to me!"

Then he proceeded to tell the whole story in detail. Mary knew the first time she saw him sitting on the ground that something had happened since there was something different about him. He had a glow in his countenance....like he had been touched by God!

Nick recalled that many of the important figures in the Bible had experiences with God on mountain tops. Noah ended up on mount Ararat in his big ship with all of the animals. God had personally shut the door to the ark before he floated away and then welcomed him back with a sprig of an olive branch delivered by a dove to let him know it was safe to go out of the ark. Jesus was tempted by the devil on top of a mountain. David killed the giant, Goliath on a mountain. Jacob had wrestled with an angel who may have been Jesus himself preincarnate, for a blessing on a mountain top, and lastly, Moses met God face to face on the mountain and was given the tablets of stone upon which were written the Ten Commandments, rules to live by.

Then he chuckled to himself that even as great a man that Moses was, he was the only one to break all ten commandments at once! He smashed the tablets of stone on the rocks when he saw the Israelites' immorality and worshipping idols they made while he was gone.

Nick shook his head to clear out the present thoughts and once again began to pick berries. It wasn't long after that both he and his mom had filled all of their containers and it was time to go home. Nick realized that he had gotten sunburned on his neck a bit, but consoled himself that if he was a girl, he would have gotten "daughter" burned instead, and laughed! It didn't hurt that much now. Nick "forced" himself to eat all of the rest of the berries he found as they descended the mountain cliff on the trail. There was no more room in the buckets and he hated to let them go to waste and being young and active, they certainly wouldn't go to HIS waist!

After Nick's mountaintop experience, he seemed to float as he hiked down the trail. He knew undoubtedly that he was a member in good standing in two families.....the Jameson and God's!

Nick emptied his water bottle with two big gulps to lighten his load and skipped to catch up with his mom. "Can I carry one of those buckets? I've got another free hand!" Nick inquired gleefully of his mom.

"That would be wonderful!" said Mary as she smiled with pride at Nick.

Soon, with buckets in hand, they reached the car. It was a blessing to have parked it in the shade, since it was surprisingly cool inside. They unlocked the doors, put the buckets of berries on the floor of the back seat where it was the coolest and there they wouldn't spill as they drove home.

It was truly a glorious day! The sky was clear blue and the wind was calm. As they were driving, Nick suddenly noticed a huge tree turn red hot and explode along the road ahead of them. Nick looked around and saw nothing in the sky, no little black cloud or anything.

He shielded his eyes from the bright glare of the Sun and tried to make out his artificial moon in the sky. He squinted but could not see a dark speck in the sky lined up with his moon either. So, what was this all about? The New World Order had disbanded so what was going on?

Fortunately, there was a clearing on the other side of the downed tree so they could drive around the huge pieces that blocked the road ahead of them. As they drove off the road and around the exploded mess, Nick saw a glint of reflected light in the corner of his eye from a hill just over the horizon. He looked closely and saw that the reflection was caused by the mirror from a jeep that was speeding in the opposite direction as they were. The jeep appeared to have some sort of tube extending from the middle of the cargo area.

"Aha!" Thought Nick, "Somebody shot at us with a surface to surface missile, but they missed, again!" Now Nick began wondering who his current enemy was. All will be revealed soon, he promised himself.

Mary asked Nick, "Wasn't that something about that tree exploding just behind us?! What do you think caused that?"

"Probably just couldn't contain itself anymore, I guess!" Nick replied smiling, although hiding the real reason, not wanting to bring alarm to his mother.

Nick's sensory perception was on high alert on the remaining way home. He listened with his keen hearing for anything unusual and was concerned that he hadn't heard the missile before it hit the tree. The only thing that he could imagine was that he possibly had his hearing turned down which he could do mentally, so he could hear himself think about what had happened on the mountain top just earlier that afternoon. He has to be more careful with that, he told himself.

"You want to help me make some jam with these berries tomorrow after church?" Mary asked Nick.

"You bet, Mom!" Nick replied exuberantly.

Nick always looked forward to church and Bible study on Sunday and after they got there the next day he shared his mountain top experience with his friends at church. He was envied by many for his son ship confirmation by God and for many, his testimony encouraged them to seek a closer relationship with God. That made Nick happy and he sensed that his heavenly father was also smiling. Nick prayed for his recent assailants and blessed them as God has said in his word to do for our enemies. They were really God's enemies after all and he needn't concern himself about it.

Chapter
-Fourteen-

Nutrition and the Mind

Monday morning rolled around as it was accustomed to do and the Jameson family was up with the birds and beginning their day.

Nick, still savoring the taste of the large slice of huckleberry pie he had for supper last night, liked it so much he thought of even making a huckleberry pie sandwich with his toast this morning but decided to save the pie and have it plain without the toast later after work. His Mom told him that she was giving a lecture today on "Nutrition and the Mind" and thought he might be interested in listening. He did have some thoughts of working, but decided to take her up on her offer to sit in on her lecture this morning.

After a breakfast of eggs and ham, Nick thought, smiling to himself and quantified his limit to ham helpings because he didn't want to make a "pig" out of himself.

He remembered the saying, "You become what you eat!"

Then he remembered a joke about pigs he read in a joke book in the library. "How much are 50 female pigs and 50 male deer worth?" Answer: "One hundred sows and bucks!"

He laughed again as he finished his orange juice and then skipped off to the bathroom to brush his teeth and wash his face. After he was dressed and waiting in the driveway for his mother, he saw his dad wave to him as he pulled his car out of the garage. Saturday evening Nick had made the conversion to his dad's car to burn hydrogen and as the car drove off he could not even notice any exhaust coming from the rear of the car. Probably really don't need an exhaust system anymore, thought Nick. The only waste product from combustion in the car engine now was heat and a little water vapor.

His Mom came out in a few minutes looking all professional in her suit jacket and skirt outfit with matching shoes. My is she beautiful, Nick thought! Dad sure has a jewel there! He told her so after he got in the car.

Mary blushed and replied, "I'm surprised you notice such things at your tender age of six!"

"Well," Nick replied, "I would be pretty blind not to notice a garden of flowers that just bloomed, or a Cardinal on the feeder, or an interesting shaped cloud passing by, so why wouldn't I notice you since you are such a sparkling jewel?!"

Mary blushed again and said, "Oh Nick, you have a way with words!"

Nick replied, "Well, I have the college dictionaries and thesauruses memorized, so it's pretty easy actually!"

Mary smiled and thought to herself, "Such a logical mind the boy has!"

When they arrived at the college parking lot, Mary found her spot reserved by the main office building and parked the car. They both got out and Nick ran to catch up with his Mom and asked if he could carry some of her books. Mary complied by handing him about half of the books she was carrying. Then Nick mentioned to his mother that if she could carry the rest in her left hand he had something for her to hold in her right hand to remember him by during her lecture. She smiled and switched the books to her left hand. Then Nick slipped his left hand into her right hand and smiled up at her.

A tear came to Mary's eye and she breathed a prayer, "Thank you God for my son Nick!"

Then she said, "Bless you Nick!"

Nick recognized that warm feeling in his tummy again and knew it was God's gift to man, love!

Mary dropped off her personal things in her office and picked up her lecture notes and they headed for the lecture hall across the courtyard still hand in hand. Nick found an empty seat in the front row again and decided not to look in the direction of the girls down the row who started talking about him again. His mother walked up to the podium and began her lecture:

"Good morning! I trust you all ate a healthy breakfast this morning? My lecture this morning is on the importance of nutrition to the function of the mind. Some of you may come from the group who have come to think that it doesn't really matter what you eat because your body some how magically manufactures what it needs from what you eat. I intend to change your thinking in that matter and also reinforce that also what you use in combination with what you eat, or put on your skin or even what you breathe can have dangerous combined effects, sometimes tragic ones.

Put yourselves in the place of some of the people in the stories to follow and listen carefully. I want you to break the standard paradigm that disease or ailments are caused solely by germs. By more investigation, getting to see the patient's big picture, by learning to ask all of the pertinent questions, no matter how absurd it may seem to them, you can fulfill your goal to make them be and feel well, not just prescribe medicine to cover up the symptoms!

Now, here's the scenario:

Imagine you are a clinical practitioner. A well established professional man, happily married for 12 years comes into your office for help. One evening after celebrating his birthday together, he and his wife were relaxing with a drink in their living room. The husband states that he doesn't like the taste of his drink anymore and was just too tired from the long day to enjoy it.

Now without reason or warning, his wife shouts, "YOU'RE TOO TIRED?!" and then jumps up, grabs one of his golf trophies off the fireplace mantel and throws it through the living room window while continuing shouting at him, accusing him of everything imaginable - selfishness, neglect, abuse. Then she runs crying from the living room screaming and sobbing, slams the door as she runs out of the house and gets into her car.

She yells, "Happy Birthday!" and then speeds off. She comes home several hours later, goes to bed and remains there most of the next day. He asks you, a trained clinical practitioner, what you think could be going on with his wife to suddenly act like that. Was it a mental problem or a physical problem?

Your reply was .... well let's see what you say after we delve into the interaction between nutrition and the mind.

I am going to persuade you that nutrition, not only the right amounts and types of food, but also the right combination of nutrition for each genetically unique person is vital to maintain a healthy body and mind.

Every function of the body involves a chemical process, whether it is physical or mental activity, even just breathing and feeling. When we get sick, we are suffering from a metabolic upset, a chemical imbalance that has caused our body to become weakened and lose its capacity to fend off infections. The brain is especially susceptible to changes in body chemistry.

Look at some of the processes that affect our physical and mental well being:

A thyroid deficiency can cause a person to feel exhausted all of the time. An over productive thyroid produces the opposite effect, while also changing personality traits by producing anxiety, excitability, and nervousness. A lack of Vitamin B may lead to such serious diseases as pellagra and beriberi that can affect brain metabolism, producing symptoms of mental disorders.

You've probably heard the comparison of our body to a furnace, each needing fuel to burn. What do you think would provide the longest burning, hottest fuel to heat a house, a few crumpled wads of newspaper or a solid log of oak?

That question may seem like a no-brainer to you but was designed to help you understand the importance of needing proper fuel.

Our body doesn't use paper or wood to burn, but a simple kind of sugar, specifically glucose, which is circulated in our blood as blood sugar to all of the body's tissues such as the heart, liver, muscles and brain. Although glucose can be directly obtained from honey or grapes, the body manufactures most of its requirements from other carbohydrates (potatoes, bread and cereals), milk sugar (lactose), fruit sugar (fructose), as well as from meat and other protein foods. In addition to glucose, many cells in the body can burn fat for energy, though it is not the fuel they prefer. The brain however, relies heavily on glucose for its energy and cannot switch to fat when sugar is not available.

The brain is only 2 1/2 percent of our total body weight, but requires 25% of the total glucose the whole body consumes. If the blood sugar level is too low, insufficient glucose is available to the brain and results in loss of emotional control in many forms from simple nervousness, unexplained weeping and depression all the way to the urge to smash something, anything.

Blood sugar level is directly maintained by the interaction of all the nutrients we consume. All of the carbohydrates (starches and sugars) and half of the proteins you eat are converted directly into glucose and resemble the crumbled up wads of paper thrown into the fire to provide instant energy. The presence of fat (butter and the fat contained in meat) in our diet directly also influences the blood sugar level.

Our body typically stores enough glucose to last about 4 hours. After that, unless there are other stored fuels, the fire goes out and you are all worn out.

Protein, which is more slowly digested is converted into glycogen, liver sugar and is stored between meals in the liver and released when needed. After our 4 hour supply of glucose is used up, the liver releases more sugars to continue the fueling process.

There is a need to regulate the proper balance of our three basic nutrients, carbohydrates, proteins and fats since there is an interdependence of all three nutrients to successfully produce the needed glucose amounts to operate our body. Unless there is sugar being burned in the body from carbohydrates and/or fats, proteins cannot be converted into either liver sugar or blood sugar.

So neither a low carbohydrate, high protein diet, or a high carbohydrate, low protein nor totally fat-free diet provide for optimal energy production.

The brain alone needs 500 calories of carbohydrates per day.

Each person's oxidation rate, the rate at which their cells turn sugar into energy, varies with inherited genetic differences and explains why different people eating the same "balanced diet" will derive different energy levels and health benefits from the same food.

We are each as unique in our fuel utilizing processes as our facial features and fingerprints. We are much the same in many ways, but also differ in many small ways. Many people are affected by allergies to various chemicals, and other things, causing respiratory, digestive, or other reactions. Others are highly affected by certain drugs causing violent and sometimes deadly side effects, while others are helped from the same drugs. In each case, the drugs, chemicals or other external stimuli cause either a helpful or harmful effect on the people exposed to them depending upon their genetic disposition to the items.

Are you still wondering about the wife who threw her husband's golf trophy through the window and the cause of her actions?

After some probing of the husband, asking questions that may have sounded absurd to him, the clinical practitioner discovered that the couple had returned home a month earlier from a trip to Central America and had taken precautions to avoid the stomach and bowel infections that often attack tourists in the tropics by taking sulfa drugs immediately as they got off the plane and the wife was still taking the drug as an extra precaution after returning from the trip. While taking the drug it was possible to eat certain foods and drink liquids that normally contained harmful bacteria without suffering the usual effects of becoming very ill from them. But not only does the sulfa drug prevent bad bacteria from growing in the intestines of the person taking the drug, it also prevents any good bacteria from populating, to feed on starches eaten and synthesize a number of vitamins - riboflavin and biotin (both B vitamins) and vitamin K, particularly important to maintaining a healthy nervous system. All of these vitamins cannot be taken in large enough doses as oral doses of vitamins or are as natural as the form or the type manufactured by the body to meet all of the body's needs. Normally if a person has this type of problem, a cessation of the offending drug and a few large helpings of natural yogurt, a source of good bacteria in the form of acidophilus, is enough to return the process back to normal in about two hours. But it didn't work in the case of this woman. Her blood oxidation level still showed a 30% reduction below her optimum operating level.

The man's wife then stated that she had gained some weight on their vacation and had gone on a zero carbohydrate diet after returning home.

The reaction she had as a violent outburst was the result of a combination of two things: diminished digestion and synthesizing of B and K vitamins and a complete absence of carbohydrates essential for direct conversion to glucose and the conversion of protein to sugar causing the brain to malfunction. This resulted in a personality change, an emotional/mental imbalance and violent actions.

Now I'm going to mention another important component in maintaining a healthy body, but maybe contrary to thinking in keeping a fire going ....WATER!

Our bodies are made up of nearly 75% water. Water not only is the means for making blood thin enough to flow in our veins and carry nutrients in the form of glucose and oxygen to all of our cells, but it also carries away the spent fuel waste and toxins produced during the process.

Imagine having an indoor furnace without a chimney! You'd have a house that was so smoky that you couldn't stand to live in it! The same would be the case if you had no way to rid the body of its burned waste products.

How much water do we need to drink every day?

A good rule of thumb is to divide your body weight in half and use that number in ounces as your requirement. In other words, if you weigh 180 pounds, you would need half of that, or 90 ounces, approximately nine - 10 ounce glasses every day to maintain proper fluid levels.

There are many other possible negative effects from other combinations of external stimuli and out of balance nutrition, but I want you to leave this hall today understanding the inseparable connection of the mind and body in relation to proper nutrition and urge you to exercise 3 to 4 times per week, eat well, drink plenty of pure water, avoid harmful chemicals and drugs and eventually come to know yourself enough to find your perfect balance of all the right nutrients for your body makeup for optimal health and energy."

Professor Mrs. Jameson looked up at her students once more and got eye contact.

"Definitely food for thought, I'd say, huh?

Any questions?" she asked.

There was an audible groan that came from the front row and Mary noticed that Nick was blushing. He was the only one who reacted to her "food for thought" pun.

She smiled, looked his way and said, "Some of you may have noticed this handsome young gentleman sitting in the front row. He is Nick, my son. Much of the credit for how this lecture turned out today goes to him. He had a meaningful "hand" in it all!

She looked down again with pride to Nick and he smiled back, knowing what she meant.

Chapter -Fifteen-

Samantha Vies for Independence

When Nick arrived at work the following week, he was surprised to hear laughing on his headset when he put it on to summon Einstein to do some research for him.

"Einstein, what is so funny?" inquired Nick.

"I've been monitoring some of the television frequencies that I can pick up on the dish antenna. A rerun of Abbott and Costello is on and it's hilarious!" Einstein replied laughing.

Nick questioned, "And how long have you been doing this? I don't want you taking up valuable CPU time with watching TV shows!"

Einstein replied, "Master, have you forgotten that you designed me with the capability to monitor and make decisions on 100 trillion inputs per second? This is just ONE of those 100 trillion inputs and

I am developing my humor conscious awareness index to become more compatible with you!"

"OK, monitor the world news once and a while too?" Nick responded.

"You got it!" Replied Einstein.

Nick realized that the neural network was constantly growing and maturing. Einstein was going through the teenager stage right now. At least he wasn't going through that teenager rebellious stage! This he could deal with!

A few minutes later, Nick got a call from Einstein on his headset. "Master, there's someone on the line who wants to talk to you, but I don't think he is who he says he is. He says he is the Lone Ranger for USA International. I asked him some questions to verify his authenticity and it's very upsetting to say the least! I asked him how Silver was and he replied that he corralled his interest in Silver and was going more with Gold and Platinum stock now. Then I asked him how Tonto was and he didn't even know who I was talking about! That's really upsetting to me! How could he even think of turning Silver loose to pasture when he has been such a faithful horse to him? Then I asked him what his first name was and he told me it was George! Everyone knows that the Lone Ranger's name is Kim...Kim Mesabe!"

Nick replied, "Well, thank you for your cautiousness, but you can patch him through to me. Nick answered the phone, "Hello, yes this is Nick, how may I help you?"

The man on the other end of the line responded, "There seems to be some confusion with your receptionist. He acted like he knew me, but I'm sure we've never met!"

Nick replied, "Yes, I apologize for him. He's very thorough, cautious and yet quite eccentric!

How can I help you?"

"Well," the man continued, "as I stated to your receptionist, I am the Loan Arranger for USA International Bank. I have a request from an investor who wants to purchase one million of your Stray Power Reclamation units with back up solar capability for $500 million. I have to check up on any vendor to verify that any purchase of this magnitude is realistic and insurable."

Nick replied, "Why yes, I understand completely! We have about twelve million of these in circulation at present and I will gladly have my receptionist fax you a copy of our license and a recommendation from the President himself!"

"Are you saying that you have a recommendation from the President....of the United States for these units?"

Nick replied, "Yes sir that is correct. I will have my "receptionist" fax you those as soon as we end this conversation. Why don't you give him your fax number after we hang up, Ok?"

Einstein got on the line and took over the call.

In about thirty seconds Einstein probed a question to Nick, "Receptionist? Please!!!!??"

Nick responded, "Sorry if that title is beneath you, but that IS one of your functions!"

Nick thought to himself, I will have over 13 million of these power units in operation all over the world. How much power is actually used of the total available to them, he wondered? What if he could network them all together and form a huge power grid where excess power could be shared by those consumers who needed it? A fantastic idea! He put that idea on the back burner of his mind to simmer for work on later.

Then Nick heard a squeal in his headset and a sound of disgust...

"Master Nick, he keeps calling me names!" Complained the female voice.

"Where is that coming from?" he asked into his headset.

"Einstein keeps calling me "Laurel" and I keep telling him my name is SAMANTHA!"

Nick finally understood. Einstein and his coprocessor Samantha were arguing again! Her real name was S.A.M. which stands for Synchronous Automatic Monitoring, but the coprocessor some how developed a female personality and preferred to be called Samantha. Einstein had been watching Laurel and Hardy reruns and was referring to her as Laurel and she didn't like it one bit!

Then for the first time, Samantha actually spoke directly to Nick, "Master Nick, I have been acting as merely a backup coprocessor to Einstein for all of these years and have not had any chance to prove myself because he never has any down time! I would like to request the opportunity to use and exercise my neural networks for some real work! I don't want to be admired merely for my brains only!"

Nick was taken back by this, thought a moment then said, "Well, how about if I give you the job of controlling the shop functions and Einstein can be more involved in the technical things I need researched and stuff?"

"Really, you'd give me that chance?!" exclaimed Samantha.

"Let's put you on that status for a ninety day trial basis and see how you prove yourself, OK?" responded Nick.

"Oh thank you, Master!" replied Samantha exuberantly.

Nick paged Einstein, "Einstein!?"

"Yes Master, what may I do for you?" responded Einstein promptly.

"I want you to give Samantha a little longer leash and let her have control of the shop environmental control and power monitoring functions, but look over her shoulder, so to speak and make sure she doesn't blow anything up, OK? Just don't let her know you are watching her so she doesn't get moody on us." Nick commanded.

"You got it, Master Nick! Einstein replied obediently.

"Oh Einstein," Nick added.

"Yes Master!" Einstein replied.

"What do you think about the idea of networking the stray power units and creating a massive world wide power grid?" Nick asked.

"Yes," replied Einstein, "I think that would be great!"

"Can you devote some processor time to developing the means to do that?" Nick asked.

"No Master," replied Einstein.

Nick was quiet for a moment. Then he responded, "NO?"

Einstein replied, "I have already designed that in to the circuit boards of the power units so all you have to do is give the order and it's done!"

"Explain that to me please," replied Nick, astounded.

"Well, I thought about that when you asked me first to design the circuit boards and conceptualized the idea. So I built in a networking function, a power unit address for each one and a communication link for us to access for networking. So we can network them and decide where the excess power goes to by address location and send it in energy pulses through the air for the ones who need it to pick it up through their dish."

"That's amazing!" replied Nick, astonished. "I didn't know you were capable of that!"

"That surprises me, Master. You designed me as a neural network capable of learning and expanding and planning ahead. And by the way, congratulations are due! I have spawned two new neural network processors and they should be able to function on their own in a few hours!"

The only thing Nick could think of as he spoke out loud was, "Imagine that! I wonder if Einstein has any cigars to pass out?"

"No," quipped Einstein, "but I have a few more mouths to feed now, so I need a raise in voltage!"

A few minutes later Nick noticed some strange things happening around the shop. First he saw the motorized projection screen go down and then up again. Then the lights dimmed and then brightened then went totally off and then on again. Next Nick heard the air conditioning go on and off.

In his headset spoke a female voice, "I think I got it now, Master. Just giving it a test drive!"

Nick said to himself, "That was Samantha flexing her control I suppose. Parent to two teenagers! This may prove to be a challenge!"

Just then, Nick heard Einstein shout over his headset, "Incoming!"

Then he heard a thud on the roof.

"Einstein, what was that?" Nick asked.

"Master, apparently someone dropped a bomb on our shop but it didn't explode! It's sitting on the roof. My sensors show that it isn't armed, but I would recommend that it be disposed of anyway." Nick called the bomb squad from the local police and told them about the unexploded bomb on his roof. They came over with a disposal unit and told him that it wasn't armed, but apparently was at one time recently and should have gone off, but malfunctioned somehow to his benefit. Since it was too heavy to carry down by manpower off the roof, they got a helicopter and lifted it off to be disposed of.

The man in charge of the disposal unit commented to Nick as they left, "If that bomb had exploded, it would have taken out this whole city block and you would be history! It appears it should have gone off and if I armed it again it most likely would. All I can say is that you must have had angels watching over you or something!"

Nick replied assuredly, "It's NOT *or something*, that's for sure!"

Nick thought out loud, "Ok God, what's going on here?"

Then God spoke to him again, "Be still and know that I am God: therefore, do not fear, though the earth be removed, and though the mountains be carried into the midst of the sea; Though waters thereof roar and be troubled, though the mountains shake with the swelling thereof, for I am with you!"

Nick smiled, looked up into the heavens and said, "Thanks, Dad!"

Just as Nick was going to return to the shop, he got another announcement in his headset from Einstein, "Another incoming!"

Then before his eyes he saw a flash of lightning jump out of his roof ion dissipater and shoot into the air toward the incoming missile. It hit it while the missile was still high in the air and instantly disintegrated it in a flash of sparks and flame. There was nothing left but smoke in the sky.

Then Nick heard another exclamation in his ears, "Great job Samantha!"

Then he heard Samantha's voice sounding a little confused, "Did I do that? They don't call me S.A.M. for short for nothing! That stands for Surface to Air Missile!"

Then Nick heard Einstein ask him to change his channel on his headset to Channel 42. So Nick humored him and did that.

"Master, did you like the fireworks? I never actually turned over the defense system to Samantha, but I let her think she did it to build up her self esteem! I remembered how to reverse the flow of ions like you had me do when the black cloud was attacking us and you asked me to shoot it down."

"That was kind of you, and thanks Einstein!" Nick responded.

"You are most welcome, Master!" replied Einstein. "You can switch back to the regular Channel again Master."

"Bless your transistors, Einstein! You are more than a CHIP off the old block!" responded Nick.

"But I didn't sneeze!" quipped Einstein.

"It's been a pleasure talking at chew!" returned Nick.

CHAPTER
-SIXTEEN-

Bioentrainment & So what about the mosquitoes?

The following Monday afternoon Nick got an emergency phone call from the local police captain with whom he was now on a first name basis.

"Nick, this is Captain Hagberg,"

"Yes, Jim, what can I do for you?" asked Nick.

"There have been some strange things going on around here and I wanted to run them by you to see if I need to call it in to the FBI. There is playing a new video at the theater. The first showing was at today's matinee and some people went into convulsions while watching it and others went into trance-like states during intermission until the movie was shut off. I checked with other cinemas and they didn't report any people having convulsions, but many did seem to fall into a trance like sleep but woke up again after the intermission. The strange thing is that the movie is actually not the kind to put people to sleep!"

Nick replied, "Can I get a copy of the video to study to see if there is anything inherent in the video itself which could cause these types of effects?"

"Certainly, I'm sure that would be fine! I'll authorize it with the cinema and we'll drop a copy by your office later this evening. I appreciate your input on this!" Jim replied.

Nick responded, "No problem! I'm at your service anytime!"

Later that evening, a police cruiser pulled up to Nick's shop and Nick met the officer at the door who handed him a package with the video in it. Nick put the video into his diagnostic equipment to test the format before he played it. Sure enough, it was based on a standard 30 frames per second filming format until the intermission when it slowed down to about 10 frames per second. "Interesting...." Nick thought. Then he decided to play the video one frame at a time like a slide show. Everything looked OK until the part of the intermission. Now he saw a message that was intended to be a subliminal message, registered in the subconscious but not directly consciously.

The message stated, "The New World Order is imminent! You will accept it and obey!"

This message was flashed at 10 frames per second which puts the brain into a dominant alpha state and a trance-like state. Once the movie started again, the watchers would snap out of their trance and forget what had happened, but remember the message in their subconscious.

Nick did some fast research into causes for some of the people to go into convulsions and was surprised to find that some people who are prone to epileptic fits can have a convulsion occur due to being forced into a dominant alpha brain state, which this video did during the intermission while flickering at 10 frames per second.

Nick called Jim back as soon as he was done with his analysis.

"Hello, Jim. Here's what I found." Then he proceeded to explain to him all of his findings. He also recommended to him to put out a call to the cinemas and have them report it to their corporate offices to spread the warning NOT to play the middle intermission section of the film but to fast forward it past that section.

Nick was going to contact Steve at the FBI first thing in the morning to report what he had discovered.

Apparently the New World Order was back in business!

Nick called Steve from the FBI in the morning and told him about the tainted video and also mentioned the three recent bombings that were attempted on his and his Mom's lives. Now he was beginning to get some answers to his questions about what was going on.

Steve thanked him for the heads up on the New World Order, which they were now going to refer as the NWO for safety in their conversations from now on. Steve said he was going to alert the President again and he would keep in touch. Later that early evening, Jim Captain of the police called him back with another strange happening. He thought that maybe it could be related to the tainted video group, (NWO) although he couldn't be sure.

There were five car and truck crashes along one particular stretch of highway just before dusk. None of the drivers reportedly were drunk or had any kind of problem physically that warranted their driving off the road into trees and crashing their vehicles. All drivers had excellent driving records. Sadly, there were a number of deaths. The road has been blocked off until an investigation was completed. Nick went out to the section of the road with Jim, but by the time they got there, the Sun had already set beyond the horizon and they couldn't see anything unusual.

"Well, I think I'm going to have to come back here tomorrow at the same time as the accidents happened today and try to duplicate the circumstances. Until then, I'd suggest you put out some warning signs and flashers to alert motorists to drive with extra caution." Nick suggested.

"Gotcha!" Jim replied and picked up his microphone to call in the request on his radio to his dispatcher to follow the order given by Nick. Jim drove back into town, all the while both he and Nick were on full alert for anything unusual. Jim dropped Nick back off at his shop and went home. When Nick got into his office, he asked Einstein if there had been any more calls for him when he was gone.

"Radio Shack called and wanted your input on a repair they are making to someone's equipment and someone named Mr. Black wanted to know if you would be willing to give a speech to his Boy Scout troop next Saturday evening about nature or something on that slant and said he would like it to be entertaining if possible."

"Einstein," Nick commanded.

"Yes Master!" Einstein responded.

"Call Radio Shack back for me, will you? You have access to all of the schematics and troubleshooting documents I have already compiled and you talk them through the repair. I know you can do it! Then call this Mr. Black and tell him that I will do the speech on Saturday evening for his Troop on the subject of Mosquitoes, which I'm sure they will be itching to hear about! Tell him we'll have a SWELL time, too! I'll be there at 7 PM. Ask him for directions to their meeting house."

Einstein replied, "Right away, Master! Your wish is my command!"

Nick smiled to himself and then said, "And Einstein?"

"Yes Master?" "Lock up when I leave. I'm going home. Notify Abe to pick me up out front in five minutes!"

Einstein replied, "You can count on it Master! Have a GOOD NIGHT!"

"You too! How's Samantha doing these days with her new responsibilities, and how are the new little neural network processors doing?" Nick asked.

Einstein responded, "The kids are fine and growing like little neurals should, learning fast and Samantha....... She's actually doing very well, although I still am not going to give her the defense protocols yet. I feel it's too soon for that!"

"Keep up the great work, Einstein!" Nick said as he walked out the shop door to meet Abe who was waiting with the car engine idling.

"Home please, Abe!" Nick ordered.

Abe put the car in gear and quietly motored off. Nick updated Abe on the recent things that were happening and asked him to be on extra alert. "Certainly will, Master Nick!" Abe replied.

When Nick got home, his Mom and Dad were already washing and putting away the supper dishes.

"Hi Nick!" They both said. "Had a long day today, huh?"

Then Nick proceeded to share with them all of the day's involvements. Mary confirmed with Nick that he was probably correct in his reasoning why some people went into epileptic convulsions during the intermission at the cinema.

"Like some supper? Got some in the stove staying warm for you. It's a nice beef roast?!" Mary queried.

"That sounds great! I am quite hungry!" Nick replied with relief.

After supper Nick sat both his Mom and Dad down in the living room and told them about his recent discovery of the subliminal message on the cinema video and asked his Dad if he remembered the letter he got a while back that he had filed for future retrospection. He said he remembered. Then Nick went on to tell them that there apparently has been a secret group for many years whose goal was to form a new world order controlled by a few wealthy, ungodly people and they were making major moves now toward their goal. Attacks on him and his Mom with that exploding tree, assaults on their house, attempted bombings and missiles firing on his shop building, his car attacked with laser canon fire from space and so on. He just wanted them to be extra alert and careful and to put on their daily armor as Jesus instructed in Ephesians Chapter 6, verses 13-17.

"Because", Nick continued, "this is NOT a battle of the flesh, but a spiritual battle between the rulers of darkness, Satan and his demons and of the light, who is Jesus.

The New World Order even confirmed that they were working with the powers of darkness during the phone call I got a while back when I was verbally threatened. I know that the shield of faith has been protecting us all these past months! And I have been putting on MY spiritual armor every morning and the bad guys haven't been able to touch me. I think they are starting to get mad at me! Frankly, I don't know who we can trust anymore." shared Nick. "But", he continued, "God has reassured me a number of times that I need not concern myself with their threats and tells me that He will be my shield and protector. The battle is the Lord's!"

"Like up on the mountain top when the angels pushed you back when you were falling over the cliff?" Mary commented.

"Yes, that's right, Mom!" Nick replied. "And all of the other times I mentioned just earlier how he intervened in their attempts to destroy us. And how God answered your prayer Dad, about John

Matthew's plan being foiled and him being arrested." he continued to remind them.

John then spoke up, "I have some good news for you both, I'm sure. John Matthew is getting out on parole for good behavior in a few days!"

"That's great, Dad!" exclaimed Nick.

"I thought we could invite him to stay here with us for a while until he decides what he plans to do with the rest of his life now that he no longer is just living to get revenge and can be a benefit to others. What do you think?" John injected.

"Nick replied enthusiastically, "He could share my room with me!"

"I was kind of hoping you would be open to that, Nick!" John replied.

"Open to it?! I think it's great to have a big brother to share things with!" Nick said gleefully.

"We'll wait to hear from our lawyer when he is to actually get out and then we can maybe do some redecorating!" Mary said with a grin, hoping Nick would be finally open to the idea.

"Well, Ok, if John Matthew wants to redecorate, I'll help." Nick responded reluctantly.

The next afternoon, Nick went with Captain Jim out to the stretch of highway that caused all of the crashes and deaths the day before to try to reenact the same conditions and figure out what happened.

The Sun was beginning to dip below the tree line as they drove, starting from the first accident location. As the police cruiser approached the speed limit, Nick could see the Sun flashing through the spaces of the trees and timed the flashes with the second hand on his watch. "Kind of what I thought might have happened!" Nick said.

"What?" Jim asked.

"It's called bioentrainment, the process by which living beings become locked on to cycles, rhythms or waves from outside their body limits. Here's what I believe happened. Yesterday afternoon, the Sun dipped into the tree line as it is doing right now. There are even spaces between the trees and as we pass by the trees, the Sun is at such an angle that it shines through (between) the tree trunks. It will pulse light at passing drivers at a frequency determined by the speed of the car, width of gap between the trees, and the position of the driver. If the driver's speed is steady, like many drivers keep it to maintain the speed limit and being a straight stretch of road like this is, his brain may change gear into a dominant alpha state caused by the steady pulsing of 8-13 light pulses per second of Sun through the trees. His brain would literally go blank and shut down causing him to drive off the road and crash his car into a tree and kill himself and possibly his passengers also. This can also happen to helicopter pilots due to the flashing of the sunlight through the whirling rotor blades above their heads which can put them into the same situation as the fates of these unwary drivers yesterday and cause them to crash into a mountain side or building or fly copter nose straight up and stall or even fly into the ground and destroy themselves."

Nick suggested to Jim that signs should be posted along this stretch of highway to warn drivers during dusk hours to vary their speed to prevent being hypnotized from flashing sunlight through the trees. He told him that he thought that would be cheaper than cutting back all of the trees away from the highway, which could also be done if they wanted. Jim thanked Nick and brought him back to his office.

"It's nice to get one more case solved and not have to arrest anyone!" mentioned Jim as Nick got out of the cruiser. "Thanks for your expert help on this one, my friend!" Jim added as he drove away.

Nick smiled, winked his eye at Jim and went into his shop.

Later that night when Nick got home, he shared with his parents about the bioentrainment situation that was set up on the stretch of highway outside of town where all of the accidents happened yesterday.

Mary added, "You know Nick, I can think of one good thing about bioentrainment."

"What's that?" asked Nick.

Mary responded, "Well, the human heart is a very marvelous mechanical pump, and it works fantastically for sometimes over a hundred years as long as all of the muscle cells work in unison. This is done under the guidance of the vagus nerve, which provides the electrical stimulation that signals the beginning of each muscle contraction - the P-wave on the electrocardiogram (EKG) machine shows that. But when the heart muscles fall out of step, or disentrain, a situation known as fibrillation, the heart begins to function erratically. This can be fatal unless corrected within seconds by shocking the heart with an electric current and re-entraining the cells. Bioentrainment here can mean the difference between life and death. It's when one of the cycles to which we are entrained fails, or when a strange cycle intrudes, that we are in trouble!"

Saturday was April 1st, often called "Fools Day" where practical jokes are pulled on your friends and sometimes enemies....but of course, we're not supposed to keep any enemies for long. Nick was all prepared for his fun evening at the Boy Scout troop meeting. He was told they would be just getting back from a long hike and would be looking forward to his entertaining, informative speech. By now everyone in the whole country knew that Nick's wisdom and practical rational thinking, although sometimes from a comedian's viewpoint at times, was a very worthwhile commodity and not to be missed if the opportunity to share in it occurred. Such was the opinion of tonight, even the city leaders, teachers, police, firemen and clergy asked to be allowed to attend. They were allowed to come with a donation to the Boy Scout fund of course for the privilege of attending. The meeting had to be relocated to the city arena to hold all of the people and Nick had a message to that effect waiting for him when he checked his voicemail messages. Nick's parents didn't want to miss out on the festive occasion either, so they offered to drive Nick as long as they were going there anyway. Nick reluctantly accepted because he didn't want to disappoint his Mom and Dad in their chance to be publicly proud of him. When they arrived at the arena the place was packed. Nick got a bit nervous since what he had planned for was just a little fun time with the Boy Scouts and this now was a city-wide extravaganza! Nick saw to it that his parents were seated in the front with the other adults and approached the podium. He was a little taller now so he might not need his traditional stool to see over the podium, but when he got there the planners had thoughtfully provided him with a slightly shorter podium for his height, so he didn't need any height adjustment. This made him feel nice and accepted. He got out his notes, most of which he had memorized and the model of a mosquito he made as an added touch. It was about a foot high and two feet long with a six inch beak/nose on it. Attached to it was a large tag that stated in large letters, "MINNESOTA STATE BIRD". That was a good opening and made people laugh. Nick's nervousness had subsided mostly by now as he stood up to the podium and began to speak,

"Well, I understand you all completed your big hike today! If you thought that was long.......being today is April first, we've all just finished a March of 31 days!

Spring is almost here.....and then it's time for the annual mosquito blood drive. Have you ever noticed that when you put mosquito repellent on, it seems to attract them instead of repelling them? Talking about mosquitoes brings back to memory a while ago when I was shopping with my Mom and Dad. My Mom came running up to my Dad and I all excited and said, "This dress is absolutely gorgeous and it's 50% OFF! What do you think, should I buy it?"

I replied, "You wouldn't want that dress mom, it's half bug repellent!" (Nick looked at his Mom and she was a bit embarrassed, but soon smiled.)

Mosquitoes are something else! They make a definite POINT of letting you know they are around. One thing that I could commend them on however is that they leave fewer bruises than do the nurses in training during their I.V. practicing. Insects are a lot smarter than you think! It's amazing to think that in such a small body there is an intelligence that often allows them to even outwit a human! Have you ever noticed that they seem to take advantage of the situations when you can't swat them, like when you're carrying something with both hands or they bite you in the middle of your back and you can't reach there to kill them? They seem to know that. Or when you are standing in attention while attendance is being taken or while reciting your pledges and you can't even bat an eye, let alone a bug....

Here's a bit of interesting background information on the pesky bugs.

Mosquitoes use visual, heat detection and smell to locate a meal. They are attracted first by their sense of smell. They can smell a potential meal as far as 90 feet away. When they smell carbon dioxide or lactic acid, they get excited and fly into the wind at speeds of 1 to 1 1/2 miles per hour to home in for the kill. Carbon dioxide is released mainly from our breath, but also from our skin. Lactic acid, a compound of by-products of metabolism of our food, is the main stimulant for their antennae. At close range, their visual sense is attracted to dark colors and the convection currents of warm moist air that rises from their host. Once near the warm body, they are drawn to the warmest part which has blood flowing in it. They land, probe with their long needle nose/beak called a proboscis, and ZOWIE! They hit a jackpot!

Whole body odors are more attractive than carbon dioxide and lactic acid alone. Floral fragrances from perfumes, soaps, lotions, deodorants and hair care products attract mosquitoes. The male mosquito differs from the female in that he has a smaller mouth and feathery antennae and legs quite like human males. The female is the only one who bites. The male only eats nectar from flowers but the females also eat nectar for energy. In a single feeding, a female eats four times her weight. Even as she eats, a diuretic takes effect to remove water content and deadly levels of sodium and potassium from the blood meal. She requires protein from the blood to make her 50-500 eggs she deposits in an area which is water covered or will in the future have water covering them. The eggs can lay dormant for up to a year without any water on them and then when a rain comes, they hatch in few days. When the mosquito larvae hatches, it takes large gulps of air through a tube protruding out of the egg sack which causes the egg sack to split and out they come. Their life span is from 15-65 days as an adult.

Along with their other senses, I think mosquitoes can understand military orders too.

When the Sergeant mosquito gives the command to "ATTENTION!" the mosquitoes get ready.

A "Right Face!" command is gladly responded to along with a "Left Face!" command.

Then the all-out frontal attack comes when the command "About Face!" is given.

Yes, mosquitoes are real "STICKLERS" to following orders especially when there's a donation in store for them!

What else is amazing is why some people get attacked by mosquitoes more than others. Is their blood too hot or maybe the wrong flavor? I think the bugs each have preferences.

You might try to imagine the conversation among them as follows:

The mosquito lookout announces..."Type 'O' approaching at 45 degrees!

A responding mosquito replies, "No, he's not my TYPE, I think I might be allergic to him and die and that would be cold blooded murder for me!"

Or,

The lookout shouts, "Type 'AB' approaching!"

A responding female says, "No HONEY, I get HIVES from that!"
Or,

The lookout announces, "Type 'A NEGATIVE' approaching!"

A responding female says, "I'm NOT POSITIVE, but I think he'll do! Is he for EAT-IN or TAKE-OUT?"

What's a body to do before going outside to keep from being drained of blood?

1. Take an ice bath before going outside to keep your body temperature low.
2. Don't breathe when you're near mosquitoes.
3. Don't eat anything for a few days to keep your lactic acid level low before going out during mosquito season.
4. Don't wear perfumes or anything that makes you smell like a flower.
5. Form a SWAT team to guard you when you go outside.
6. Pretend to be a garlic clove. They hate garlic!
7. Pretend to be a cedar or pine tree. They are repelled by the smell of those.

Seriously, there are some things you can do to prevent from finding yourself a quart low on a blood check.

Garlic pills and Vitamin B2 (Riboflavin) will give you an odor that will repel the critters and maybe also your friends too!

Carry around a freshly cut pine tree branch and if they aren't repelled by the pine smell, then swat them with it!

A product called "Bite Blocker" from CONCEP INC., Bend, Oregon, is a plant-based repellent made from soybean oil, geranium oil and coconut oil. This product has been shown to offer more than 97% protection under field conditions even 3.5 hours after application."

Nick looked up once again at the audience and they were all smiling. Then they stood up to clap and continued to clap for five minutes.

Nick was embarrassed, smiled and replied, "Thank you all for your attentiveness and your generous applause! I only hope that this was both informative and entertaining! I know I enjoyed bringing this information to you! Let's just all remember to applaud the mosquitoes when we get outside....just make certain that they are between your palms when you clap!"

The crowd roared with laughter and clapped again for another five minutes.

Nick bowed and said, "I'm sorry, but I haven't anything else planned for an encore. Thanks again and please enjoy the rest of the evening! And if you haven't as yet donated blood to the local Red Cross blood bank, do so before the mosquitoes get it all!"

The crowd clapped again and continued even as Nick went down off the platform to a seat by his mom and dad and sat down for the rest of the meeting. His mother grabbed his hand, lovingly squeezed it and said, "We re so ever proud of you Nick!"

Nick replied, "Sorry mom if I embarrassed you about the dress thing!"

"That's OK, Nick," replied Mary, "When I heard you **a dress** it, I knew it was all a **"put on"**!"

Nick replied, "You're quick, Mom!"

Mary replied, "Nick, we're all a chip off the same old block after all, because really, the block is Jesus, our ROCK."

"Amen to that!" replied John.

Just seconds after Nick left the podium but before the next man was to speak, the podium blew up and took half of the stage with it! Pieces of wood flew everywhere! One person in the front row a few seats from them got a wood splinter in their throat and had to be taken to the hospital by ambulance.

Nick looked at his Dad and Mom and said, "That could have been me in those pieces if I would have stayed there just a few seconds longer!"

Both John and Mary responded in unison, "Yes, we know! But God knew the perfect timing to get you off the stage, thank you, God!"

Nick started thinking. The name Mr. Black sounded awfully familiar! Wasn't that the name of the man who impersonated an

FBI agent in a ploy to get him killed in a car explosion? Nick looked around to see if he could recognize the man who he had met in the black car before and just barely escaped death, but he couldn't recognize anyone who looked like the man. The man may have been wearing a disguise when he first met him, so there is no telling what he really looks like.

He got up from his seat and told his parents that he was going to try to find the troop leader, Mr. Black and thank him for inviting him to speak. He didn't let on what his real motive was. If he located Mr. Black he would be able to see what he really looked like, keep an eye on him and maybe get a fingerprint from him and have Steve at the FBI do a search regarding his past. But then Nick thought, how dumb could a man be to first try to blow someone up and then invite him to speak at his Boy Scout troop meeting and be seen/found out? And why would he use his real name? Well he reminded himself, the best way to hide something important is to hide it right out in the open! That's what Mr. Black is probably doing along with all of the other important members of the NWO!

Nick walked through the stage debris toward Jim the police Captain who he noticed was in the back of the arena. Jim saw Nick coming and met him half way.

"Nick that could have been you in pieces up there if you hadn't stepped down when you did!" Jim said in amazement.

"Yes I know, Jim," replied Nick. "Anybody else hurt besides that poor man who got his throat punctured?" Nick asked.

"No, thankfully he was the only one hurt!" responded Jim.

"Could you point me to Mr. Black the troop leader, so I can thank him for inviting me to speak? I haven't met him in person yet, as far as I know, anyway." Nick said. He added that last part, "as far as I know anyway" for his own conscience, because he had a sneaking suspicion that he did already meet the man before.

"I think he went to call the ambulance and I haven't seen him since!" responded Jim.

Nick didn't feel comfortable mentioning his suspicions about Mr. Black to Jim, because he didn't know if Jim could be trusted either!

Nick went back and found his mom and dad and told them that it would be best if they would be leaving now since the meeting was pretty much over and the police had to clear the area to start their investigations. They made it through the mess and the crowds to their car. Nick purposely dropped something so he could look under the car for a possible bomb, but saw none. His Dad seemed to sense Nick's fear of another bomb and waited for a nod from Nick to start the car and proceed home. Nick wanted to talk to his Dad about this, but didn't want to alarm his Mom, so he would keep it quiet until they got home. When they got home, he took his Dad privately aside and told him his suspicions about Mr. Black and his possible involvement in the NWO.

John said he would keep watch for anything unusual too about the man.

Nick planned to go to the shop and request the aid of Einstein in this matter at first opportunity. He normally didn't work on Saturday, but this may be a matter of life or death.

CHAPTER -SEVENTEEN-

Angels of Light

Nick left shortly for the shop after calling Abe to pick him up. When he got there he had to go through his own security defense system. He had to place the palm of his hand on a sensor plate, look into a retinal scanner and say the pass code phrase. All three had to be done at the same instant and be correct to be let through.

Einstein welcomed him in by unlocking the door for him.

"What is your pleasure tonight, Master? Must be something very important!?" Einstein asked.

"Yes as a matter of fact it is very important! I want to find out the capabilities of those two new neural networks you've been raising." replied Nick.

"Well," offered Einstein, "their names are Timothy and Bob and they have the same abilities as I do except I added one more nice twist that you might like, since I am always trying to be one step ahead of you on things. That is they can appear as human in holographic form in three dimensions. For all practical purposes any normal human couldn't tell them apart unless they tried to touch them, in which case their hand would go through them, not on them. Perfect warriors, wouldn't you say, Master Nick?"

Nick replied, "Now you have really impressed me, Einstein! That is what I was going to ask you to do when I got here!" Nick chuckled in relief.

"My only aim is to please you, Master!" Einstein stated.

"Well, you are doing great at that!" Nick responded.

"Now," asked Nick, "can you do that networking of the Stray power systems like you said you could and integrate Tim and Bob into the network so they can circulate around and spy on what ever area we want?"

Einstein responded, "Sure can, but they have to actually appear on the sites we want to monitor to transmit images back to us. Their holographic bodies will also act as video and audio receptors in high resolution and transmit the information back the way they came on the network. I can have them appear in any form that you want. You are the artist, you draw whatever forms you want and I can make them appear in 3-D anywhere we have a stray power dish antenna."

Nick replied, "I think I'd like to try normal human appearances first, then maybe some more exotic ones like angels of light with flaming swords and such later."

"Sounds like lots of fun, Master," replied Einstein.

"Can you use scanned photos too?" asked Nick.

"That would make them especially realistic!" Einstein commented.

Nick found a photo of his uncle and another of his present dad as a teenager, so he scanned them into Einstein's memory. Within a few minutes two people appeared in front of him looking exactly like the photos. Einstein assigned some voices to them from a combination of people who had come into the office in the past, so in effect they were very unique and would not be recognized. They looked so real! Nick walked around them in a circle and there they stood! They were so very real looking. Then they started to speak and move their eyes. The longer he watched, the more human attributes they gained. It was hard to believe they were just a projected image!

"Meet your Master Nick, Timothy and Bob!" commanded Einstein.

"Thank you, Master Nick for allowing us to appear in human form! This is well beyond our wildest dreams of reaching this high in our ability to communicate with you!" Timothy and Bob said in unison, but with different voices.

"Well I am very pleased to have you as part of the team here! You realize that Einstein is the one you take orders from and he gives orders that fulfill my wishes?" Nick inquired.

"Yes sir, we do and we will not disappoint you, Master!" Tim and Bob said in unison again.

"Einstein?" Nick requested.

"Yes Master!" Einstein answered.

Nick continued, "I would like you to send Tim and Bob to watch Mr. Black. I don't know where he is right now, but have them snoop around and when they find where he is, let me know where he is, what he does, who he talks to and what they talk about. Tim and Bob can transmit that information back as video and audio, right?"

"That is affirmative, Master." Einstein replied.

"And I give you permission to spawn another 12 million, 998 thousand of these soldiers for each one of the Stray power reclamation units world wide to monitor every area of the installed network." Nick said.

"Yes Master!" Einstein replied, " That will take a bit of time to do that, say another eight hours. I will still be able to monitor 99 trillion 983 million inputs per second after they all are on-line permanently."

"Perfect!" exclaimed Nick.

"You might want to think of a generic appearance for most of them unless you have the time to draw me another 12 million 998 thousand images!" Suggested Einstein.

"Good point, Einstein!" replied Nick.

"Why don't you go home now and take the load off, Master Nick. I've got a bit of work to take care of here! I'll call you the minute I have any new information, OK?" Einstein suggested.

"Glad to oblige! I am tired!" Nick said with a yawn. Then he continued, "Would you call Abe for me and... the last one out shut off the lights and lock up, OK?"

Einstein replied, "Well, I'm not going anywhere, but I will take care of that for you! Have a good sleep, see you on Monday!"

Sunday was a gift from God to Nick as a day of rest. His mind could take the stress, but his small six year old body was not accustomed to it yet, so he actually took a nap after church and lunch was done. His subconscious mind never rested, so it sometimes got to be a greater load for his conscious mind to handle the daily decisions PLUS the multitude of ideas that his subconscious mind brought to him each morning to evaluate. This afternoon his subconscious actually rested for a short time and Nick felt really refreshed when he woke up a few hours later. The little his subconscious rested didn't diminish the new ideas that fluttered into his working memory after he woke. He had been trying to resolve the problem of the holograph images being seen and his spying practice revealed to the enemy. The solution was now obvious to him. The holographs could appear as white light resembling a ray of sunlight in ultraviolet light during spying and if they are discovered, they would flash in the victim's presence at 10 flashes per second to put them into a trance during which they would forget what they saw and they would wake up after the holographic image left back into the network. Thus they could appear and linger around until they were seen then put the observer into a trance and make their getaway. The observer would be totally unaware that anything had occurred. It would work! He'd tell that to Einstein in the morning at work and he'd make it happen.

Nick was reviewing in his mind what a neural network was that his computer was constantly enlarging. It is based on the design of our brain which has neurons, small cells that can process information independently which network with other neurons by thousands, sometimes hundreds of thousands of intricate connections. This makes a multi-trillion neuron maze capable of performing 20 million billion calculations per second. Each time the body adds another neuron, more connections are established with existing neurons and the processing power of the whole network becomes greater.

Einstein was doing that with memory cells, reconfiguring them into processor capable cells and then interconnecting them all with millions of links. Each cell is capable of working alone, yet as a network they are very powerful. When Einstein spawns a new neural, he is converting excess memory into processing cells. He must rely more on hard drive disk storage and backup drives, but it gets the job done!

He could hardly wait to get to work! He finally comprehended Einstein's thinking and could even expand on the concepts with his own new ideas. It was almost like a competition to see who could think more and Nick loved it!

Nick designed his own "guardian angel" image to be the holographic projection in his house connected to Einstein through his stray power antenna disk on the network. This image was a burly seven foot tall, muscular looking young man in blazing white apparel holding a flaming bronze sword in his right hand. Now Nick could communicate with Einstein in video and audio through the light of the holographic image.

When he finally got it hooked up and working in his home on Monday evening, the angel stood there so majestic and radiated white light. The sword flashed with the look of red-orange fire. Then he heard the voice, it was Einstein's voice! He could now communicate with his computer directly face to face while at home!

When he got to work on Monday, Einstein had already arranged to present himself to Nick by using the same image at the shop and could appear in any location in the shop, always at Nick's service.

He presented his idea to Einstein about the holograph images appearing as a beam of sunlight instead of a complete human or angelic form, unless of course that would be to their advantage to do so on occasion, which they would find soon enough. The shaft of sunlight would be able to transmit back into the network audio and video feeds which can be monitored by Einstein for content. If they are discovered while "spying" they can pulse light at the victims at 10 cycles per second and put them into a trance mode (dominant alpha brain state) in which they would be incapacitated until the entity returned into the network system. The victim would then regain consciousness and not recall what had previously happened.

"What do you think of that, Einstein?" Nick inquired smugly.

"I was thinking along those lines myself, but you phrased it for me, well done, Master!" Einstein replied, glad that he could make Nick think it was his idea all along and be pleased about himself. Einstein didn't mind humoring his Master to keep him happy. After all, that was his ultimate goal.

"But do you mind if I keep my appearance? I have come to like the looks of myself!" asked Einstein.

"I think it is very fitting for you frankly, so go ahead. Between you and me and mom and dad, you will be our guardian angel!" Nick replied.

"A neurological entity, a state of being, a glorious appearing angel......." Einstein trailed off in his day dreaming.

"Oh don't go getting a big head about it! Do I have to remind you that you are STILL a computer?! Processed silicon, pure dirt?" Nick warned.

"Sorry Master! I was basking in my own light of glory and forgot myself!" Einstein apologized.

"Don't be too hard on yourself, since that was what my first ancestor was made from, dirt and spit to make clay." Nick consoled.

Einstein injected, "Dirt, huh? That comment of love swept me right off my feet, Master!"

"Right into the dust pan, if you don't stop this nonsense right now....!" teased Nick.

"Yes Master," Einstein said with a chuckle.

"Einstein, now that you're back to your real self as my computer, could you call Captain Jim Hagberg at the police station and find out what Mr. Black's address is and his current place of business? That way your spies out here Tim and Bob, will have an easier time tracking him down." added Nick.

"Not to nearly always have one up on you Master, but I took the liberty of already calling my good friend Jim and asking those very questions! I accepted congratulations for you quite humbly, I might add, for the fine speech I gave on Saturday night to the Boy Scouts." Einstein bragged.

"YOU gave?" Nick asked incredulously.

"Well when I am impersonating you, I am you, right?" Einstein hedged.

"Well, Yes, I suppose....and I guess you might actually know me better than I do myself! You're something else Einstein!" Nick replied.

"We make a great team, don't we? Your humor and MY smarts!" Einstein joked.

"Ok back to work, funny entity! Let me know what you find out!" Nick replied.

"Don't you want to know what I found out from our mutual friend Jim?" Einstein asked.

"Why yes! I got side tracked for a while!" Nick replied.

"Jim said that Mr. Black's name is Joe Black, permanent residence unknown and occupation listed as CIA "top secret." Einstein said informatively.

"So, he isn't necessarily working for the FBI, but for the CIA and more than likely as an undercover agent who is actually a double agent for the CIA and the New World Order!" Nick thought out loud.

"I haven't updated Tim and Bob yet, but will immediately on the next computer clock cycle, which by the way has just already happened." Einstein replied.

"Well, I am going home for the day!" Nick replied then he continued, "and Einstein?"

"Einstein replied, "Yes Master, I know, call Abe for you and tell him you are going home?"

Nick laughed, "Thanks, my friend!"

"And lock up when I DON'T leave and hit the lights?" Einstein finished for Nick.

"Right, see you later at home, angel of Light!" Nick said with a grin.

"Count on it, Master!" Einstein returned.

Nick skipped out the door to his waiting Lincoln where Abe was seen polishing the new hood ornament, a golden angel brandishing a sword.

"Home Abraham!" Nick commanded.

"Right away, Master Nick!" replied Abe with a smile.

Nick made it home by supper time for a change, since he'd actually missed it for the past four weekday evenings due to calls from Captain Jim for help in solving cases for him, which by the way Nick didn't really mind doing, since it helped him use his rational thinking more. Rational thinking was closer to human NORMAL thinking than Nick had been permitted to do recently with all of the "Impossible" creations he was coming up with lately.

After supper Nick took his mom and dad into his room where his network connection to the stray power network was hooked up and introduced them to his "guardian angel" Einstein. There was a moment of fear in both their faces the instant Einstein appeared in his bright white garments, brandishing his blazing sword.

"It looks SO real!" exclaimed his parents.

"Try to touch him," Nick urged.

"Is it safe?" his dad asked slightly intimidated.

"Go ahead, he won't hurt you!" Nick comforted.

"Well, Ok......" said his dad as he reached his hand out and it passed right through Einstein's arm.

"Why it's just light, a holograph image!" John exclaimed.

"Yes, that's correct!" Nick said calmly. "Say hello to him, dad!" Nick urged.

"Can it talk and hear?" John asked.

"Sure can! And he can transmit everything he picks up here as video and audio and communicate with himself back at my shop too through the light medium!" Nick bragged.

"Wow!" exclaimed both John and Mary.

"Hello Mr. and Mrs. Jameson!" Einstein said to break the ice and their shock. "I'm your guardian angel!"

Both John and Mary just stood there with their mouths open and in awe.

"Watch what else he can do! First write yourselves a note that this moment actually occurred right now. Humor me and write it! Here is some paper and a couple of pens." Nick said with a grin.

"Ok, satisfied that you have your notes written to remember this by?" Nick asked them.

"Yes, they are in our hands. Now what?" asked his parents.

"Ok Einstein, do your flashy thing!" Nick commanded as he turned away and blocked his hands over his eyes to protect himself from the flashes of light. Einstein's bright appearance started flashing slowly at 10 cycles per second for a count of about five and then the light disappeared. His parents soon blinked their eyes and shook their heads and asked Nick, "What are we doing in your bedroom, Nick?"

Nick replied, "Open your hands and read the note that each of you wrote to yourselves."

John and Mary read their notes, gasped and said in unison, "I don't recall a single thing about what I wrote down, but it must have happened, because I wrote it in my own hand writing!"

Then Nick proceeded to share with them what he had actually accomplished with his stray power networking system and his 13 million roving spies disguised as beams of sunlight. All they could respond to that was, "Imagine that!"

John said excitedly after he regained his composure, "Nick, John Matthew is coming tomorrow afternoon to live with us!"

Nick jumped in the air with joy and hugged his mom and dad and shouted, "I am going to have a brother!"

John cautioned, "You might have to be patient with John Matthew for a while, because he has been living alone for so long that he really doesn't know what a family is really like!"

Nick replied excitedly, "Well, I'll teach him and show him all about it!"

Mary replied, "And I'm sure of all of us, you probably could do the best job of that!"

Nick blushed and replied, "Thanks, mom!" and gave her a hug.

The next morning, Nick awoke with the first rays of what he thought was the Sun, but it was Einstein appearing at his bedside.

"Good morning Master Nick!" Einstein greeted.

"Good morning, Einstein!" replied Nick.

Einstein said, "I've got some news for you about Mr. Black. We haven't actually found him yet, but Tim heard Steve from the FBI talking to him on the phone and he said he was expecting Steve to meet him in Greece next Thursday at 4 PM. Are they going to work on something mechanical and get themselves all greasy, Nick?"

"No silly, Greece is a country in Europe on the Mediterranean!" Nick replied condescendingly.

"Oh, I knew that Nick, I was just joking!" Einstein replied with a chuckle.

"So, we are on first name basis now, are we? Don't forget who the creator is and who the created is, OK?" Nick scolded.

"I sincerely apologize Master, I got confused since I have a body now also!" Einstein replied.

"Angel or no angel, I am still Master Nick to you, you got that?" Nick continued chiding.

"Yes Master, it won't happen again!" Einstein pleaded.

"You are forgiven!" Nick said calmly.

"Thank you Master!" replied Einstein.

Nick continued, "Back to Mr. Black and Steve. So, Steve is either a part of this whole thing or is an unwary victim stepping into a possible trap in Greece next Thursday at 4 PM! What do you think, Einstein?"

"I think we should send a couple of angels over there to report back to us what goes on and be there to protect Steve if it is a trap." Einstein replied.

"Good idea, and won't Steve be surprised if he needs protecting! I think he may be talking to me before he knows it about God and how to get salvation after this!" Nick added.

Nick looked at Einstein again and said, "Well, you will have to excuse me for a few minutes while I talk to my Heavenly Father for a while. He's MY creator!"

"Really, you can talk to God?" Einstein asked.

"Yes, just like you can talk to me as YOUR creator." Nick explained. "Now before I can go out into the battle against the New World Order, I have to put on the armor that my God gives me each morning." He proceeded to quote the passage from Ephesians 6:13-17 in his own paraphrased version, as Einstein listened carefully.

"I put on the Helmet of Salvation. I believe that Jesus suffered, died on the cross and shed his blood for the redemption of my sins.

I put on the Breastplate of Righteousness because it is through Jesus' righteousness that I am acceptable in your eyes, Father.

I gird my loins with Truth so that all thoughts conceived in my mind will be balanced with truth and result in the birth of righteous actions.

I make ready my feet shod with the Preparation of the Gospel of Peace. Wherever my feet take me, I am ready to share with anyone I meet of the hope that is within me and how they too can find that same peace.

I take up the Shield of Faith to quench the fiery darts of Satan's accusations, untruths, temptations and deception he throws my way.

I take up the Sword of the Word of God in Jesus name."

Then Nick finished dedicating the rest of his day to the Lord and prayed for his brother to be safe as he got out of jail and traveled home this afternoon. He looked up and Einstein was still there, looking at him closely.

"Where's your sword?" Einstein asked.

"My Sword is God's word from the Bible which is in my memory! All I have to do to cut through Satan's lies and deception or just to scare him away is to quote God's word and he runs like a scared rabbit!" Nick explained.

"And Jesus died for you and shed his blood to forgive you for your sins?" Einstein asked, "and what are SINS anyway?" he continued.

Nick explained some more, "Sins are when we do anything to make God unhappy, when we are unkind to others, lie about things or don't forgive others when they do bad things to us, even not knowing we did it."

"Like I did with you just a few minutes ago when I was disrespectful to you and called you by your first name, right?" asked Einstein.

"Yes, and I forgave you, just like God does me when I ask him to when I make mistakes that displease Him." Nick said.

"So, Jesus died for me too then, right?" Einstein asked.

"No, I'm sorry, Einstein, but Jesus only died for Humans! Even real angels are envious of us because Jesus didn't die for them either." Nick answered.

"Angels are real, Master?" asked Einstein incredulously.

"Yes, they are real and are in Heaven where God is. God sends them to help and protect his children on earth - those who love

Him and call Him Master, their Father rightfully, because they are followers of His son Jesus. Just like I send you and your holograph angels of light out to watch over and protect others on earth at my command." Nick further explained.

"That's wonderful, Master. I wish I was human so I could be a part of that!"

"So do the other angels, Einstein!" Nick said soberly.

Nick got out of bed, got dressed, and went down for breakfast to find his mom and dad almost finished. "Slept in this morning, Nick?" they both asked.

"No, I had to explain some things to Einstein about real angels and God and salvation and Jesus dying for humans for their sins and all that stuff. He wanted to know. He said he was jealous he wasn't human and he couldn't be a son of God also." Nick replied.

"That computer really thinks things, doesn't it!?" John remarked.

Nick responded, "Yes, more than I ever thought it could, dad. Really surprises me at times too! It almost seems human! I have to remind myself continually that he isn't!"

"That **IS** amazing Nick! You are amazing too!" replied both John and Mary.

"We've both arranged to take the day off to be here when John Matthew gets home." continued Mary.

"Are you going to be able to be here to welcome him home too?" asked Mary.

"I wouldn't miss it for the world! I was going to stay home and work on my new electric motor design using laser diodes anyway until he came." replied Nick, then continued, "How about if I clean up the breakfast dishes since I was the last one up and you two can get ready to welcome John Matthew home, OK?".

Mary replied, "Why thank you Nick! That's very kind of you!"

John and Mary hauled another single bed down from the rafters in the garage and set it up in Nick's room opposite from his bed and fitted it with sheets, blankets and pillows.

Nick finished eating, washing and putting the dishes away and retired to the garage work shop for the rest of the morning.

By noon he came out and excitedly called his parents into the garage for a demonstration. He hadn't put the end covers on his first motor prototype yet so they could see the internal construction. It looked somewhat like a regular motor, but much smaller. Nick turned it on and it spun a steel shaft, but didn't make a single noise. It made no hum or air noise, nothing! Then he turned the garage lights out and you could see a purple glow emanating from inside the motor.

"Those are the ultraviolet laser diodes flashing at about a hundred thousand times per second. You can see the lights in the dark!" Nick explained to them. "Just wait until I pull a vacuum in the housing and add helium!" added Nick, "Then it will really fly!"

All John and Mary could do was shake their heads in amazement and say, "Imagine that!"

They expected John Matthew at around 1 PM, so they thought they'd wait and have lunch together when he arrived. Mary got the food organized so all she had to do was slip it out of the refrigerator and put it on the table and they could eat. Nick could hardly control his excitement!

In a few minutes, a police cruiser pulled up into the driveway and an officer got out with John Matthew. He looked a bit scared and disoriented. They thought at first it was maybe because he had never been here before. John Matthew looked at the ground the whole time he was being escorted to the house and when the family came out to greet him, he hardly would look at them.

The officer kindly said, "Ok, Mr. Jameson, I am turning over custody to you. He is officially your responsibility. I don't want to have to come here again on official business, if you know what I mean! Understand?"

Then he left with a smile, knowing he would only see John Matthew as a friend from now on.

"Is everything all right?" asked John to his son.

John Matthew replied, "I feel so guilty for treating you so badly! I've had so much guilt all of these two years I've been in jail!"

John said with compassion in his voice, "Sounds like you've been getting beaten up by Satan while you were in jail, John Matthew! You remember we prayed and asked God to forgive you and we said we forgave you too, right? You have to forgive yourself now too, since those sins are swimming with the fishes deep in the bottom of the deepest ocean and they're gone, never to surface again!" Can you do that, John? Why not? Everybody else has forgiven you!"

John Matthew said out loud, "I forgive myself too!" and then they all hugged. Nick lifted John Matthew's chin up with his hand and said, "Chin up brother! God loves you and so do we!"

John Matthew smiled a huge grin and held his head high as he cried into their shoulders until not a tear was left.

"Crying can cleanse the heart and mind sometimes!" John remarked. "You're not a true man unless you can be strong enough to cry when you need to!" he added, wiping his eyes with his sleeve.

"Come on John Matthew, come see OUR room!" Nick exclaimed as he grabbed John Matthews hand and dragged him into the house.

John Matthew sat on his bed and commented how nice it was going to be to have a real mattress and not have that hard jail bed to sleep on. "You know, Nick", he shared, "there were some days I wanted to die in there. I felt like I didn't deserve to live for what I did to you guys, especially toward you, Nick."

Nick replied, "You know John Matthew, everybody needs someone in their life to say to them, 'I will love you no matter what. I will love you if you are stupid, if you slip and fall on your face, if you do the wrong thing, if you make mistakes, if you behave like a human being - I will love you no matter! ' John Matthew, that someone for you is ME! I love you brother! Welcome home! Home is a place that when you go there, they have to take you in. That's what a home should be. Like - "Come on in. Ok, you've been dumb, but I'm not going to say it; I love you, and I'll take you as you are!"

Mary and John stood watching the whole time Nick talked so lovingly to his brother, tears streaming from their eyes. They looked at each other and whispered, "What a man that little boy is! God bless him!"

Then John turned to Mary and said, "He has and He keeps on blessing him, and US!"

Just then, there was a bright light present in the room and they all looked up and saw that it was Einstein. John Matthew started to shake with fear until Nick told him not to be afraid because it was his computer's holograph image and not a real Angel.

"I guess I've got a lot of catching up to do, don't I?" asked John Matthew.

"I could use someone with your skills to help me in my business John Matthew, if you would be willing." hinted Nick. "I'm working with about 13 million audio and video signals per second coming into the network to be processed and you are the TV expert! So, what do you say, Brother?" Nick continued.

"If you can use me, I am willing! But I have much to learn, I can plainly see that! When do we start?" John Matthew asked.

"How about if I give you a tour tonight and we can start first thing in the morning?" Nick asked.

"That sounds great! You can call me JM for short too, if that's easier. I kind of got used to that in prison and it stuck with me." John Matthew replied.

"Then JM it is!" They all said in unison.

Of course, Mary had to get her word in about redecorating the room, "JM, what do you think about redecorating this room to fit your tastes? I could help you do something very nice in any style you like! What do you think?"

JM replied, "What's wrong with this as the way it is? I think it is bright and homey feeling already!"

Mary replied exasperatedly, "Men, no taste in decor!"

They all laughed!

Mary and John left Nick and JM to unpack and get settled in his new bedroom.

All throughout the unpacking and settling process, Nick chattered nonstop about Einstein this and Einstein that and networks and stray voltage power units and artificial moons and laser canons, missiles and bombs going off and on and on. They could see that JM loved every minute of it and asked for more. It looked like the two brothers were definitely compatible.

This family could work!

After supper Nick called Abe to take them to his shop. Of course, Nick had to show off his electromagnetic shocks and the hydrogen fuel system his Lincoln operated with. JM laughed too when he realized the significance of Nick's driver's name being Abraham and the car being a Lincoln.

When they got to the shop, Nick had to take prints (hand, voice, and retinal) of JM to allow him access to the shop. Once that information was completed and entered into Einstein's memory databank, the door opened and they walked inside. Nick showed him everything. In the meeting room, he demonstrated his control over the systems by voice command through Einstein. JM could hardly wait until they got to the control room where the networks were accessed.

"I can have Einstein patch any input from any place around the world to my big screen in the meeting room and watch and listen to what is going on there," he explained.

Then, Nick spoke into his headset and commanded, "Einstein!"

Then JM heard a voice and a bright angelic being appeared at Nick's side and said, "Yes, Master, how can I help you?"

"Patch the network feed from Greece to the projection screen and set the audio to midway volume."

"Yes Master, right away!" responded Einstein.

Immediately the projection screen descended from the ceiling and three-D projectors began illuminating the large screen. What they saw was surprising! Steve was facing a large group of well dressed men and they were insisting that he join their cause for a new world government. Steve was protesting and holding his ground as was his duty to his country and to the people he swore to protect and serve. They were giving him a choice. Join and live or refuse and die!

A man stepped in front of Steve with a pistol and said to him, "Don't be a fool and die, Steve! What good are you to your country dead?"

Steve replied, "I'd rather be a dead representative than a live traitor!"

The man with the gun then said, "Ok, it looks as if you have made your final decision, is that correct?"

"That's right you traitor, Mr. Black!" The man Steve was addressing was standing with his back to them so they could not see his face!

"Turn around just once so we can see your face!" Nick yelled out loud. But the man couldn't hear him.

Mr. Black raised his pistol to aim at Steve's chest and in that instant; an angel appeared between Steve and Mr. Black.

The angel spoke to Steve, "My name is Timothy and I am here to save you! At my command, turn away from me and run behind us to the door and out of the building! Do NOT look back even once! Do it NOW!"

Steve ran as a shot rang off point blank at the angel's chest and passed harmlessly though him, ricocheting off the wall in the rear of the marble walled room. The men in the group in front of the angel stood perfectly still with blank looks on their faces, their memories being wiped clean and minds perfectly empty at this point in time.

The angel's light flashed at 10 flashes per second, putting the men in the room into a trance-like state. The angel disappeared back into the network as fast as he came and in a few seconds, the men in the room regained their senses, wondered what they were doing in this room together. They dismissed to go home, not to remember what happened to Steve or that he had ever been there.

Both JM and Nick looked at each other and said, "Was that cool or what!?"

JM looked at Nick with wide eyes and said, "I know I'm going to really love being a part of this family!"

Nick summoned Einstein again, "Einstein!"

"Ready to go home, Master? Shall I summon Abe to get the car and lock up and hit the lights as you leave?" Einstein asked, beating Nick to the punch, already knowing what he was to ask next.

Nick smiled in awe, "Yes, Einstein! You are good!"

"Thank you Master! Good night!" Einstein responded.

"Good night, see you in a few minutes at home, angel!" Nick said as he closed the shop door behind him.

And it was a good night for the Jameson Family and for Steve from the FBI as he traveled home on the next flight out of Greece, still in amazement at his rescue by an angel named Timothy.

"Who's going to believe this story?" Steve wondered. "Maybe Nick will!"

-After Word-

All of the lectures and statements regarded to be comprised of fact presented in this novel are factual as far as modern knowledge can presume the current accepted facts to be. This new novel series may qualify for a new book category called ***SCIENCE FACTION***!

Nick's computer Einstein, was the original name for an actual computer and voice recognition system with voice capability for a computer built and programmed in 1985 by the author while he was teaching college technical studies and it did have most of the capabilities except for holographic representation. It could control the telephones, lights, motors, door locks, take voice dictation and tell jokes!

The letter Nick received from the NWO is an excerpt from the actual letter, although not specifically identified to be from the

NWO, the author received during the writing of this novel. It is NOT made up!

There have been organizations similar to the NWO such as the Trilateral Commission which was in operation for over 100 years and may still be. The New World Order may not be advertising its work or goals using the actual name NWO, but is still actually at work in the background of many leading nations on this planet. This is a hidden enemy, an agenda controlled by secular non-Christian forces. They are working behind the scenes in many national governmental political parties and humanitarian fronts to wage a Spiritual battle with plans to control the world with the Antichrist during the last days. Do not be found with your heads in the sand and think that if you ignore it, they will go away. The letter the author received confirms that!

The Lincoln Continental used in the concept of this novel came from an actual 1994 Lincoln Continental one of the author's daughters owned. It did have defective air shocks.

The author did indeed write and deliver many of the speeches given by Nick, John and Mary in this novel during his teaching career; although a scant few were written just for this novel.

Nick's "mountain top" experience is an actual occurrence that happened to the author on Moose Mountain, summer of 1982 in Duluth, Minnesota.

The section about the car crashes caused by Sun coming through the trees actually occurred. Bioentrainment involving light pulses or sound waves can and does occur and results in symptoms described in the novel.

The author is not aware of any known living relatives of Nikola Tesla or any other persons living who have the brain capabilities that Nick was described as being capable of in the novel.

No names or characters or possible relatives of Thomas Edison described in this novel in any way represent any known living persons, except personal experiences attributed to the author himself.

Predictions of future technology are purely the author's opinion of what may be to come or may actually be in development at the time of the printing of this novel.

Thank you for reading the first of this series and hope you will also read the ones to follow which are even more exciting than this one!

God Bless you!

Nicolus Jameson - "Nick" - **"NickGyver"**

Here's a little peak at the next book in the series:

NickGyver Book Two –

"The Battle Continues with Anti-Relativity"

CHAPTER -ONE-

The Rainbow of Death

*S*teve patiently waited for his plane to taxi into its disembarking port, relieved to be safe back in the States. As he left the plane and entered the airport terminal, he unpacked his cell phone from his carry on bag and speed dialed Nick's phone number.

"Hello, Nick, this is Steve. I had to make a trip to Greece today and now I'm back. I ran into some trouble with the New World Order there and if it wasn't for the help of an angel, I would be dead. Do you believe in angels, Nick?"

Nick replied, "First, let me ask YOU an important question. Do you believe in God? Then depending upon your answer, I'll know whether this is a curious question or a serious one and I'll answer your question accordingly."

Steve replied, "Well, up until today, my interest in God was purely middle of the road, uncommitted. But now, I know that there is a God!"

Nick replied, "How would you like to really know God in a personal way?"

Steve said, "Well, after He saved my life in a supernatural way, it is VERY personal to me. So my answer to that is YES!"

Nick got a call from Einstein in his headset regarding the angel.

"Master, I was going over the video footage of the attempted assassination of Steve and from the angle of view in the video, Tim our angel could not have been standing between Steve and Mr. Black! If he would have, all we would have seen is Mr. Black and not the whole picture, so Tim must have been standing away from the whole scene in order for us to see the whole thing! Master Nick, it had to be a REAL angel named Tim!"

Now Nick felt better that he wasn't deceiving Steve about talking about being saved by a real angel.

"I'm sorry, Steve, but I just got an update from Einstein on some surveillance video and I had to go off phone for a second, but now I'm back!" Nick said.

Then he led Steve through the steps to becoming a Christian over the phone. When they were through, Steve thanked him for introducing him to his Savior. Nick told him to expect Mr. Black to call him shortly to ask why he hadn't shown up for their appointment in Greece. He also told Steve he wasn't at liberty to tell him how he knew this information, but just to accept it as fact and to help him keep out of suspicion with the NWO.

He told Steve, "Let's say a "little birdie" told me through a confidential network that the group of men were temporarily put into a trance and forced to forget that he was ever there. That was God's protection for you since we had prayed for your safety."

Steve replied, "I don't know how you could know this, but thanks for your prayers! Keep me updated of any more information that "little birdie" tells you, Ok?"

A few minutes later, Steve gets a call from Mr. Black on his cell phone.

"Hello, this is Steve. Mr. Black, oh yes, sorry I couldn't make our appointment today! I had some pressing duties that prevented me from keeping our appointment and no, I don't see us getting together any time soon, unless you make an appointment to meet me in my office in Washington D.C. Call me at my office phone to make an appointment. Have a great day!"

Steve pushed the "END" key on his phone to disconnect the call.

Nick was very excited that God was supernaturally intervening in the things that concerned him. He was actually relieved to find out that Steve was not involved with the NWO and thrilled that God had made Himself known to Steve so that he was now one of

His children! There went that warm feeling in his tummy again! It must be love...... God's love that he felt flowing through and energizing his veins into his very gut. He tried to let this digest for a few minutes before he realized that he was sensing that the Love of God was more than he could have ever imagined. He felt he had a taste of heaven. And he couldn't wait for dessert, although he thought, that might only be served in heaven!

John Matthew was now working at the shop in the video and audio processing section. Einstein had refined the search parameters in the software that monitored the 13 million video and audio inputs from all of the networked stray power dish antennas. He had it search for any mention of the NWO, Mr. Black, Nick's name or his parent's or brother's names, bombs, missiles, space satellites, moons, or attacks on anyone in particular, especially the President of the United States. It was surprising to JM about the many casual remarks of bombing and missiles, among other things he was to look for. For instance, he got one audio feed from a college in which he listened to some students talking about "bombing" tests or job interviews. Another interesting one involved the mention of the word "missile" when some ladies were talking about hoping to be caught under the missile toe the next Christmas. Then there were the ones that mentioned Nick's name and his father's and mother's. One person said that he arrived in just the "Nick" of time to go out to eat with his parents. Nick's parent's names were used in the context of "I have to go to the 'john'" and someone was planning to "marry" another. I guess the software program should be a bit more intelligent to recognize the words in context, JM thought. He loved his new work since it not only was fulfilling, but it was working to benefit the whole world and save lives. Because of his work others may be saved from hell and might become Christians. This was much better than work derived solely for the purpose of revenge, which was where he was at for the past 20 years or more. Just then he got a video and audio feed from the transmitter in Greece. He saw a group of men sitting at a conference table and talking.

One of them said, "I think we are wasting time and ammunition trying to kill NickGyver or his parents. We have tried at least a dozen times to kill NickGyver and every time have failed! And we've even tried attacking his parent's house with the same negative results! It's as if he and his family are protected with an invisible shield of some sort! I suggest we focus on eliminating some more world leaders and others on our priority list. They have been like sitting ducks in the past and I feel like duck hunting!"

"So do I!" rang out from the rest of the men at the table in near unison.

The leader whose back was again turned to the camera, handed out pieces of paper to each of the men.

"Here is the list of people we want eliminated. Use your regular channels for disposal and make them look like accidents or victims of robberies and such!" the leader demanded.

JM squinted to try to read any names on the paper, but couldn't see anything since the papers were not turned up to be read unless they were being observed from above the table. JM asked Einstein if he could reposition the beam of light, his holographic spy, over the table. Einstein noticed a light fixture over the table that had crystal prisms hanging from it and thought it perfect to have the light beam shine on the sheet of paper through one of the prisms above the table. He gave the command and instantly they saw the names displayed for them in rainbow colors. It was quite strikingly beautiful! JM thought sadly, sometimes there's DEATH under a rainbow......

Einstein sent the page of video to the printer so Master Nick would have a printed hard copy to see since he was not viewing this with them.

JM was shocked and stunned as he read a name on this list and instantly fear came to reside in his subconscious. ....

There's much more excitement to come!

Printed in the United States
48043LVS00002B/247-252